THE
MARBHAVEN
REAPER

MAILE STARR

Cover Designed by Maldo Designs.

Formatted by Maldo Designs.

Edited by EJL Editing.

Paperback ISBN: 979-8-9914306-0-9

eBook ISBN: 979-8-9914306-1-6

To Sweet Peas and Knuckle Heads everywhere,
grief is the weight of a nickname never to be spoken again.

Chapter One

She talked often about where we'd go if we ever lost each other.

Whenever we were anywhere more crowded than Marbhaven that is. Marbhaven, Oregon: home to a mere 2,300 souls, a harbor that smells perpetually of fish, and cliffsides that spiral up and up and up, gatekeeping the only pathway out.

Marbhaven is home to one of everything and nothing more. One grocery store, one restaurant, one candy shop.

I remember the chewy saltwater taffy that Mom let me try free samples of when I was a kid, only the free samples, never a whole bag. The stories she told me to distract me from heavy rain pounding against our roof. The sound of the waves calmed everything around us.

I hear them now, the waves. They don't calm me today.

Today, as I sit on the bench where I last saw her, the waves are ominous whispers. It's as though I'm being watched, listened to, talked about.

"Go to the place where we last saw each other, Jade, and we'll find each other." Mom said this every time we entered a crowded place, the occasional mall, a museum, anywhere.

Well, I'm here. Where is she?

The last few days are a blur of colors and streetlamps, crashing waves and headlights. First, Mom called on Sunday to tell me that Father Iraci had stood in for Father Rodriguez's usual service.

I wasn't that bothered, figured he was sick. When Mom went to check on him, he wasn't home, or anywhere. Then three days later, my little sisters called in a panic because Mom hadn't come home from her job as a scientist three towns over.

My eyes are fixed on the waves, but my thoughts are elsewhere. A steady ticking has taken residence in my head. Ticking as the hours wear on. Ticking until, statistically, Mom is most likely never coming home. Thirteen more hours and that's it. We'll have hit seventy-two hours, and the police will start searching for her body instead of her.

I'm stuck in purgatory, perpetually waiting.

Waiting for Mom, waiting for my sisters, Raina and Anisha, to come home from school. They'd be home if I hadn't had to speak to the most unhelpful person in the world. Officer Meyer, our only police officer, offered no hope at all. Too much for a couple of ten-year-olds.

"Jade!" Deanna calls from the house. Her black hair is pulled back into complicated braids that only Deanna can manage. A light blue sweater clings to her as she beckons me, pale skin red from the wind chill. "School bus!"

My heart pounds in my chest and tangled black hair gets caught in my eyelashes. I'm fighting the wind all the way back to the house, through the still messy kitchen, and out into the front yard.

I reach Raina just in time to catch her in a whirl of blond curls. She wraps her arms around me fiercely.

I didn't realize how worried I was that they wouldn't make it home.

Anisha's dark blue hair hangs limply around her face. She's subdued coming down the school bus steps. Her eyes are empty, they have been since I came back from college.

She walks straight past my outstretched arm.

I wish I could say I was holding out hope, but when someone like Vanessa Zaveri goes missing? You have to wonder who was confident enough to mess with her, and then you doubt that she's safe.

"How was school?" I fight to keep my voice even. Anisha snorts derisively and walks past me. Raina smiles weakly and tries to reassure me that her day was good, but I know it was a stupid question, anyway.

They toss their backpacks down in the entryway and collapse on the couch. Deanna shoves two steaming mugs of cocoa into their hands and busies herself cleaning the kitchen.

She's dropped everything and called out of work for the past two days for us. All the Cherishés have. I've never been more thankful to have her as a friend, but I wish she didn't have to do this. She's still saving up for college. I'm hoping Mr. Jones at the diner doesn't fire her for the amount of work she's missed. I stand to help her, but she practically pushes me back down onto the sofa.

"Jade Zaveri, you sit back down and wait for your hot cocoa." Her tone is so mom-like that I obey her out of reflex. We don't sit in silence for long.

"Mom?" Raina asks expectantly.

I shake my head solemnly. "Not yet, kid." She usually hates it when I call her kid, something that would typically goad me into doing it more. We've all let a lot slide lately.

"What happened to her?" she asks, more insistently.

I bite my lip, trying to figure out what ten-year-olds would understand. Maybe understand isn't the right word. I'm more concerned with what won't shatter them. "We know she left work but didn't make it home. Something happened to her in the middle."

"Do you think someone killed her?" Raina's voice is high-pitched but controlled. More controlled than Anisha, obsessively biting her nails.

"I"—my voice stops. The air simply refuses to come. I force myself to take in air, then let it out. Father Rodriguez, then Mom.

Why?—"I don't believe that. No matter what anyone says."

Anisha takes a sip of her cocoa. Her dark blue curls spill over her shoulder on one side. "What makes you so sure?" Derisive, but hopeful. She doesn't want to get her hopes up, but God, don't we all want to get our hopes up?

"I know that you guys have only known her as a pretty normal mom, but when I was a kid? Things were different. Mom's tough."

A memory of Mom on this very couch plays in my mind. She's reckoning with a pile of bills and staring a social worker down with a fiery blue-eyed glare.

"She's gonna be okay." I turn back to them. "We have to have faith that she'll be okay."

They nod slowly, sipping their cocoa. I hand them the TV remote and retreat to the kitchen. I know how to play with them, clean up some scrapes, and occasionally discuss the fifth-grade drama. I'm not equipped for this.

"Deanna?" I whisper. She pauses her feverish scrubbing of the wooden counters. "Your dad. He didn't happen to see Mom before she went missing, did he?"

"No." Deanna makes to wipe her hands off on her sweater and reconsiders, using the kitchen towel instead. "Why would he?"

"Oh c'mon!" I scoff. "You've seen them flirt. At church?"

Deanna smirks reluctantly. "I have. But he didn't see her." Her brow furrows. "Like you said, Jade"—she clasps my hand in hers—"we have to have faith."

I nod, my lips tightening in an effort to hold back the tears that are threatening to spill over. Not in front of Deanna. She's doing enough already.

"That's the same thing you've been wearing for the past two days, isn't it?" Deanna's grey-eyed gaze passes over me. "I remember you arriving in that."

"I . . . yeah," I sigh.

"Go upstairs and get changed. I've got it down here."

"Are you sure?" She waves me off insistently. I make my way through the living room and up the stairs. They creak.

Usually, I know the path that doesn't make noise up and down the stairs, but I'm too distracted.

My room is in the corner farthest away from the stairs. Mom's is the closest. The entire reason I know how to get down the stairs without making noise.

I've only been back for a few days, but my room is already messy. It certainly doesn't help that I threw some stuff around after stupid Officer Meyer asked me if my dad could have had anything to do with this.

I told her that I'd never met the man, and he hadn't spoken to Mom since shortly after I was born. She made quite the show of explaining that this happened with men like my dad. It wasn't hard to read between the lines.

Mom is white. I'm not. I have a good idea what my dad must have looked like.

My hand forms a fist around the hoodie I've chosen from my closet. It's a light green that brings out my bright green eyes. Mom gave it to me on my fifth birthday, telling me that it used to be my dad's, and she wanted me to have it. I run my fingers along the soft inside of the hoodie, remembering how it used to swallow me up to wear it.

I throw it on along with a pair of thrifted jeans that I let Deanna embroider with leaves and blueberries back in high school, then drag a brush mercilessly through my wind-tangled black hair. It's down to my waist now, and every day that the wind gets to it, I want to chop it off.

I make my way to the bathroom, hoping to wash my face and be somewhat presentable for the rest of the day. I'm tired of feeling dirty and sad already. I want to get rid of one of them. Plus, Deanna's older brother takes over tonight.

Which is nice of him. Out of that whole family, Aaron's the best cook. If I can stomach eating tonight, I know I'll eat well.

I meet my own eyes in the mirror, trying to steel myself to go back downstairs. An outcropping of zits is forming on my chin, but I can't bring myself to care. My feet drag the rest of my body downstairs and into the kitchen to help Deanna. Instead, I end up asking her to do my hair.

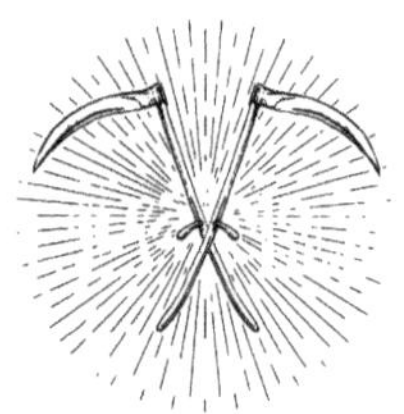

My hair is pulled up into jet black knots and braids, wrapping forever around the crown of my head. Deanna spared no effort. I hardly ever let her do my hair and it's much longer than hers. I'm glad, if only for the brief distraction it gave Raina and Anisha when Deanna tried to show them how to do a rope braid. Raina's hair is now pulled into knots all about her head.

"To bring out the curls tomorrow morning," Deanna said.

Anisha's blue hair is pulled back into what Deanna called warrior braids.

Deanna's gone now. The house is loudly empty without a fourth. The clock continues to tick by.

Nine hours. Where is she?

Anisha is twisting her hair in worry, biting her lip, and staring at the door. Raina is buried deep in her homework, but she hasn't moved past problem one. I should be doing my own homework, but I can't bring myself to do it. Not when I think—I know that I'll have to drop out soon.

There's a knock at the door, gentle but firm. "Upstairs!" I hiss.

"Go."

They drop their things without a word and scurry up the stairs. What if they've come back? What if Father Rodriguez and Mom weren't enough? I have to bend down to properly see through the peephole.

A pale man in his early twenties with flouncy black waves holds three bags of groceries in his hands. I open the door hurriedly, but the metal latch stops it after only a few inches. My face burns.

"Hold on," I mutter, closing the door, undoing the latch, and opening it again. "Aaron! It's good to see you again."

"You too, Jade." He wraps his free arm around my shoulder.

I shut the door behind him and pull the latch again. "Raina! Anisha! You can come back down." Footsteps thunder down the creaky steps. They clearly haven't had cause to learn the path of least resistance yet.

"Aaron!" they shout, barreling into him. They've been hugging everyone more frequently and harder lately. The danger certainly hasn't slipped past them.

One of the grocery bags falls to the floor as Aaron attempts to hug them both back. "Let go, guys." I laugh shortly and pick up the fallen groceries. Aaron follows me into the kitchen, and we unpack the meal for tonight.

"How was college?" Aaron asks carefully.

Aaron was years ahead of me in school, going off to college when I was only a freshman in high school. He babysat the girls on a number of occasions when I was busy, and I'll always be grateful that because of him I was allowed one after-school club.

"It was alright." I shrug.

"You were going for . . ." He waits for me to answer, turning on the stove. At least he's accepted the past tense when it comes to my schooling. It's a lot easier than Deanna's persistent hopefulness.

"Math." I toss him a freshly washed tomato. "Calculus was a lot of fun, actually."

"You can always learn online, Jade." He chops with a practiced finesse that I can't help but stare at. "I know it's going to be tough with the girls, but we're here for you. You don't have to give up yet."

"I hardly had time for myself in high school." I laugh humorlessly, burying down the seed of resentment that is building in me. I'm happy to do this instead of them going into foster care. I won't let it happen, not after what Mom went through before Nani Anisha adopted her. "Speaking of, do you know anywhere that's hiring?"

"Flower shop down the street." Aaron points his knife in the direction of the front door. "Remember Amy? I set up prom with her for you guys?" I nod. "She's a great boss. She'd treat you right, give you the time off you need. It's good pay."

"Thank you."

"Maybe I'll send you a math problem a day from my grad school textbooks, huh? Keep those skills sharp?" I roll my eyes. "Jade, I'm serious. If there's one thing I learned from Dad when everything happened with Mom, it's not to forget to take time for yourself."

I nod somberly. Raina and Anisha weren't even born yet when Lauren Cherishé died. It wasn't exactly a surprise with her in and out of the hospital for months, but the blow was devastating. Especially the realization that we would never again taste her marionberry pie or—or—

Sobs issue from my mouth completely unbidden. My elbows catch me on the counter as my legs give out underneath me. I hear the clatter of the pot being dropped onto the stove and then Aaron's arms are around me.

Before I can compose myself, small footsteps pound into the kitchen. Through my bleary eyes, I see Anisha's bright blue braids. "I'm sorry. I'm sorry——" I say, gasping for air.

Aaron relinquishes me and turns to them for a split second. "Can you do me a favor and run a bath upstairs? I think it would really help her."

I hiccup in confusion, trying to shrink away from their little faces. They do as he says, the stairs creaking on their way up.

"That should keep them occupied for a while," he mutters. "Come here." I bury my face in his neck, shaking uncontrollably. "Hey. Hey. I know, Jade. Believe me, I know how this feels."

"How did you do it? God, I can't do this."

"Yes, you can." He smooths my hair back. "And my situation was completely different. I was a kid. I barely knew what was going on and we still had Dad to take care of us."

I'm all alone.

"You're not alone," he whispers, somehow reading my thoughts. "I'll be here to cook dinner every night until the end of time if you need me to. Deanna will never stop helping you clean up when you get behind. Dad won't hesitate to clear out our spare bedroom for the three of you."

I sniffle. My eyes finally run dry. "God, I'm sorry," I whisper. "I don't usually do this." I gesture to my face.

"It's alright."

I make to back away from him, but my eyes land on something black on his neck. I reach out to brush it away, but it doesn't rub off. I'd say it was a tattoo, but there's something off about it. Maybe an art style I'm not used to. Two crossed scythes rest below his ear. "How long have you had this?"

"Oh!" He jumps back in surprise. "Sorry. I forgot about that for a second. It's . . . new . . . ish. I've only had it for like a year and a half." He rubs it gingerly. "It's a band thing."

"What band?"

He turns back to the stove. "The Scythes? Metal band, pretty obscure."

I sniffle again, wiping my eyes. "What are you making?"

"Mulligatawny soup. Deanna said you loved when your grandma made it, right?" I nod, my eyes brimming with tears again. I wipe them away with the sleeve of my hoodie. "I'm sure I don't do your grandma justice, but I'm willing to try."

He turns, leaving the pot to simmer. His hair is the tiniest bit frizzy from the steam. It's kind of cute.

The water upstairs stops running. "How about you go upstairs and have that bath? I think it would make them happy."

"I know what you guys are doing. Trying to distract them." My voice cracks. "I don't know how to have the—the emotions talk with them."

"You three are going through the exact same thing. You already know what to do. Trust yourself."

I lower my head in acknowledgment and make my way upstairs to take that bath. Piping hot water does sound nice. Hopefully, I can make it through the silence without thinking too hard about the ticking clock. Eight hours.

I snort at the amount of their own bubble bath mixture that Anisha and Raina threw into the tub. They stopped the water just shy of the overflow point. I roll up my sleeves and drain some of the water, nearly burning my hand in the process.

The perfect temperature.

By the time I dry off and come downstairs, the heavenly smell of mulligatawny soup fills the kitchen. Simmering chicken, curry, and thyme. There's also some form of baked good. It smells like a Sunday, when Mom sets the entire afternoon aside to cook a special dinner for Father Rodriguez and the Cherishés to come over.

The soup warms my entire soul right down to the bones. I can tell it has the same effect on Raina and Anisha. Their shoulders drop down from their chins. When Aaron pulls out whatever is in the oven, they jump up in excitement.

"Look, Jade!" Raina says excitedly.

"It's a starfish!" Anisha finishes.

Sure enough, Aaron brings an entire pie to the table, and the crust on the top is a misshapen, but adorable, starfish. "Oh wow!" I marvel at it. "Mom would love it!"

"You think so?" Raina asks.

"Yes. She'd be very proud." I carefully stay in the present tense.

"Take a picture for when she comes back," Anisha says, sticking her chin out. She's daring me, daring me to say that Mom isn't coming home. Daring me to break her heart with the probable truth. Her eyes swim with a doubt and fear that her usual dares don't have.

I take out my phone and snap a picture of the pie.

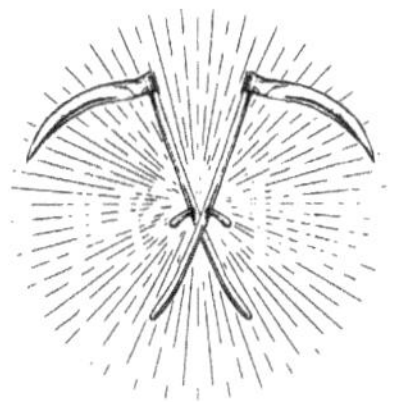

I'm lying in bed as the morning sunrise leaks through my blinds. The old clock by my bedside ticks.

Tick. Tick. Tick.

Seventy-two hours. She's gone.

Chapter Two

It's Church Day, and my first day of work. Mom has been missing for almost a week now. We go to church every Sunday, 8 a.m., on the dot. I only broke tradition twice while at college for finals. We usually meet the Cherishés there, but today they're escorting us over.

Mom always treats—treated it as an event.

We all had to dress up, but she never made Anisha wear a dress. Anisha prefers vests and colorful ties. I was all too happy to help her pick one out this morning, a purple to pink gradient tie with her hair in those warrior braids again.

As for me, all my church clothes are still at college. I didn't think to bring them back with me. I didn't think to bring much of anything.

I'll have to send in an official withdrawal soon and clear out my dorm. I'm delaying the inevitable and I know it.

Mom's dresses wait expectantly in the closet. I stare at them, my heart pounding. "You're only borrowing," I whisper to myself. I'm not and I know it. This whole house and everything in it, it's mine now. Not hers anymore.

"Knock knock?" Deanna's voice comes from the doorway.

"Hey!" I feign a smile.

"You gonna pick a dress out? You don't have to, but you'd better hurry either way. We're gonna be late." Her tone isn't stern. In fact, it's all too gentle.

"I can't choose," I whisper.

"Your mom wouldn't blame you if you didn't go." She plops down onto Mom's bed, beckoning me away from the closet. Her nails are painted periwinkle to match her gauzy dress.

"She could," I mutter.

"She wouldn't. She's not"—Deanna takes on an entirely different posture, straight-backed and pompous, and adopts that high-pitched rickety voice we know all too well—"Mrs. Tabitha Anne Gibson, dear. Goodness gracious, I cannot believe you three grew up without a man in the house. It's no wonder you turned out this way, Jade Ayla dear! Off to college and partying, I'm sure! You must redirect yourself to the ways of the Lord."

I snicker against my will, adopting the same voice. "Out of wedlock! All three of you? Goodness gracious, it's no wonder Father Rodriguez took pity on you. And poor dear Deanna, you'll find a husband soon, I'm sure of it!"

Deanna cackles mercilessly. "Should've worn a rainbow dress the Sunday after that."

"Rainbow? What a lovely dress on you!" I continue in the voice, relishing the joy of our shared laughter. "It's a shame those gays have ruined it, isn't it, Deanna dear?" Deanna snorts. "What did you say?" I wrap my hand around her shoulder. "Lesbian? I was sure those were made up. Like Unicorns or women who don't want children."

Her laughter rings through the room, making Mom's absence all the more apparent. My laughter dies in my throat.

Deanna notices, her laughter dying too. I straighten up. "Dress. Help me pick one."

She goes to the closet, scanning the rack of dresses. All of Mom's day-to-day clothes are folded in the dresser. "This one." Deanna plucks a cream dress printed with pink and peach roses from the closet. "It's calf length on your mom, so it should be about knee length on you."

"Perfect." The dress is not made for me. I'm borrowing it. "I'll be down soon."

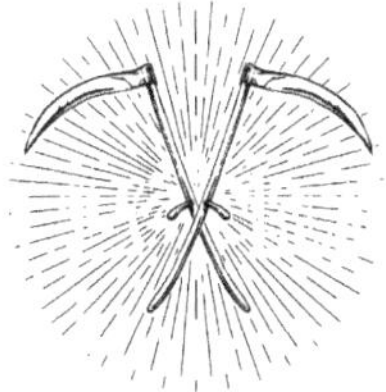

Raina and Anisha are in the backseat of Carl's car. Deanna occupies the passenger seat while Aaron and I sit in the truck bed watching the early morning fog envelop the trees. The rain stopped around sunrise. I fell asleep to it last night. Sometimes I'm worried that the roof will cave in on my room, but not last night. Last night it was soft, relaxing. So repetitive I could forget.

Now it's gone.

We pull up to the white wooden building, its paint worn down by the wind. They built it at the top of this cliff a century or two ago when Marbhaven was first settled. No one would ever dare to move it. Even with all the small children running around, no one has constructed a fence.

Carl Cherishé puts the car into reverse and backs into a parking spot, a skill I think I'll envy until the end of time. Aaron and I clamber out and join the rest.

Carl turns to Deanna and Aaron, with a look in his eye that I can't quite decipher. "We clear on the plan?"

"Crystal." Deanna nods.

"Got it," Aaron mutters, practically launching himself forwards.

"What plan?" I follow, waiting for a response that doesn't come.

My heart beats loudly in my ears as we enter the church.

Everyone is staring at me. Prying eyes prickle against the back of my neck. Women shoot pitiful glances towards Raina and Anisha, children they now consider mine. If we can get into the chapel quickly, we'll hopefully avoid most of the questions and condolences.

A woman walks towards us, eyes soft and pitying. I brace myself.

As she opens her mouth to speak, Aaron shoots her a glare that could kill and pushes us ahead of him. I turn just in time to see her back away in shame.

"Gibson," Carl mutters out of the corner of his mouth. A middle-aged woman with a pension for wide brimmed and flower adorned hats approaches us. Today, she wears a peach-colored one with a matching knit dress. Deanna practically dives out of formation towards her before she can get a word out.

"Mrs. Gibson, I was hoping I could discuss something with you."

Anisha snorts hard. "Anisha," I mutter, trying to contain my own amusement. "That's not polite." My voice cracks. Raina tries to keep her own mischievous smirk under control. "Quiet, kid." I poke her shoulder as we dip our fingers in the holy water.

"Alright, adult." Raina bites her grin down.

We make it into seats in the corner of the chapel without any more issues. The ceiling is adorned with fading gold leaf and chipped blue paint. I inhale the familiar scent of our church and smile. Old wood and incense. All is right with the world. Mom could be right outside the chapel in the lady's room. Calm washes over me for the first time all week as the crowd shuffles into their seats.

The chatter is more subdued than usual. Two people are missing since the last service. I can't blame them. This is Father Rodriguez's usual service.

All is not right with the world.

Father Iraci steps out wearing a green and gold robe. His

wrinkled skin is even paler than usual, and his eyes are sunken. He clearly hasn't been sleeping.

"Welcome." His voice echoes bleakly through the congregation, not nearly as stern as usual. "It has been quite the week, has it not?" Muttered agreement greets his words. "We come together this day for comfort and companionship under the eyes of the Lord."

"Amen," a few whisper, but most remain silent.

"I'd like all of you to join me in a prayer for the Zaveri family." I freeze, my heart hammering wildly as the entire congregation turns towards us. Anisha and Raina sink further into their seats, trying to become invisible. My face burns.

Father Iraci lowers his head as does the rest of the congregation. Raina, Anisha, and the Cherishés do the same. I can't make myself move, instead I fixate on the crucifix directly in my line of sight.

Why did they have to give Him so many abs? I wonder. I can practically hear Mom telling me to pay attention, but I don't want to. I don't want to hear the words he is saying. I don't want to know if Father Iraci believes Mom is alive or not. I don't want to know.

The crown of thorns is lodged deep into His skull. Much deeper than the church near my college. Stone blood trickles down the bridge of His nose. It was once painted red, I think. I can't tell.

Eyes are on me again, and they know that I haven't lowered my head. My breath catches as the entire congregation whispers, "Amen," at me.

I can't sit here anymore. I make a careful and quiet exit out of a side door and into the lady's room.

Mom is gone. She's not coming back. Not a single person knows who took her, from where, or to where. All we have to do now is wait for a body to show up and then for me to identify it.

I twist a lock of my hair, examining it in the mirror. I could cut it. Deanna might even do it if I let her braid it one last time. The door squeaks open. I freeze.

I recognize the peach-colored hat, and my heart sinks down to my stomach. "Jade Zaveri! Just the girl I was looking for." Her high-pitched rickety voice grates at my bones. "I wanted to say how sorry I am about your mother."

"That's very kind of you, Mrs. Gibson." I detach all emotion from my voice.

"To just up and leave like that? I can't imagine doing that to my babies."

My brain grinds to a halt. "Excuse me?"

"Oh, I just hate to see two young girls alone without a mother! And to leave a girl of only nineteen to do her job. But the role suits you quite well! I can tell you'll make a great mother."

My teeth gnash together, but I steady myself before speaking. "Still just their sister, Mrs. Gibson. Now, what you said, about my mom leaving? She didn't—"

"Oh, I know everyone is treating it like a missing persons case, but really, your mother. She came to church every Sunday like any good woman should, but her history with men. It was bound to happen eventually Jade Ayla dear, it's not your doing."

My blood boils. This emotion I know what to do with. "I don't think I'm hearing you correctly Mrs. Gibson." My voice is careful and measured. "Are you trying to imply that my mom, who is missing, isn't missing? She just left us?"

"Well, of course you shouldn't blame yourself dear! But every Sunday with three children outside of marriage? She had something to atone for. It's a terrible thing for her to do to you three of course. Bound to only hurt you further than growing up without a father. Tell me, have you been—"

"You know, you're being really rude, Tabby." My arms are crossed so tightly I don't know if I'll be able to uncross them.

"Tabby?" Her affronted gaze only fuels me.

"Actually, you're rude most of the time. But today, of all days, you have to yet again slut-shame my mother, as you have countless times before, to my face."

She splutters for words, growing red in the face.

"And not only that, you are using your incorrect judgment as always, to assume the worst, again, about my mother. And here we are in a bathroom, that I suspect you followed me into, five days after my mom went missing, Tabby! She didn't leave. She's a dutiful and caring mother. Kind of badass, considering."

Gibson opens her mouth in shock at my curse word.

I speak before she gets the chance to chastise me. "She could have left at any time, like my dad, but she stayed. Because she loves me. She loves her daughters Tabby. We aren't trophies to her, symbols of her womanhood. We aren't here to give her grandchildren. She would *never* leave us, but by God I would not blame your children for leaving you."

I leave her trembling in rage next to the sink and storm past her, out of the bathroom, and back into my seat next to Deanna. "Are you alright?" she whispers.

I smirk triumphantly. "Never better."

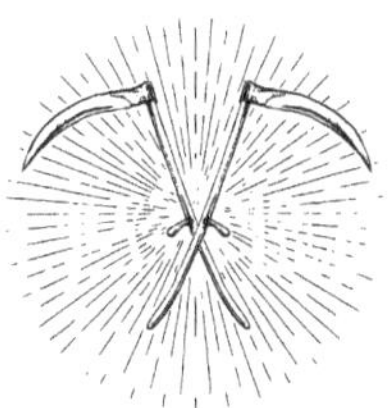

We hurry out of church. I need to get to my new job on time. They drop me off at home and take Raina and Anisha out for something sweet. Maybe ice cream, but considering the temperature, probably donuts. Mom always takes us out for something sweet on Sundays. "A treat for getting your butts up early!" she always says . . . said.

I sit in the front seat of our car trying to make myself turn the key. It smells in here, it always has. Some strange mixture of cigarette smoke and salty air. This was Dad's old car.

We're going to need money soon. I can't take anything out of Mom's bank account. The police are watching it. If it gets used anywhere, they'll have a lead. On the bright side we don't need to pay rent thanks to Father Rodriguez buying our house out from under the landlord.

I was seven years old when we were facing eviction. Mom worked three minimum wage jobs at once, getting through college online. It wasn't enough.

Father Rodriguez saved us. Now he's gone too.

I sigh heavily and slam my head back into the headrest. I let out one long drawn-out curse word in a low gravelly voice.

A sharp rap on the window. I straighten up, staring straight into the face of Aaron Cherishé, and roll down the window. "Did I forget something in the car?"

"Nah." He shakes his head. "Figured with all the missing family members maybe you shouldn't go into work alone is all."

"Oh." Father Rodriguez is the closest thing I've ever had to a father, and now my mom. What if I'm next? "How will you get back though?"

"They're going into town too." He jerks his thumb back at Carl's truck. "Do you want me to drive?" I shake my head. I need to do this. Me. I need to get it together. "Shotgun it is!"

The rain picks up again as we get near the bridge. Aaron turned the radio on, but they've only been playing advertisements the whole drive over.

"So, I saw that Mrs. Tabitha Anne Gibson left for the bathroom the same time that you did during mass?" His voice sounds teasing, but there is a hint of concern that betrays him.

"Oh yeah. We had a lovely chat in the lady's room." I grit my teeth. "She's under the impression that Mom left."

Aaron's mouth drops open in shock. "She thinks what?"

"Thinks Mom just up and left us. Isn't missing at all." I pause. "Isn't missing us at all either."

"That bitch!" Aaron shouts.

We turn down an empty side road. The rain gets worse. I turn the wipers up to full speed, squinting ahead. "Come on. Give me a break," I mutter to the weather itself. Turning my attention back to Aaron, I say, "Yeah. I told her off though."

"Oh boy. *You* told her off? I'll bet she's crying in her attic as we speak."

I snort, peering through the rain drops. "Might have told her that I wouldn't blame her kids for leaving her?"

He roars with laughter. "I think her youngest is graduating this year, right?"

"Yeah. Mary's a year behind me and trust me when I say that she is out of there." I bite my lip. I can hardly see.

"Oh, I'll bet. Hasn't she got a secret—Jade, look out!"

I slam on the brakes before I have time to think. We jerk forwards in our seats.

We've stopped mere inches away from hitting someone. Peering through the windshield, I can just make out the figure of a woman cloaked in red standing in the middle of the street. She's holding something that glints. The heat of her glare burns through the windshield.

I open the car door, rain soaking my hair instantly. "Sorry!" I shout. "Didn't see you there. Are you hurt?"

She's wearing a red hooded cloak and is still glaring, but not at me. Her gaze is fixated on the windshield. The shiny something that she's holding . . .

I stumble backwards, my eyes landing on the curved metal blade at the end. A scythe.

She breaks into a run in the opposite direction. I scramble back into the car, locking the doors. By the time I look up to hit the accelerator, she's gone. Water pools around me.

"What was that?" I turn to Aaron. His eyes are wide and shell-shocked. "You saw that too, right? She was carrying a—"

"A scythe," he finishes for me. His shaking hand brushes against the tattoo behind his ear.

Chapter Three

It smells like a Sunday again. Meat is braising and soup is simmering.

"I'm telling you," I hiss. "You have to go to the police." Aaron shakes his head fervently. "What if this has something to do with Mom?" Nothing. "Or Father Rodriguez?" He doubles over the oven, stirring the soup. My voice turns softer. "She was glaring at you, wasn't she?"

"Yes," Aaron whispers over the sizzling beef. "And I don't know why."

"Why aren't you going to the police, Aaron? They'll listen to you." Not me apparently.

My blood boils thinking back on my most recent interaction with Officer Meyer. I asked what evidence they'd found. She told me to be patient. These things take time.

Yeah. Sure. If she's even looking.

"Who in their right mind is going to believe that there was someone holding a scythe and staring at me in the middle of the road?"

"Will you at least tell your dad?" I grab his hand, forcing him to turn towards me.

"Jade, drop it."

"Aaron, seriously, why not? What's going on?"

"You wouldn't understand it's——"

Deanna floats into the kitchen. We freeze. Aaron and I are

practically nose to nose and holding hands. Heat spreads across my face.

"What's . . . going on?" Her eyes flit between us. "Are you two . . ."

"No," I choke out, dropping Aaron's hand. His face burns red, and he turns back to the stove.

"Jade, could I have a minute alone with my brother?" I nod, ducking out of the kitchen.

Carl is in the living room with Raina and Anisha, turning a rosary over and over in his hand. Raina and Anisha are reading their chapter books for school. It's due tomorrow, but no teacher is going to fail them, anyway. I'm glad for something to keep their minds occupied.

I sit on the floor in front of the couch, pretending to be enraptured by the prayer framed on the wall. Deanna embroidered it when we were in high school, and Mom was all too happy to hang it up where everyone could see.

"The rain came down, the streams rose, and the winds blew and beat against that house; yet it did not fall, because it had its foundation on the rock."-Matthew 7:25

"I know you like her, Aaron, but now is not the time! She's vulnerable," Deanna hisses. To her credit, her voice is barely audible, but no one else is talking.

"That isn't what was going on." His voice is low and agitated. "And of course, I know she's vulnerable. I would never."

"Oh. Never?" she scoffs. "You mean you'd never decide to drive with her to work completely unprompted?"

"That isn't—Deanna. I'm not—"

"Something happened on that drive. You two have been whispering all night."

"Yes. Something happened on that drive, but it's not what you think. I promise."

Deanna's skepticism seeps out into the living room. "I'm not saying that you can't ever date her. I can't tell either of you what to do. But if you guys start dating now, she will regret it. You know she will."

Deanna can't be serious. One car ride and a moment of holding his hand and she thinks we're going to date?

I'd think she'd be mad at me. Aaron deserves someone who's ready to settle down. All he's ever wanted is that white picket fence life. I'm the one who snuck out to see people in the dead of night. Sometimes different people in the same week. Mom pretended she didn't know, but she left things in my room, nonetheless.

I catch Carl's eye. He smiles at me sadly, as though he's read my thoughts.

With Mom and Carl being an item, I really, *really* couldn't. God no. I'm being ridiculous. This is ridiculous. Deanna's like my sister, Aaron, not quite as close as that. But still. No.

No. Absolutely not. Deanna is reading into things.

Aaron stands in the doorway and clears his throat. "Dinner's ready."

The whole dinner happens under a blanket of awkward silence. Everyone heard Deanna. Everyone. On the other hand, the beef and vegetable soup warms me down to my bones. "Soup is delicious, Aaron. Thank you." He nods, running his hand over his tattoo again. "Something did happen on the drive," I blurt out.

"Jade," Aaron whispers nervously. "Don't."

"Oh my God, I knew it!" Deanna slams her spoon down. "What was it?"

"Please," he whispers, blue eyes boring into mine.

"Did you kiss?" Raina perks up.

Aaron opens his mouth to speak but is interrupted by Anisha. "The little boy and girl in our book just kissed."

"Alright. Alright. Everyone, quiet." Carl's voice is calm and commanding. "Let Jade speak."

I make eye contact with Aaron, and oh God, the puppy dog eyes.

He isn't intentionally doing it, but Deanna does it too. Bit of a family trait. Luckily, I'm immune. "Nothing." Okay, maybe not exactly immune.

"Boo!" Anisha shouts. "Tell us!"

"You're the one who brought it up!" Raina says.

I shoot an apologetic glance in Aaron's direction. "What was it?" Deanna tosses her hair over her shoulder, staring me down. Her grey eyes pierce my soul.

"Just that——" I shovel soup into my mouth to buy myself some time.

"I kissed her on the cheek, okay?" Aaron shouts above the noise. "She stopped at work, I kissed her on the cheek, we went our separate ways. That's it."

Carl narrows his warm brown eyes at us. "That isn't much to tell."

"It was just really awkward, Dad." Again, Aaron runs his hand over the tattoo, a nervous habit he's developed since I last saw him. "Anyway, let's drop it."

I meet his eyes across the table. We need to tell someone. The way she glared through that hood was . . . unnerving.

"How was work?" Carl turns to me.

"Good," I mutter into my soup. "Not much to report. Pretty empty with all the rain. One guy apparently comes in for a bouquet every Sunday though."

"Mr. Clarke, right?" Aaron's head perks up. I nod. "You'll see those flowers in the graveyard tomorrow. They're for his wife."

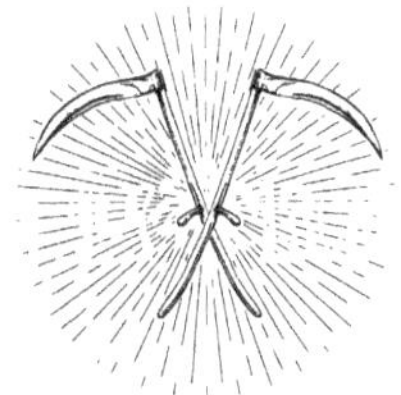

"Any news?" Deanna asks. Two whole weeks Mom's been missing now. We're scrubbing the dishes after a Sunday lunch instead of dinner this week. Deanna has work at the diner tonight.

"No." I sigh. "No one's heard anything about her. No activity on the bank account either."

"I'm sorry," she says, only half-heartedly scrubbing at her plate. "We have to have hope that she'll turn up."

"I know." There's a silence that is only filled by the sounds of scrubbing and plates clattering. "I'm just glad church wasn't as bad today as last week."

"Oh yeah." Deanna snickers. "Mrs. Tabitha Anne Gibson avoided you like the plague today. Lucky."

"She'll be back. Mark my words, she'll be back."

Aaron, Raina, and Anisha break into laughter in the living room. I smile. He's teaching them a card game and they keep accidentally slapping each other instead of the cards. I haven't seen the girls laughing this hard since winter break.

"You're sure it was just a kiss on the cheek last week?" Deanna asks.

"Hmm?" Deanna stands beside me and has one thin black eyebrow raised. "Yes Deanna. That's all." We haven't seen the woman I've been referring to as the Red Reaper since last week, but she certainly hasn't slipped my mind. Why was she staring at Aaron that intensely? And why won't he just report it?

"You're being careful?"

"Of course, I am. I don't have anything going on with your brother. I promise."

"I mean, it's fine if you do. Well, not exactly *fine* fine. It'll be a little weird, but I promise I'll get over it. I mean, you're both family."

"Deanna?" Her mouth clamps shut. "I have no interest in your brother, and I doubt he has any interest in me. Don't worry about it."

"I wouldn't count on that," she mutters.

"Hey Deanna!" Aaron calls. "Can you take over with the girls for a second?" Deanna gives me a knowing look and exits the kitchen. Aaron enters on her heels. "How are you?"

"Fine, I guess." I shrug.

"You wanna go for a walk on the beach? Clear your head?" I wonder if he knows that Mom and I would do that every single day after school before the girls were born.

"But the girls——"

"Deanna's got them handled. Don't worry."

Maybe I can finally convince him to tell someone about the Red Reaper. "Alright." He fidgets with his hands, moving them into his pockets when he catches me watching. "I need to get changed first though, it's chilly."

"Right. Yeah. I'll meet you down there?" I nod. "Hold on." He laughs. "Three guesses what you're gonna wear . . . Is it, drumroll please, your pretty green hoodie?"

"No, it's in the wash." I chuckle, turning towards the stairs. "For once."

I'm back down in the living room minutes later in a pair of ripped light wash jeans and a black and white flannel. I smile, throwing my hair up into a bun to counteract the inevitable wind. "Where are you going?" Deanna raises her eyebrow mischievously.

"Just on a walk with Aaron. I'll be back within the hour."

"Oooooh!" Raina and Anisha giggle.

I roll my eyes, but I can't help smiling at them. "Shut up you two."

"Is he gonna kiss you?" Raina asks.

"And not on the cheek this time?" Anisha crosses her arms.

My face burns. "No! We're just going on a walk."

"Do you even know how to kiss?" Anisha asks.

Deanna and I meet each other's eyes, snickering. "You might not believe it, but I've kissed a lot of people," I say.

"Who?" Raina perks up. "Do we know them?"

"Just some boys at my high school." I shrug. "And some girls."

"Who?" Raina asks again.

I wink at her. "I'm gonna go on that walk now. I'll see you later, okay?" I walk out the back door before they can get another word in.

The sound of the rolling waves beckons me, the promise of sand and peace. The wind cries as it whirls past my ears.

The bench that overlooks the beach is empty. Mom and I would sit here for ages and soak in the sunset. I look out over the afternoon waves. Someone is lying in the sand. I start to smile, but—

A shock of red. The sand below him is red. His hair is soaked in it. Blood. My heart drops into my stomach, fueling my legs into a dead-on sprint down the path towards him.

"AARON!"

Chapter Four

My knees give out as I slide across the sand next to him. There's so much blood, he's covered in it. I search frantically for the source of the bleeding. A faint gurgle comes from his throat.

My gaze travels to his neck in horror. It's been slit open. Blood flows from it in a steady river.

I meet his wide, panicky blue eyes. My hands move of their own accord to cover the wound. "It's gonna be okay, Aaron," I whisper, not really believing it. "HELP!" I shout to the empty beach. "HELP! Someone please!" I don't have my phone. I should have brought my phone. "HELP!"

An imitation of a cough rattles through him. Blood bubbles beneath my fingertips.

"Somebody help, PLEASE!"

No one is coming. My eyes sting as I watch him struggle to cling to life. My hands and clothes are soaked in warm blood, his blood. There's too much of it. He's choking on it.

"Aaron." My voice breaks.

He coughs in that same way again, thrashing beneath me and struggling for air. God, he's suffocating.

He gathers just enough energy to reach up and cup my face in his hand. Weak and shaky fingers brush behind my left ear. His touch burns like a red-hot iron. A choked sob escapes my lips.

His hand falls to the sand with a dull thud. His eyes are empty, but his face—

His face is frozen, wide eyed, and in pain. I watch him desperately, hoping against hope that he'll come back.

"Aaron?" My voice is hoarse and raw. I lay my hand across his chest and raise my gaze to the sky. "Please, God, please." His body remains lifeless and frozen. "Aaron, please." I bury my face into his chest, I don't care about the blood.

The spot where he last touched pulses. Wave after wave of pain and heat engulfs me. The world is hazy, filled with nothing but sand and red and the taste of iron. Tears burn my face.

Someone screams. I jerk up, searching for the next victim. Or the killer.

Aaron is standing right in front of me. Or, at least, I think it's Aaron. He has Aaron's face, his blue eyes, his flouncy black hair.

But there's no slash through his neck. His hair is clean.

I look back down at Aaron's body beneath me, then at this Aaron standing next to me.

The Aaron standing above me clutches at his neck and breathes heavily, eyes darting around wildly. I inspect the body beneath me. Aaron's face, his neck, his blood.

"Is—Please tell me this is some kind of joke." Anger wells inside of me, but God, I hope it is.

"Jade." He locks his eyes onto me. "You have to get out of here. Run." I can barely process his hurried words.

"But—but you're right here. You were right—wait. What? You're right here. I . . . " The world fades in and out around me.

"Jade, you have to run, or she'll get you too. Go!"

"I can't leave you here," I whisper to the hazy sand.

"Go!" he shouts, even more panicked than before. A glimpse of red fabric in the corner of my vision spurs me into action.

I'm not in control of my body. I'm somewhere outside of it. But my feet are sprinting back up the hill, across the grass, towards the house. Wet hair sticks to the side of my face and neck.

"HELP!" I scream as loud as I can. The word rips through me.

The weight of it all sends me to the ground outside of our back door.

Deanna bursts outside, shoving Raina and Anisha behind her. She slams the door shut with them inside when she catches a glimpse of me. Her mouth drops open in shock and her steps falter before she can get to me.

We're both on our knees several feet away from each other. "Why are you covered in blood?" Her words come out flat and monotone. I can't bear to meet her eyes. "Jade." Her hands shake. "Why are you covered in blood?"

I inhale deeply, speaking to my blood-soaked hands. "Call someone. Please."

"What is it?" God, she knows.

"I'm so sorry. I tried. I"—tears are pouring down my cheeks again. Air isn't coming properly—"Deanna I'm so sorry," I choke out.

"Who——"

"Aaron."

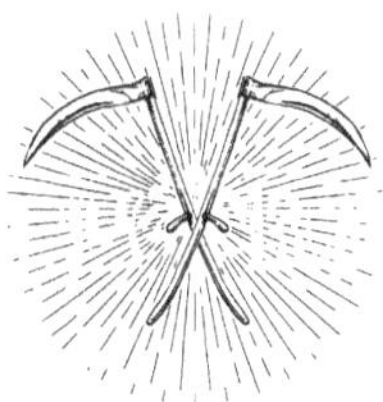

We hear the sirens echoing off the cliff sides not too long after Deanna comes back out. She ordered the girls to stay inside and away from the doors. Her arms shake uncontrollably around my shoulders.

Police pull up to my house for the second time in a month, closely followed by an ambulance. They head straight for me. I shake my head, trying to form words, trying to point them to the beach. Where Aaron is.

"Beach," I choke out. "He's on the beach."

"I got her." One of the EMTs catches me in his arms as Deanna finally releases me, sprinting after the others as they head to the beach.

"No," I whisper hoarsely after her. "No, Deanna, don't." I turn to the EMT frantically. "She can't see that. It's horrible. Stop her." My vision goes dark, and I fall forwards.

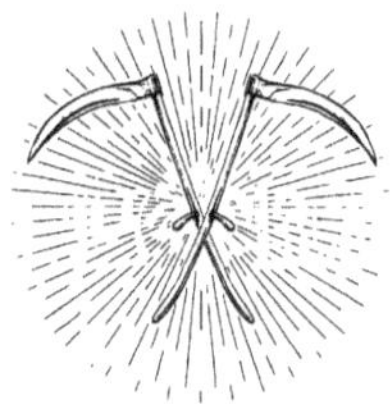

My feet are elevated. I'm lying down. The man is speaking to me in a quiet reassuring voice, but I can't make out his words. My head is light and fuzzy. My eyes dart around from object to object. He lays a blanket over me.

"It's not me. It's him!" I speak in short gasps. "On the beach. Aaron! He's——"

The man shushes me. "We got him. Don't worry." I open my mouth to speak, but he doesn't let me. "Breathe in . . . and out." He has to repeat it several times before I can make my body obey.

My surroundings become clearer. I'm in an ambulance. It's moving. "Where is Deanna?"

"With your sisters," he replies. "They'll join you later."

This man looks familiar. Well, everyone in town looks familiar, but I can't place him. Did he go out with Mom once?

I fixate on a pair of blue eyes above me.

"Aaron," I sigh in relief. He's alive. Aaron smiles weakly at me, still fidgeting with his neck. My head pounds. That spot where he touched me burns again.

I shift my focus to the man who is again telling me to breathe. He doesn't react to Aaron's presence.

"He's not here," I groan.

The man doesn't answer. The pounding in my head reaches a fever pitch and I allow my eyes to close as hot tears pour out of them.

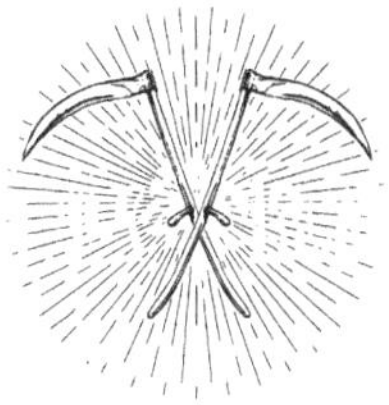

My eyes fly open. I jerk up, flailing away from the hand that tries to restrain me. A strong steady hand pushes me back down again. "Lie back down now, Jade." Carl Cherishé is speaking, but his voice doesn't carry its usual strength.

The walls are covered in cartoons and happy little rainbows. I recognize it. Mom took me to the ER when I had an allergic reaction to peanuts. I remember the swelling, how hard it was to breathe, just as it is now.

I'm in a hospital room for children. A small, bearded leprechaun on the wall is smiling jovially at me, taunting me. I glare at it.

My clothes are gone, replaced with a hospital gown. When did that happen? Who saw me? I vaguely remember someone peeling the blood-soaked clothes off and helping me into this. "Carl?" My voice is barely a hoarse whisper. "Where's—where's Aaron?"

I meet his soft brown eyes. "Jade." Something breaks in them.

I squeeze his hand. God, please let me have had a psychotic break and hallucinated everything. Please. "There was nothing they could do." His lips quiver. "He was dead"—a weak and high-pitched whimper escapes his lips—"before they got there, Jade."

I tighten my lips to stop them from trembling.

"You were so strong today, Jade. There was nothing"—he squeezes my hand—"nothing anyone could have done."

My sobs break loose in a silent scream. "I want my mom." The words fall out of my mouth unbidden.

A knock sounds from the door. I straighten my back, body still shaking, tears dripping down my cheeks. I wipe them away, but they just keep coming.

Officer Meyer, her red hair clipped at her chin and her brown eyes a poor attempt at sympathetic and motherly, enters. "Did she just wake up?"

Carl nods. I force myself to sit up and face her, swallow the tears, determined to be presentable. My voice comes out hollow and numb. "What happened to me?"

"You went into shock, and you passed out. But your vitals are fine now, so I'm told." Her voice is clipped and businesslike. "I know how horrible this must be for you. But I need to know everything you can tell me."

Whoever did this to him will pay. I nod at her.

"If you could step out Mr. Cherishe?" Carl gets up, his movements like molasses. "I'm sorry for your loss Mr. Cherishe," she adds, almost as an afterthought. He nods curtly at her before exiting the room. The door shuts, revealing a cartoon frog with a crown on its head.

I give her an account of how I found him there, how I tried to stop the bleeding, how he was coughing, gurgling, then dead.

"And then——" I pause. And then, Officer Meyer, I most likely hallucinated Aaron talking to me twice. What do you think of my testimony now? "I saw a red cloak, and I ran."

"Do you remember seeing anyone near the scene? Any details?" God, we should have told them about the Red Reaper. Why didn't he tell them about the Red Reaper? I let my head fall into my hands. "Anything?"

"The reason I ran, when I saw the red cloak"—I pick at my hospital gown—"last week I was driving with Aaron in the rain. I stopped right before I hit someone. She was wearing a read cloak and holding a scythe. Like the Grim Reaper." I shut my eyes briefly. "She was staring at Aaron."

"You're sure," she says doubtfully. I nod at her notepad, and she reluctantly writes it down.

"And when I ran there were footsteps. Whoever did this is nearby. Whoever did this—knows where I live. Are my sisters okay?"

"They're here in the hospital, they'll be fine."

"But what about when we go home?"

"We'll have someone waiting outside for the evening. You don't need to worry."

"Officer Meyer, I'm telling you. Someone is after us. First Father Rodriguez, then Mom, now . . . this." Are Mom and Father Rodriguez somewhere in a ditch with their throats slit too?

"Jade Zaveri." She drops her notepad into her lap exasperatedly. "Can you think of anyone who would want to get to you? Your father perhaps?"

I shake my head, shrinking back into myself. "No."

She rolls her eyes and jots something down onto her notepad. My eyes fix on the scrawled word. "Uncooperative."

Chapter Five

I stare at my bedroom ceiling. If I fall asleep, maybe I'll find out this was all a dream. I can start Sunday all over again.

I need to stop being practically catatonic. Deanna and Carl need me.

My hair is a knotted mess, still stuck to me in places. I haven't showered since I got back. Sleep isn't happening anyway.

My feet pad against the carpet as I make my way down the hall and into the bathroom. We've all consolidated into one house now. Carl and Deanna are in Mom's room.

The water rushes from the shower head, crashing against the tub. I'm afraid it will wake everyone up. I don't think anyone else is sleeping, anyway. I duck into the shower, adjusting the shower head up like I always have to. My grey nightshirt sticks to my skin, eliciting a humorless snort from me.

I peel my now soaked nightshirt off before getting back into the shower. The water runs through my hair in rivers that usually relax me. I lather shampoo through my tangled hair and allow my eyes to drift shut.

All I see is Aaron, gasping for air. Aaron, covered in blood. Aaron, miraculously okay and screaming.

I open my eyes and he's standing in front of me, quickly moving a hand to cover his eyes. I yelp, stumbling backwards towards the other end of the shower.

"I didn't see anything!" He turns away. "I'm sorry. I thought you'd be in bed." His clothes aren't soaked, with blood or water. In fact, he appears perfectly fine.

"You're not real. You are not real," I repeat. "I'm still in shock. I'm hallucinating."

"Listen. I'm just gonna go stand out there until you're finished. Again, I am so, *so* sorry. I promise I'm not using death to be a creep." He steps out of the shower. No. He floats through it. I blink several times. What is going on?

It must have been a hallucination. A sleep-deprived, shock-driven hallucination. I scrub every inch of my body until I'm sure there's not a speck of blood on me or in my hair. That'll get rid of him.

Right?

I step out of the shower onto our fluffy bathmat with the yellow ducklings on it. My toes dig into the softness, every inch of my body craving comfort and warmth. I wrap myself in a large fluffy beach towel, allowing my hair to drip onto the floor.

Apprehensively, I open my eyes. He's still there, turned towards the corner with his hands in his pockets. He looks so real. I tip toe towards him, my hand outstretched.

"Are you covered yet Jade?"

I reach out to tap his shoulder. My hand slides through him. "Yes." I cock my head to the side.

He turns around and meets my eyes. I gaze into them in shock, unable to look away.

A flash of metal through the air. I clutch frantically at my throat. There's blood everywhere. Blood is pouring out of my neck. A woman, her face mostly obscured by the red cloak, stands in front of me. She holds her scythe over me, a satisfied smile on her lips. Those eyes, a light amber brown and incredibly striking. The Red Reaper sprints away as I bleed out.

Someone else comes running towards me, screaming, "Aaron!" at the top of her lungs. She puts her hand on my neck. I meet my own terrified eyes, feel the sand and blood washing over me.

Then unbidden, a shriek issues from my mouth, unending and uncontrollable. It rips at my lungs. I'm looking back into Aaron's blue eyes, which are wide and watery before he clenches them shut.

"Shh." He reaches out to grip my shoulders, but they slide right through me. "I'm sorry. Jade. I can explain. Shh."

"Jade!" Carl's voice is outside the door, more panicked than I've ever heard it.

"Jade?" Deanna shouts, banging on the door. "Jade, are you alright?"

I take gulps of air, trying to collect myself. I'm imagining things. "I'm fine!" My voice breaks. "Sorry. I'm just—I'm fine."

The door bursts open and Deanna engulfs me in a hug, quickly joined by Carl. Raina and Anisha's door squeaks open. "Is she okay?" Raina squeaks.

"I'm fine." My voice is hollow as I turn back to Aaron. He stands in the corner of the bathroom, looking at his sister and dad longingly. I blink and he's gone. I'm imagining it. I must be.

They walk me back to my room not too much later, Carl tucks me into bed as though I'm not a nineteen-year-old woman, and I'm fine with that. I can't imagine what he's going through.

Bleakly, I stare at the ceiling. I used to put little bobbles up there when I was a kid: glowing stars and moons, drawings I did. It's empty now.

Everything is empty.

I roll onto my side, facing the window. The distant sound of waves crashing jolts me into a seated position. Will it ever relax me again? I rub vigorously at the last spot where Aaron touched me, trying to remove the sensation of his weak, dying fingers from my memory.

It burns again, like a hot iron. I furrow my brows. My hand pats my nightstand until I find the lamp and flick it on.

Mirror. Mirror. Where is the mirror?

Under the bed. I knew I forgot to bring it back to college. I peer into it, greeted by bleary green eyes and a haggard face. Is my skin duller than normal? Is it showing through everywhere? I've got to get this under control.

Stop. Focus.

I peer past my face to the spot where Aaron last touched me, behind my left ear. I adjust the mirror until I can see it clearly. That's not right. I've never had a birthmark there. I don't have any birthmarks.

I rub the spot again. Maybe it's a blood stain? "OW!" I inspect my hand. Nothing came off on it. I squint at my reflection. "Is that?"

Two crossed black scythes. The same tattoo Aaron had.

"Don't scream this time," Aaron whispers. I jump up, gaping at him. He stares at the ceiling. "And maybe don't look into my eyes either. You don't need to see that again."

"You're not real," I whisper. "You can't be real. You're dead. I saw it, Aaron. You're dead."

The tattoo can't be real either. If I'm seeing him, it stands to reason that I'm hallucinating other things. "Just let me explain, okay?" he whispers. "Why don't you sit back down. I'll explain everything."

"Why do I have your tattoo? No. No. Why am I asking a dead guy questions?"

"Listen—"

"You're not real. There's no logical way that you're real. I'm just freaking out, that's all." I heave a deep breath in and out. "Do you know what would happen if anyone found out I was hallucinating? They'd take Raina and Anisha away!"

"No one is going to take Raina and Anisha away," he whispers. "No one. You haven't even been assigned a social worker yet."

"But—"

"Listen, Jade, please."

"No one else could see you!" My brain hits a wall. "No one. Not your dad, not your sister. They didn't see you. You're. Not. Real." I turn away.

"I am." His voice takes on that same soft quality that Deanna's has. I turn back to face him, hungry for more, another few seconds to pretend I didn't watch him die.

I lower my head and bite down on my lip. I will not cry. Not again. "What's going on Aaron?"

"I'm dead but—"

"But you look so solid. So real. Like I could"—I reach out for his hand. It slides through him yet again—"You're not, you can't be real."

"I'm dead, there is no coming back from that. But there's something you didn't know about me, Jade. It has something to do with that mark. Your mark now." He tilts his head, showing me his neck. His tattoo is gone.

"But how—"

"I was a Reaper."

Chapter Six

My feet carry me away from him as fast as they can. I'm imagining all sorts of things now. He follows me, but I can't look at him. I refuse. I will not. He isn't real. I'm done kidding myself.

"Jade!" he shouts. I can't hear him. I won't hear him. No.

I need to calm myself down. I need to do something else, think about something else.

I push all the living room furniture closer to the walls like I used to. I haven't done this in years. I clear everything off the shelf in the middle of the wall and wrap my hand around it.

First position. I straighten my back and tighten my abs. Arms forwards, deep breath in. Demi plié. 1,2,3,4—

"Jade. Don't ignore—"

I clench my eyes shut. 5, 6, 7, 8. Again. 1, 2, 3—

"Will you please listen to me?"

6, 7, 8. Relevé and back down. Back up onto the tips of my toes.

"Ballet isn't in your toes, it's in your whole body." I don't remember my ballet instructor's name, but I remember her words, her hands guiding my chin up. She told me how to feel each movement rising through my spine as though I was being drawn up with a string.

"Jade."

"I am attached to a string," I whisper to myself. Nothing else outside of that string matters. Third position. I bring my arm out to my side. Keep it rounded.

"Jade, Listen to me."

"I'm attached to a string. I'm attached to a string."

"I'm attached to a string!" he screams. "That string is you!" I stumble, leaning too far forwards. "You're a Reaper, Jade. My Reaper. I can't stay here. It hurts. Looking at my family and they can't see me. And I have to leave them. Do you understand how much that hurts?"

"Do you know how much it hurts to look at you?" I hiss. "You died! Your throat was slit open, and I was thinking that maybe we'd have a moment of peace for a goddamn second, but you died in front of me. Not even yesterday, Aaron."

I meet his eyes, heartbroken, wet, and piercingly blue, and—

A flash of metal through the air. I clutch frantically at my throat. There's blood everywhere. Blood is pouring out of my neck. A woman, her face mostly obscured by a red cloak, stands in front of me. She holds her scythe over me, a satisfied smile on her lips. Those eyes, a light amber brown and incredibly striking. The Red Reaper sprints away as I bleed out.

Someone else comes running towards me, screaming "Aaron!" at the top of her lungs. She puts her hand on my neck. I meet my own terrified eyes, feel the sand and blood washing over me—

My scream dies in my throat. Aaron shuts his eyes. I'm back in my living room, gripping the shelf on the wall for dear life.

"Do you know how much it hurts not to be able to look into your eyes anymore?" His voice is hoarse and low, eyes still shut. "I love your eyes. They're one of my favorite things about you."

I swallow hard. "You have favorite things about me?"

"Yes," he confesses, staring at the wall. "I love your eyes. Deanna isn't the only one that loves your hair. You're determined. You're funny. I love cooking for you."

My lips part in surprise. "How long?"

"Ever since you came home last summer. When we—"

"Fell asleep on the beach after Deanna's birthday party. Right."

I smile. "We were both so drunk."

His smile is pained. "I know that I'm not, that I wasn't, the type of guy that you just date for fun." He shoves his hands in his pockets, staring at the carpet, either out of kindness or nervousness or both.

"You're practically a housewife." I try to smile. My heart aches at the way his bottom lip trembles. "Maybe I could have been." I take a step towards him. How bad could it be to pretend for a moment?

"It wouldn't have been right to ask that of you. Not when you already had to deal with your mom and sisters."

My legs fold beneath me as I practically collapse to the floor. "The Red Reaper killed you." He nods. "Who was she?"

"I have no idea." He sighs heavily, sitting down across from me. "And I don't know why."

"You said you were a Reaper?" My heart thuds.

"Yes." He rakes a hand through his hair.

"Was she also a Reaper?"

"I don't know."

"You were afraid of her."

"Of course I was. You're a Reaper for a year and a half and someone with a scythe stares you down through a car window. How else was I supposed to feel?"

I don't know what to say. What to ask him. Part of me is still screaming that this can't be real. That this makes no sense.

"Jade, I would have marked anyone"—his eyes almost meet mine, but he averts his gaze at the last second—"anyone but you. But you were—"

"Jade?" Deanna calls. Aaron looks longingly at the stairwell. She appears at the bottom of the stairs, her usually tamed hair in knots. She's wearing my pink pajama set and the shorts are quite long on her. "Were you talking to someone?"

I turn to Aaron, his gaze fixed on Deanna. "No. Just myself."

Deanna can't see him. I was stupid to think, even for a moment, that he was real.

She takes in the disarranged living room with empty eyes. "Ballet?" I nod. "Can't sleep?"

"Nope."

Deanna's empty eyes meet mine. Guilt washes over me, threatening to drown me. I should have gone down there with him. I should have made him wait. I knew there was danger. I knew he was hiding something.

"I'm glad that"—she takes a deep breath before continuing—"I'm glad that we teased you so much before you left. Otherwise, we would have—I could have lost you both."

I engulf her in a hug. "I'm sorry Deanna. I'm so sorry." She shakes in my arms, as though she's trying to cry, but simply can't. We stand in the disarray of the living room in thick silence. The air itself is empty without Aaron here.

I close my eyes, determined to forget his face right in front of me.

"He made Mom's marionberry pie almost exactly like she did," she says. I run my fingers through her hair. I'm useless in these situations.

"He did," I whisper back.

"He hated"—she hiccups, trying her best to do the voice—"Mrs. Tabitha Anne G-Gibson almost as much as we do."

"He called her a bitch on the car ride to work."

She laughs weakly. "God, he was so annoying too. He always told Dad whenever we snuck out together."

"Does that mean that Mom knew too?"

"No." She laughs again. "Maybe. I don't know."

"Come on," I mouth, glaring at him over Deanna's shoulder.

He shrugs. "I wanted to make sure she was safe," he says. Deanna doesn't react.

Of course, she doesn't. Because I'm hearing and seeing things.

She breaks free of my arms and backs away, wiping her eyes more out of habit than to get rid of tears. "We should—we should make breakfast. For the girls. Before school."

"They're not going to school today." I hadn't considered it until this moment, but they aren't. I can't put them through that. "I'm gonna call in right now. Breakfast after. I'll make it. You sit."

She sits at the round table without protest.

I dial the school as I put a kettle on to boil. When I turn around, Aaron disappears. One moment he's staring at Deanna, his hand hovering above her shoulder. The next moment, he sighs heavily and is gone. I blink several times, trying to clear my head.

God, I wish Father Rodriguez were here. He'd help me understand.

I'm greeted with a voicemail, telling me to leave a message after the tone. "Hi! This is Jade Zaveri calling for Raina Zaveri and Anisha Zaveri. There's been a family emergency and they won't be coming to school today. This is their . . . " I've heard Mom make this call dozens of times. She always simply says mother. What should I say? What am I to them now? "Guardian calling. Again, Raina and Anisha Zaveri will be missing school today. Thank you."

The kettle whistles, drowning out any doubts I have about that title. Guardian is fine. I pour out two cups of chai for Deanna and myself and set to work on breakfast. Normally, I'd make a bowl of cereal or oatmeal and that would be it. And maybe I should. Either way, a bowl of cereal or a fancy breakfast and Aaron's absence is loud. Too loud.

I set to work on box mix pancakes. A balance between the two. Aaron would never settle for box mix, even on his worst days. His pride wouldn't be able to bear the hit. I work in silence.

Milk instead of water and butter instead of vegetable oil.

Deanna quietly sips her tea. Her gaze is fixed on the window, where, if she looks hard enough, she might see the ocean.

Raina and Anisha are the next people to enter the kitchen. Their eyes are sleepy, and I can tell that they have just woken up. At least they got some sleep. I hope it was peaceful and not overwhelmed by the sound of my screams.

What was that, anyway? My imagination isn't that vivid. From elementary to high school, I've been known to be the math and science girl. History sometimes, but never English. I couldn't ever forget that the characters weren't real. I haven't ever been known to be good at storytelling or being in someone else's shoes. So how in hell did I imagine myself as Aaron in his dying moments? How did I imagine that level of pain, pain that I have never come close to in my life? And most unlikely, how did I imagine myself from the outside?

The pancake batter crackles in the skillet.

What if I didn't imagine it? There's only one way to find out. I brush my fingers over my new mark. It barely stings now. It would be easy to turn around, ask Deanna if it's really there.

And what would I be admitting? That I've been seeing her brother all night and she can't ever again? Too selfish a price to pay for my sanity. No. I'll take the hallucinations. They're bound to calm down at some point.

I pull my hair over my left side, letting it fall over my grey nightshirt and the new mark. The mark of a Reaper . . . I guess.

Pancake after pancake flips over. I serve them as they come.

Carl comes downstairs last. My heart shatters at the emptiness that his presence carries. The air is instantly too thick again. Carl carries a rosary loosely in his grasp as he takes a seat around our table, muttering prayers under his breath.

I could have saved his son. If I had just gone with him.

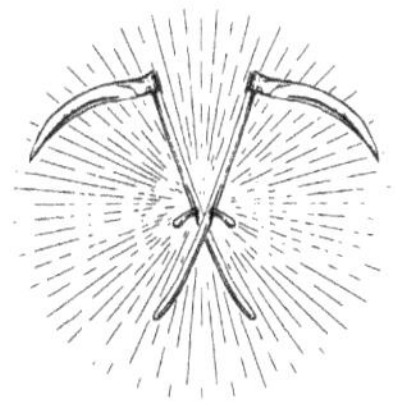

A week later, and I've only seen Aaron twice. Both times he begged me to listen, but I buried myself in whatever I was doing at the time and drowned out his voice.

The living room hasn't been moved back to its normal layout yet. I've been doing so much ballet in there that Raina and Anisha have begged me to teach them the basics.

"Alright. This is first position." I demonstrate. "Heels together, feet turned out." They follow my instructions exactly. "Good. Back straight, Anisha."

"My back is straight!" she says indignantly. Her shoulders are curved forwards towards the floor. I gently grasp them and pull them back in line with the rest of her spine. She pouts.

"Chin up, Raina. Trust your feet. You don't need to watch them." She gazes ahead dutifully at the wall.

The funeral is in an hour and a half. Anything I can do to get their mind off it before we go.

"Alright," I say sometime later. "We need to get dressed."

I'm zipping up one of Mom's black dresses with sheer half-length sleeves and skirt pockets when he appears again. "Today's the funeral, isn't it?" he says. It's all I can do to be silent. "Jade, I'm telling you that I am real. I need you to listen to me."

No. I can't acknowledge this. Deanna at least needs my sanity.

"Jade, please. You're a Reaper. You have to send me on. You. No one else can do it. And if you don't do it soon, I'm going to fade away and I don't know where I'll go."

I choke on the air. "Why didn't you wait for me?" I spin around to face him. "You knew she was here. You knew she was close. Why didn't you wait?"

"Seriously?" He raises an eyebrow. God, exactly like Deanna. "You're upset with me because I got murdered?"

"You didn't go to the police," I whisper in anguish.

"And did they listen to you about the Red Reaper?" I shake my head. He folds his arms. "How is this my fault?"

"It's not, okay? But I don't know if you're real. There's no logical way for you to be real and I have to be mad at you or you're never going to go away."

"This isn't logic." He takes a step towards me. "It's pure madness. It doesn't make sense. But it is real." I don't speak. I don't even know what I would say. "That mark. It's real because it's still there. You can still see it."

I pull my hair aside and find the mark in the mirror. I've checked every morning, and it's still there. Clear as day.

"What does being a Reaper even mean?" I shake my head. "Deanna can't see you. You're not real."

"Deanna can't see me because she isn't a Reaper."

"And I am."

"Now you are."

"Then how come I haven't seen any other dead people coming to me?" I turn to meet his gaze again, but he averts his eyes, carefully fixing them on my forehead.

"Marbhaven is a small town. You're only responsible for people who die within a certain radius of you. No one else has died within that radius yet. Why do you think I decided to do grad school online?"

"Deaths are infrequent here."

"Yes."

"But what even is a Reaper? I mean, what do I do with you? Why do they exist?"

"At the beginning of time when the first thing died there was one Reaper, a child of Life and Death."

"Aaron." I glare at him. "I don't want some kid's fairytale. I want the truth."

"This is the truth. Or at least the one that I was told."

"Oh c'mon. First Reaper, child of Life and Death. It's a kid's story."

"Will you just let me tell it?"

I plop down onto Mom's bed. "Fine."

"At the beginning of time, there was one Reaper, a child of Life and Death. The population grew until there were too many for one Reaper. The Grim Reaper recruited more Reapers, enough to lead all of Life's beings to Death."

"So, I have to, what? Take you to the land of Death?" He nods. "I don't even know where that is. This isn't real." I hear a car pull up front. "And I have to go to your funeral."

"Jade!" He follows me as I march from the room.

I shepherd Raina and Anisha into the Cherishe's car.

Deanna is wearing her Wednesday Addams costume from many Halloweens ago and Carl is wearing an ill-fitting suit. At least I'm not the only one who didn't go shopping for something new.

I pull my hair over my left shoulder, waiting for someone to notice that I've been pulling it over the wrong shoulder all week. A stupid thing to worry about—they never will.

We're back at church again, but not for mass today. For once, it isn't raining all that much. I make pointed eye contact with both Raina and Anisha. We nod somberly at each other.

Every step towards the entrance seems to lengthen the distance rather than shorten it. He's being buried after this. It doesn't feel real. Especially not with him walking in line with the rest of us, staring at the back of Carl's head.

Raina and Anisha fall towards the back of the group, and I edge towards the front, flanking them. For the most part, people are leaving them alone as we approach the next set of doors. They whisper as we pass, but no one intervenes. We're about to enter the next set of doors when Deanna groans resignedly.

I turn to see who is approaching us. Of course, it's Mrs. Gibson. She's wearing a black knee length dress with a matching short coat. Her box dyed blond hair is done up, and there is no hat in sight today. At least she has some semblance of respect.

I dive out of our formation at the same time as Anisha.

"Hi, Mrs. Gibson!" Anisha's steps are purposeful and measured. I follow close behind, determined to not let her face this woman alone.

"Hello, Anisha Marie!" she speaks in a high-pitched baby voice.

Anisha makes a face, but soldiers on. "Jade said that you don't like rainbow people?"

Oh God, why? Why is she doing this?

"There's no such thing as rainbow people, dear. They're simply—"

"Mom said it's okay if I like girls too," she says. I disguise my snort as a cough behind my hand. "And I think you're wrong. Rainbows are pretty."

Mrs. Gibson glares at me. The Cherishe's and Raina are safely inside. "Is your family determined to be unpleasant?" She narrows her eyes at me.

Pride swells inside of me as I beam at Anisha. "Yup!" Anisha nods happily and runs back to join us.

Father Iraci makes a rather touching speech about Aaron and his effect on all the people that loved him. He mentions grad school, and a life cut short. But he doesn't mention his cooking, or the way he laughed.

Aaron stands behind me and Deanna, peering up at his own coffin. It's a closed casket. Sewing his neck back together wasn't a task the local mortician was up to. I clench my eyes shut and shake that memory out of my head before it has time to resurface. My brain has been alternating between what I saw and that same scene from Aaron's perspective every time I let my mind be quiet for too long.

I glance at Aaron out of the corner of my eye. He looks at his dad and sister longingly, holding out a hand for them, but it shakes. He's too scared to touch them and have his hand slide through. Too scared to accept that he's dead.

I shake my head again. I'm imagining things. I have to be. There's some neurological explanation for suddenly gaining an imagination. I'm sure of it.

I can't take my eyes off him. He's right up there in the coffin, but he's right back here, with his family. Surreal, too strange.

He takes a shaky breath behind me and reaches forwards those extra few inches to lay his hand on Deanna's shoulder. It slides right through her, as expected. "I love you," he whispers.

She gives a choked gasp and raises her eyes from her hands to the ceiling. Deanna's chest heaves and tears finally spill over for the first time since Aaron died. "Aaron?" she whispers. My mouth drops open. She might not have seen him, but she felt him. That was no coincidence.

I reach over and grip her hand tightly.

He's real. That's Aaron behind me. My other hand runs absentmindedly over the mark.

I'm a Reaper.

Chapter Seven

I'm back at work the next day. The burial itself was a quiet affair. Only ten people came to watch his coffin be lowered into the ground. But the gathering afterwards . . .

Why does tradition dictate that the grieving family spend that much of their day expending energy? It doesn't make sense to me.

I haven't seen Aaron since the funeral either. I think he's given up on me, thinking I won't ever believe him. And I wouldn't, except that there is no way Deanna reacting that way was a coincidence. She felt him. I know it.

"Jade?" Amelia, my boss, leans up against the counter next to me. She's got a lot of grey hair for a woman in her forties, but she wears it with pride, allowing it to intersperse through her chocolate brown hair. Her face is adorned with faded freckles and her warm brown eyes are narrowed in concern. "Are you alright?"

"Of course!" I say. "Why?"

She jerks her head to my workstation. My hands are filled with rose petals separated from their stems. Not a single flower in the arrangement was spared.

"Did—did I do this? I'm sorry. I promise I'll pay more attention."

"It's alright. You've been through a lot. I can't imagine"—she shakes her head sympathetically—"if you need to take a break, that's okay."

"I'm fine." She crosses her arms doubtfully. She wasn't

suggesting. "Yeah okay." I set the rose petals down. "Amelia? I have a question." I flip my hair behind my shoulders. "Do you see anything there?" I point to my neck. I just have to double check. Someone else has to see it.

"Besides your tattoo?" she asks.

A strange mixture of relief and dread washes over me. "Yeah. Besides that. It's been itching all morning and I wanna know if it looks funny."

She inspects it closely. "Nope. Looks like a normal neck to me."

"We're trying out this cheaper laundry detergent and I think I might be allergic is all. Thanks!" I break away and practically sprint for the storage area in the back.

Peonies, roses, lilacs, and all types of greenery fill metal buckets that line the shelves. I'll go through the buckets later today and ensure that each flower is properly cared for and fed enough flower food. I inhale deeply, letting the scent calm my nervous system.

There's a bench in the back that Amelia keeps for her breaks. I've seen her sitting crisscrossed on this bench eating lunch with her eyes closed.

I sink into the bench, sighing heavily.

"Aaron?" I whisper. "I know you're real. I'm sorry." He was talking about time running out. What if it did? What if I'm too late? I bury my face in my hands.

I'm too late. Again.

"Hey." His voice is soft and sweet like the surrounding flowers.

"You're here!" I jump up. His hair is that same dark, wavy, fluffy that it always is, and his hands are in his pockets yet again. "I believe you. You're real. I'm sorry. God." My elation dies in me. He's real. He's dead. "I should have gone with you. That day. I should have—"

"Don't." He throws a hand up to stop me. "Maybe she would have killed us both. I don't know."

"Where do you go? When you're not here?"

"I can travel anywhere within your radius that I want. None of the rest will know that though. I was trying to give you space. To process. To think. I didn't—I don't want to haunt you, Jade."

"I was worried. You said you didn't have much time left."

"I don't," he says. "I have a day at most."

"I have to send you on now or you stop existing?" My voice comes out in a whimper that I am not proud of. "But you-you have things to—"

"I have nothing more to do. The only thing left is to teach you how to use that." He points to the mark, my mark, the crossed scythes.

"No."

"Yes." He sighs, edging closer to me. "I'm sorry that it has to be you."

"Aaron, I can't."

"You can and you will. You're the only one who can." He reaches a hand out and runs it along my hair, not quite touching it. "We never got a chance," he whispers.

"We didn't," I mutter. I don't even know how much of a chance it would have been. What I could have given him.

"Don't wait up, okay?" His smile is pained. "I don't know if you did, um . . . if you were maybe starting to have—it doesn't matter. Don't wait up." I furrow my brows, opening my mouth to speak, to reassure him. "Okay, press your fingers to your mark."

"What?" I stagger back. "Aaron I can't."

He sighs, pressing his lips together. "I don't want to either."

"What happens to you if I don't?" I press.

"I don't know," he admits. "I don't know where they go. I ignored my first one, and I never did it again. They disappeared. They never came back. I don't know if they stop existing or if they go somewhere. Either way, I don't want to find out."

"But—"

"Do it now before I lose my nerve." His voice trembles. "Please."

I meet his bright blue eyes and find them swimming with fear and determination. I make up my mind.

Flashing metal. Blood. Clutching at my throat.

My knees crash into the bench. It takes me a moment to remember my surroundings. Flowers on the shelves, soft smells, Aaron. "Why am I seeing that?"

"You won't see it with everyone. It's my death, from my point of view."

"Yes." I stand, dusting myself off. "I gathered that."

"It only happens for people with particularly traumatic deaths because we—I can't stop reliving it." He shoves his hands into his pockets. "You wanted to know where I kept going? I kept going to the beach. I wanted to see if she would come back, if I could get a good look at her, to warn you."

"You didn't find anything."

"She didn't come back." We're both staring at the floor. I never noticed that his laces were undone that day.

"Why did you mark me?" I ask. "And how? Can I mark someone else?"

"No." Aaron shakes his head. "Well, yes. You could mark someone else when you die. Otherwise, you're stuck with it. It's how I became a Reaper."

"Who?"

"You remember when I volunteered at the nursing home during college?" I nod. "One of the women marked me while I was by her bedside." He fixes his gaze onto the floor. "I never sent her on. I don't know what happened to her." He sighs heavily. "As for why I marked you. I didn't want to. I wouldn't wish this on you. You don't deserve it. But you were the only one there and—"

"Did you have to mark someone?"

"That's what the woman who marked me said."

"Okay." I nod.

"You're ready?" he asks. Everything inside of me is screaming no.

To find a way for him to stay. To bring him back. I nod. "Bring your fingers up to your mark." I do. "Now look me in the eye."

"But what if—"

"It won't. Not now." I inhale deeply and meet his gaze.

A fuzzy feeling envelops me, as though we're the only two people in this bubble I've created. My lips part and my breath hitches. We stare at each other for far too long, reveling in this moment. His eyes are beautiful. Blue and bright and full of kindness and warmth. I wouldn't be able to look away if I tried.

A small orb of light flits through the corner of my vision. I blink in confusion, but I still can't stop staring. And neither does he. His gaze turns hungry, and he takes a step towards me. He falters, planting his feet and returning to business. "So, this"—he plucks the light from the air—"is an afterlife."

I examine it curiously. "It's pretty."

"Some people have a lot of choices, and others, like me, just have the one. It's based on what they believe in."

"What they believe in?"

"Well, me and you, we believe in Heaven. I don't believe in Hell, so I can't go to Hell."

"Hell isn't real?"

"To some it is," he says slowly. "But it doesn't exist for me."

I furrow my eyebrows. "But it does exist?"

"Everything exists." I open my mouth to speak again. "And nothing exists."

"And if they don't believe in anything?"

"I've never encountered someone who doesn't believe in anything."

He holds out the light for me. An orange glow settles over a set of gates and the faint sound of singing. I can smell all sorts of wonderful food.

"Of course, you believe in an afterlife with good food," I tease. He chuckles. "This is the most beautiful thing I've ever seen."

"Isn't it?" He smiles and holds it out to me. "Take it." I hold out my hand reluctantly and he drops the little ball of light into my hand.

"It's warm!" I exclaim. I hold it to my chest, letting it consume me entirely. Warmth and light and brightness. Everything is right. Here it's always Sunday.

When I raise my eyes back up to Aaron's, I find his gaze trained on me. My eyes drift down to his lips. The smile is gone.

I bite my lip. Was I too excited? Did I make it worse?

No, that's not it. His eyes are shining, not sad. There's a tremor in his right hand. The hand that marked me.

"What?" I ask.

He charges forwards and brings his lips just close enough to brush mine without going through me. I feel nothing except for a cool breeze as he exhales. My heart plummets.

"You'll be happy here." It isn't quite a question, not quite a statement.

"Hopefully." And he does sound hopeful. His hand hovers near my face. I want his hand to cup my cheek. I want him back. But I can't have that.

I nod, gathering my resolve. "Alright. Teach me."

"You'll have to crush that light and throw it over me."

"Aren't there people in there?" I peer into the ball of light.

"No. It's more like a window for you to open." He shakes his arms out. "And do it quickly or we'll have to do this all over again."

"That wouldn't be so bad." I'm tempted to lift my fingers from my mark. "Don't go."

His eyes are swimming. He's so close. It feels as though I could touch him, bring him back, make Deanna happy. Maybe I could give him a real kiss, just once.

"I can't stay."

He's right. He's right, and he's dead.

I grip the orange ball in my hand and take another step closer to him. My legs shake. I resign myself to it with one deep breath. My fingers tighten around the globe. I raise my hand over his head. His eyes stay locked on mine. He's trying not to show his fear, but I can see it.

A desperate urge to hold him washes over me, then disappointment because I can't. I resist the urge to shut my eyes.

I squeeze until my fingers meet.

Liquid light oozes from between my fingers and over his head. It pours over his face like honey, brightening every square inch of him. The light drips down his shoulders and onto the floor, making a circle around him. His eyes are still fixed on mine, afraid.

"It's going to be alright." I smile, reaching out to him. He nods, relaxing his shoulders.

The light is traveling back up him in strings of gold. "Take care of Deanna?" he asks frantically. "And Dad?"

"Of course. I promise."

He nods, relaxing into the warmth of the light that surrounds him. "Goodbye, Jade."

I swallow hard. His last moments will not be my tears. "Goodbye, Aaron."

There's a flash of blinding light that knocks me back a few paces. I blink several times, trying to see where he went. There's not a trace of him, nothing to suggest he was ever here.

Everything around me is drained of color. I collapse onto the floor, leaning against the shelves. He's gone.

Aaron Cherishé is dead.

Chapter Eight

MARBHAVEN'S STRETCH OF ROAD is usually quiet, but in the early hours of this morning, it's bustling with cars. After ensuring Raina and Anisha's safe arrival at school, I follow the cars to the edge of town. A large crowd mills about under the bridge. It's as if everyone gathered is holding their breath.

I slam the car door shut and sprint towards the crowd.

Don't be my dead mom. Don't be Mom. Don't be Mom. "Excuse me!" I shout, shouldering past a group of men twice my size. They let me through, out of pure shock. I burst through the last ring of people.

A man in his fifties is curled on his side wearing worn jeans and an old flannel coat. His dark brown hair is caked with mud. Usually warm and soft brown eyes are vacant. His dry and lined hands shake as he turns a rosary over and over in his hand. I drop to my knees beside him.

"Father Rodriguez?" He sees me, recognition crossing his features.

"Jade." He cracks a smile.

"Are you alright? What happened to you?"

"Why are all these people here?" He squints at them. "Just enjoying a sit by the seaside and they're all staring at me."

"Tony." I close my hand around his, slipping into more familiar terms. "You've been missing for almost a month."

"I—what?" His eyes are suddenly wide and fearful. He squeezes my hand as tight as he can. "Vanessa. I saw Vanessa. She was—"

"Hey! Out of the way!" Officer Meyer appears at the edge of the crowd. "Father Rodriguez, do you remember who I am?"

"Yes." His voice sounds bitter. No, I must be imagining it. Father Rodriguez doesn't hate people.

Officer Meyer hauls him to his feet. "Alright. Come with me, we need to get you to a hospital."

"Can I come with him?"

"Don't you have work to go to, Miss Zaveri?"

"Yes, but—"

"We'll take good care of him. I promise. I'm sure you have a lot of questions, and you will get to ask them *later*." She fixes me with a glare. "Once we've made sure he's alright."

"But he was going to say something about my mom!"

"Ask him later." Her voice is brisk and stern. She shakes her head and mutters, "Selfish girl."

I don't dare to defy her again. Questions burn a hole through my tongue as the crowd parts for them.

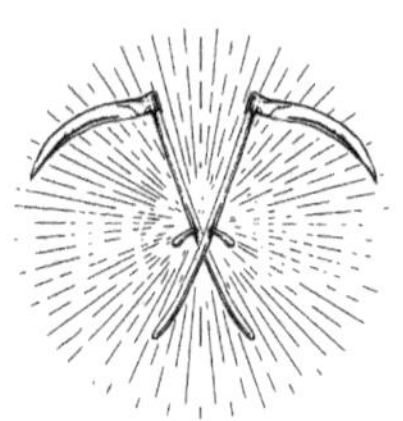

Work passes by all too slowly. We've got a wedding coming up next week and Amelia is obsessing over inventory while I tend the front.

Far more people than usual come in today. And all of them want a bouquet to leave for Father Rodriguez. They engage in speculation with me while I put their bouquets together, but it's useless. No one actually knows anything. No one has any information about how he's doing or if anything is wrong with him.

On my break, I sit in the storage area surrounded by the flower buckets. The last place I saw Aaron.

I close my eyes, trying to form a prayer for Father Rodriguez. Who do I pray to now? If everything exists, do I still pray to God? Or do I pray to everyone and everything? Or nothing at all? Does it even matter? Will it help Father Rodriguez at all?

I groan in frustration. This is useless. I need to be with him. When I open my eyes, someone is standing in front of me.

I blink several times before I register that it's Father Rodriguez smiling at me. I leap up from my seat, grinning from ear to ear and throw my arms around his neck.

I fall right through him. The smile slides from my face. My heart is as heavy as lead. I can't speak. My voice is gone, replaced by a crushing tightness in my throat. Not my father too. I'm too afraid to look back at him, opting to brace my hands on the shelf in front of me instead.

"Jade?" His voice sounds different from Aaron's. Oddly resonant. "How did I get here?" I open my mouth to respond, but nothing comes out. "I was lying in bed and then I closed my eyes and now . . . "

"You were fine the last time I saw you." My voice breaks. "You're only fifty-five. Please." I turn to face him, my heart aching at the sight of him.

"Am I dead?" His brow furrows. "Not how I thought the afterlife would be, but I do like the flowers." The bemused expression slides from his face. "You're not dead too are you, Jade?"

I shake my head. "I'm a Reaper." I pull my hair to the side, showing him the mark. His eyes widen. "What?"

"I saw that mark. Wherever they took me. They showed me the mark, asked me what I knew about it. I didn't know anything."

"Aaron Cherishé marked me when he was killed."

"Aaron Cherishé was—what?" His shoulders slump forwards. "No. He's so young. He's not—" I hold up my hands to calm him and look him dead in the eyes.

I'm a teenager, and I'm kissing someone. A girl. She smiles at me with striking amber eyes and burrows into my flat chest. Happiness and some kind of love I've never known fills my heart. Then I'm running a hand over her swollen belly, and I know that it's mine.

The scene changes. I'm holding a baby girl and rocking her back and forth. I hear a door slam, but by the time I reach it, it's too late. My love is gone.

I'm a man, handing my baby over to some man in a suit. I want to curl up in a ball and die.

I'm older, chasing a little girl with golden brown skin in her mother's garden. Jade Zaveri. She toddles around and giggles. That same warmth from rocking the baby washes over me.

"Jade?" Amelia's voice breaks through my thoughts and I'm surrounded by flowers again, back in my own mind and body. "Are you alright? You need to go home?"

How long was I staring off into space? "No." I shake my head. "Lost in thought. Sorry, Amelia."

"It's alright." She rubs my shoulder lightly. "I can recommend you a therapist in town if you want to see him." Her voice is kind, concerned, motherly. My shoulders melt into the feeling of being cared for.

"Might take you up on that. Later?" I ask. She nods and leaves me alone in the room again.

But I'm not alone.

"What was that?"

"Your life." My break ends in five minutes. "You said you saw Mom. Where? What happened?"

"I"—he closes his eyes tightly, a crease forming on his

forehead—"I don't remember. I'm sorry. I don't know where she was. It hurts."

"It's okay," I whisper. "Just breathe. It's alright."

"Send me on," he begs.

"But you just got here. I just got you back—"

"I want out of my head. Please Jade." His voice breaks.

I close my eyes, swallowing down my tears and protests. I'm doing him a kindness. He's tired. My fingers find their way to my mark, and I open my eyes. Two little orange balls of light float between us. "You choose one," I mutter, fighting every impulse to take my fingers off my mark and make him wait.

He reaches for one with a trembling hand as though being pulled by a string. As his fingers close around the orange ball of light, it turns a deep blood red.

"Wait no!" I gasp, rushing towards him. His eyes are wide and afraid. "Let go!"

"I can't." His voice shakes horribly. The light swallows his arm in a bath of red. Father Rodriguez screams in pain. I take my fingers from my mark to stop it, but it does nothing. His arm gets sucked further inside still. My mouth hangs open in horror.

I'm trapped in this spot, rooted to the ground.

He tries to pull his arm out, but the light only engulfs him quicker. His arm disappears completely, his expression contorted into nothing but fear and pain.

A strange noise issues from the light, like a garbage disposal. He screams in pain again, fighting harder and harder to remove his arm.

The light eats its way up his neck, slowly engulfing the right side of his face. His head disappears and the light rapidly zips down his body, issuing a horrible grating sound, until it's only his legs, his feet, then nothing.

I stare at the spot where he stood, hand clapped over my mouth. Did he go to hell? Did I accidentally send him to hell? He doesn't deserve that. Nothing I saw in his memories was worthy of that.

I'm not seeing this. It's not real. It can't be. Father Rodriguez isn't dead. Aaron isn't dead. This is some extended nightmare. A dream. A horrible dream that won't end.

All the air leaves my lungs. "Amelia?" I charge from the storage room. "I need to go see Father Rodriguez in the hospital."

Chapter Nine

THE HOSPITAL IS MILES from the main road. It's a small hospital, with only two wings: a children's wing and an adult wing. People mostly go here for childbirth and emergencies. For everything else we have to travel several more miles to get to a hospital with fuller facilities.

I still remember Father Rodriguez driving Mom here when she was having Raina and Anisha. They dropped me off at Deanna's and brought back two little sisters that cried for nights on end.

I hated Mom for months for bringing them into the world. I was old enough to know that there was no stork. No blessing from God. Just good old-fashioned sex and that this was her fault, her decision.

Although it certainly wasn't her decision to have their dad move states away in search of a new job conveniently after learning of their existence. I hated him even more. Peter. God, I hated him. He barely tolerated me. He was under the illusion that I was standing in the way of a perfectly good relationship with Mom. Peter thought I was a sassy smartass. I was.

I park the car, trying to prepare myself. I'm going to go in there and he's going to be dead. And I'm going to apologize to him, for failing him, for going against my better judgment and sending him on immediately.

The walk into the waiting room is far too long. It seems to only get longer as I approach the receptionist. Her blond hair is pulled back into a loose bun. I think she might be the one that we're setting up the wedding for next week. I peer at her cheerful yellow name tag. It's her: Kate.

"Hi!" She speaks in the cheerful customer service voice I know only too well from watching Deanna work. "How can I help you?"

"I'm Jade Zaveri and—"

Her face settles into sympathy instantly. He really is dead, isn't he?

"—I was hoping I could visit Tony. Um, Anthony Rodriguez, sorry. They said I could drop by after work."

"Oh of course!" she says. "Let me go check and make sure he's ready for visitors." I blink in confusion as she leaves the desk.

Ready for visitors? He's dead. Haven't they noticed yet?

"He's feeling much better now." Kate returns to my side. "Follow me." I follow her through a short hallway until we reach a door with a whiteboard outside that says Anthony Rodriguez. "You can go in now. I'm sure he'll be happy to see you."

"Right." I stare at the door apprehensively. How do they not know that he's dead? They must have him hooked up to monitors or something. Did it not alert them?

My fingers close around the door handle, and I turn it.

Father Rodriguez is wearing a white hospital gown and sitting up in bed. He's still as shell-shocked as earlier, but he doesn't appear to be on Death's door. He's eating pudding.

I close the door behind me and all we can do is stare at each other for ages. "You're not dead," I say simply.

"I was," he mutters. "Apparently I flatlined for a bit there, but I'm not dead anymore."

"Flatlined? Were you in surgery?" He shakes his head. "What happened?"

"Stress?" He shrugs. "Will you sit, Jade?" He is far too blasé about this for my taste. I take the available seat by his bedside. He reaches out and brushes my hair behind my shoulders. The moment he sees the mark he reaches out for me and engulfs me in a hug.

I almost immediately start crying. Every single muscle relaxes in relief. Thank God. Thank God he's not dead. I sob into his chest until my eyes run dry. His arms tighten around me.

"I—I thought—" I stutter.

"Me too," he whispers. "Aaron is dead?"

"Yes." I focus my gaze on my hands. "I watched him die. She slit his throat."

"She?" His voice shakes.

"There was this woman. She wore a red cloak and had a scythe. The Red Reaper." He furrows his brows, in worry or something else, I don't know. "The funeral was two days ago. He's buried next to Lauren if you want to visit him when you get out."

He nods solemnly. "I will."

"How are you alive? You were dead, I—"

"I don't know." He runs a hand through his brown curls, a crease forming between his brows. "What's going on Jade?"

"You died!" My voice breaks. "You died, and you were going to leave without properly saying goodbye."

"I'm sorry. Jade, I'm so sorry."

"You have a daughter?"

He shushes me hurriedly. "I have four."

"What? When?"

"You, Jade. You and your sisters." My shoulders relax. Of course, the ones he practically raised. "And Lucia, wherever she is."

"No one knows?"

"Not a soul. It was a long time ago." Silence passes between us. An implied promise for my silence. "Now will you please tell me what's going on?"

I nod several times, bracing myself for a story that I never intended to tell. I tell him how Aaron died, how he marked me. How I ignored him. How I sent him on only yesterday. How the last time I slept for more than three hours at a time was weeks ago.

"And that red light. I don't know what it was. Maybe that's what happens when you're brought back to life?" He nods, taking it all in. His brown eyes are full of concern. As he turns his gaze to meet mine, I realize that it's for me. "How did it feel?" I ask.

"It felt"—I can hear every heartbeat that passes between us—"awful. Like being pulled through a shredding machine." I bite my nails, waiting for more. "Then there was this loud pounding. And when it got so loud, I couldn't stand it, it stopped. And I woke up."

"I wish—"

"I thought it was a dream until I saw you. You're really marked. Two scythes." He waves. "Sorry. I interrupted. Go on."

"I wish that"—God it sounds pathetic now that I'm thinking about it—"I wish that Aaron was still here so he could tell me if that's normal."

He sighs heavily. "We'll say a prayer for him together?" He reaches out his hands and I take them. Warmth flows through my veins as he speaks, praying that Aaron has a garden of fresh herbs and vegetables in Heaven with which to cook. He prays that Aaron gets to continue learning as he always wanted to, that he gets to look down on his beloved sister and see her happy every day. By the time he finishes speaking, the emptiness that has plagued me since last week is much smaller. My heart slows to a steady and calm beat. "Amen," he finishes, gripping my hands tightly.

A moment, a beat of silence passes between us. "Tony?" I scoot my chair forwards. "Earlier today, before you died, you said something about Mom?"

"I did?" He blinks slowly.

"Yes. You said that you saw Vanessa, she was . . . what?"

He squeezes his eyes shut and tilts his chin towards the ceiling for a full two minutes before exhaling in defeat. "I can't remember. I'm sorry."

"But it means I was right." I almost dare to smile. "I thought your cases were connected. I've been telling the police for weeks. Officer Meyer keeps asking about my dad. That's all she ever does, ask about my dad."

"Oh," Father Rodriguez groans. "That woman. I met your dad, just once mind you. He was the most gentle, sweet man you could have possibly fathomed. Not at all like you."

"Hey!" I gasp in mock indignation. "I'm sweet."

"Almost as sweet as you are sour," he teases. I snort. "He doesn't have something like that in him. Never mind the fact that he hasn't shown up for about nineteen years now?"

"I don't even know what he looks like," I mutter.

"Quite a bit like you." He smiles, gripping my hand.

The nurse comes in with medicine on a tray. When he sets it down next to Father Rodriguez, I see a swooshing red logo that reads Genesis, the same company Mom worked for. "What are those?" I ask.

"Beta blockers," the nurse supplies. "For his heart."

Father Rodriguez swallows the pills with a glass of water. I catch a glimpse of the clock and curse. "Jade," he says sternly.

I apologize hurriedly, scooping up my car keys. "The girls will be home within the hour. I can't leave them home alone, not after what happened to Mom, to you, now Aaron." Panic rises in my chest again. Who's next? "I'll come visit again tomorrow?"

"If I'm still here." He shrugs.

I lean down and kiss him on the cheek. "You'd better be. That should warrant an overnight stay here."

I practically sprint out of the hospital in my rush to get to the car. It's raining again. And hard. Winter used to be my favorite season before I had to drive this much.

I pull my pink hood off and slam the car door shut. Red whips around in the corner of my vision. I turn to find it, find her, the Red Reaper. She isn't there. She's nowhere. Nothing but rain.

I exhale heavily, leaning back in my seat. That's it. I'm definitely losing it.

I turn the key in the ignition and buckle my seatbelt. The wipers are going at full speed, but my vision is still on high alert. After all, if I wasn't imagining Aaron and I wasn't imagining Father Rodriguez, then logically, the Red Reaper is watching me.

All the more reason to get to Raina and Anisha before anything else happens. I will not leave them alone and we are not going to miss dinner with the Cherishés tonight. I promised.

The highway only makes the rain worse as it pelts the windshield due to the increased speed.

I have to get back home. I have to get back home. I have to get back—

I yelp and slam on the brakes. The car in front of me comes to a screeching full stop. "What is your prob—" I falter. Their problem immediately becomes apparent to me. My blood runs cold.

There's a man sprawled across the windshield of the car in front of me. I take the keys out of the ignition and sprint towards the car, arriving at the scene only a few seconds after the driver.

The driver, a middle-aged man, is cussing repeatedly and running his hands through his drenched hair. "You!" I shout and point directly at him, drawing on the single first aid class my high school made me take. "You call an ambulance." Obediently, he whips out his phone and dials.

I turn my attention back to the bloodied body of the man. My fingers rest on his wrist trying to find a pulse. It beats once, and not again.

"Oh c'mon," I whisper at the man. "Don't. I don't need another person dying in front of me. Please wake up." No pulse. "I'm cursed," I conclude.

"You think you're cursed?" a man's voice whispers. I whip my head around and meet the incredibly dark eyes of a man who is only slightly taller than me. Unkempt black curls curve around his too big ears and his nose looks like it's been broken several times. His cheekbones are so sharp I think they could cut someone. And I could get lost in those brown eyes . . .

I do a double take between him and the fact that he isn't the driver. The driver is still on the phone and much shorter. I clear my throat. "Will they be here soon?" I ask. The driver nods, his eyes vacant.

I return my gaze to the man on the windshield. Black hair, drenched, but probably curly. Incredibly long legs. Sharp cheekbones. And his nose is definitely broken. I don't dare to lift his eyelids.

I turn back to the man standing at my side. He's completely dry. "You're the—" I gesture to the man on the windshield.

"Can't seem to die." His smile is strained.

"I—what?"

"This is the fifth time I've died this month." He shrugs. "Tell you what, I did not expect my Reaper to be this close."

I blink at him through the rain, shake my head, and turn back to his body, running a hand up his yellow sweatshirt to inspect his chest for any breaks. A visceral crunching sensation greets my fingers, like walking on gravel. "Like what you feel?" he laughs.

"No." I turn back to him indignantly. "Your freaking ribs are broken." His face is mere inches away from mine. God, he's almost inhumanly good looking. I shake my head. Tendrils of my wet hair slap my face and stick there. He snorts, reaching to brush it away then thinking better of it. "What do you mean this is the fifth time you've died this month?"

He sighs heavily. "You ever been suicidal before?" I shake my head. "Well, here's hoping you don't find out." I open my mouth to speak, but he continues. "Alright. Let's get this over with. Hand to your ear or whatever. I guess they'll fix my ribs."

"What?"

"Try to send me on. Do it, you'll see what I mean."

I stumble and hesitantly put a hand to my mark. I meet his eyes again. He blinks several times and his lips part as his gaze bores into mine. He schools his expression back into one of careful indifference. The air is filled with hundreds of orange twinkling lights.

"You believe in this many?" I gasp.

I turn back to find that his gaze hasn't wavered. "Being agnostic has its perks. I'll give it that." He shrugs and reaches towards me. For a moment, I think he's going to touch my face or something, but he simply plucks a light from next to my ear. It immediately turns red in his grasp.

"Wait. Let go," I whisper hurriedly. "I don't know what's going on with—"

He breathes in deeply, bracing himself. "The worst part." He grits his teeth as the light engulfs his arm. Heat emanates from him. His eyes squeeze shut. I want to reach out to him, help him somehow, but I know I can't.

I hear the ambulance in the distance as the red light zips down his body. He's gone.

There's a shaky gasp from behind me. I spin around. Beneath his yellow sweatshirt, his arm twitches. I reach for his hand and grip it tightly. "Holy—" I gape at him.

"Can't die," he wheezes. "You were right. Broken ribs."

"Is he?" The driver rushes forwards. "He's alive?"

My mouth hangs open. "Barely. Yes," I manage to whisper.

The ambulance arrives. The man reaches a hand up and pushes my wet hair from my face, his fingers grazing over my Reaper mark. I make way for the paramedics.

He mutters, "Thanks, Green Eyes," as they transfer him to a stretcher.

Chapter Ten

Dinner is a quiet affair. I cook and we say a lengthy prayer for Aaron at dinner. Deanna grips my hand under the table as hard as she can. I squeeze back.

We talk about Father Rodriguez's return, speculate on what happened to him. I tell them about my visit to the hospital, but not about why I went there in the first place. I tell Deanna that he's doing fine and that I'm visiting him tomorrow. That it will be fine.

It will be fine. My thoughts whisper to me as I read the girls to sleep.

"It will be fine," I growl as sleep eludes me yet again.

I roll away from the window to keep a watch on my closed door, as if a closed door will keep anyone out, will stop anyone from killing me.

The floor drops out from underneath me as I spot a silhouette by the doorway. Someone is already inside. I hold my breath, clenching my eyes shut. They already saw me roll over. They know I'm awake. It's too late.

Minutes pass as I stay in my feigned sleep position, my heart thundering in my ears. If they want to hurt me, if she wants to hurt me, why hasn't she done it already?

I peer through my eyelashes. They haven't moved. Not even an inch. They haven't even shifted their stance.

My feet touch the ground as I sit up, moving slowly and keeping my eyes trained on the figure.

It's a man, not a woman. Lanky. He's familiar. Curly hair.

"Hello?" I wrap my hand around a pair of scissors on my bedside table. No response. "I know you're there. Who are you?" My voice trembles, but at least my legs are strong.

I tiptoe silently across the carpet, scissors poised to attack. There is still no movement from the man.

I reach my unarmed hand out for his shoulder. My hand slides straight through him.

My thundering heart rate calms itself. I exhale slowly. It's another dead person. That's all. An unresponsive one at that. I know I've only had three, but they always speak.

"Listen." I make my way around him, peering through the dark. "I can help you. Just talk to—" The scissors fall to the floor with a dull thud. Father Rodriguez is staring back at me for the second time today.

But his eyes aren't his eyes. They are a bright, glowing, awful red. "Tony?" He doesn't speak. His mouth hangs slightly open. "Father Rodriguez?" His face is blank, completely unresponsive. "Anthony? Anthony Rodriguez?" I whisper hesitantly. Nothing.

Maybe I am going insane.

I reach out for him. He doesn't move, only stands there, mouth slightly ajar, red eyes glowing. Father Rodriguez only in appearance, not in soul.

Whatever this is, it isn't Father Rodriguez. I wrench my gaze away from him, making a beeline for the living room.

I grip the shelf in the living room tightly, a makeshift barre, shifting my thoughts to ballet lessons.

Father Rodriguez would take me to dance lessons when Mom had work. I clench my eyes shut and move to first. Air fills my lungs on counts one through four and exits on counts five through eight. That's all I need, something to reset my nervous system.

A shudder courses through my body. Slowly, I peer through my eyelashes.

He's right in front of me, no more than six feet away. I bite back a scream and close my eyes again. Ignore him. Whatever that is, it isn't my father.

I lose myself in practice trying to remember a dance from ages ago. One that went to some strange operatic tune I haven't heard since. I try to imagine it growing louder and louder in my head, drowning out every other sense that I have.

I can't remember the dance. I sigh in resignation and open my eyes, jumping again at the sight of Father Rodriguez's glowing red eyes.

The staircase beckons me. Maybe he'll stay here. I walk up the quiet path of the stairs and turn back around once I reach the top. He's halfway up the stairs. I didn't hear him move. My heart thunders in my ears.

My feet continue padding backwards. He—it, jerks forwards with every step, as though pulled by a string. The movement is not coming from him. It's coming from me, pulling him without realizing it.

I'm attached to a string.

Maybe I'll get lucky, and the boundary will extend past my bedroom door?

No such luck. When I get to my bed, he's standing by the closed door, casting a red glow over the whole room.

I can't pretend that the glow isn't there no matter how hard I squeeze my eyes shut.

With great pains to make the transition silent, I pull my bed one foot away from the wall, sprint downstairs and back up, his body following me the whole way.

I jump beneath the covers and turn towards the door. Nothing. I allow myself a small triumphant smile and close my eyes in relief.

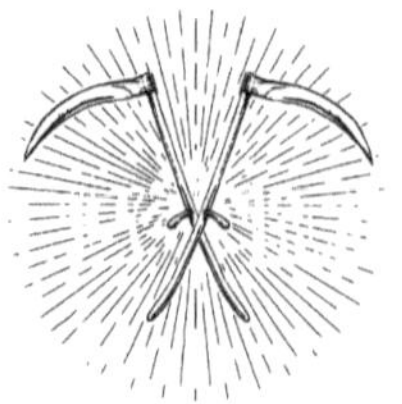

A thick liquid covers me from head to toe. The waves are clashing violently, pummeling the sand. My hands hurt from putting pressure on something. Roses, dozens of them, surround me on the sand. They are blood red. Their thorns are embedded in my hands. It stings. The smell of metal fills my nostrils.

I awake with a start. The sun shines at exactly the right angle to get through the blinds and into my eyes. I groan and turn to hide against the wall, then practically tumble out of bed into the foot-long gap I created.

I gasp and blink rapidly. There's a man at the foot of my bed, squinting through the blinds. "I wish she'd open these," he whispers, turning back to me.

I find myself staring into a set of beautiful brown eyes. He blinks in surprise and stares back at me in bewilderment. My breath hitches as he moves in closer. "You're that man from yesterday," I whisper. "Did you die again?" There's a twinkle in his eye. Almost triumphant. "What?" I ask.

"You." His voice is barely a whisper as he smiles. It's a good look on him.

"Me." I nod.

"You can see me?" I nod again. "That's"—he approaches my bed and sits on the edge—"unusual."

"How are you doing that?" I ask. He exhales and slides through my bed and onto the ground. Then he stands and sits back down. I blink slowly.

"I just have to concentrate, and I can do it." He shrugs.

After a moment I conclude that it isn't the strangest thing I've seen this week. "And why unusual? Can't all Reapers see dead people?"

"See. That's the thing," he whispers conspiratorially, leaning towards me. I lean forwards on instinct. "I'm not dead."

"You look dead. Didn't you say this was, what? The fifth time you've died?"

"This month. Good memory, Green Eyes." I blush, staring at my lap. "If you don't give me your name, I'm gonna have to call you that."

"First explain to me how you're not dead, Brown Eyes," I counter.

"Have you become acquainted with the um . . . " He gestures around his eyes. "Can't miss 'em. I've only seen a few. Glowing red eyes, stand completely still? I just call them Red Eyes."

"Father Rodriguez," I gasp, scrambling from the bed and towards the door. I fling it open. He's gone.

"So, you have seen them." I turn to face him. "I haven't met a Reaper who can yet. Not until you."

"Explain," I say shortly.

"Red eyes are like me," he says. "We die, but not really. So, we come back to life, but we have to come back to our Reapers when we sleep."

"Your Reapers?"

"Whoever we died nearest to. We're tied to them forever."

"So, I'm—"

"Stuck with me. Yeah," he says.

"Do the other Red Eyes know? Do they know this is happening?" I think of Father Rodriguez. I didn't think he could see me.

He shakes his head. He knows more. I know he does. I motion for him to continue. "I don't know why my eyes aren't red like theirs. I've always been aware of my surroundings. But you"—he points at me, rising from the bed—"you are the first Reaper to see us."

"It can't be that unusual."

"Well, the first Reaper I've seen." He sits back onto the bed in a huff.

"How many Reapers do you have?"

"Just one at a time. It's all anyone can have," he says. I open my mouth to ask something else, but he beats me to it. "I've died a lot. In a lot of different places. I've had my fair share of Reapers."

"What happened to the other Reapers?" He sighs, opens his mouth, closes it. I cross my arms. "Any day now." I fix my most intimidating stare on him.

"One day," he starts, almost against his will. "One day I ended up in a mortuary."

"They died." Visions of Aaron thrashing beneath me in the sand flash through my mind. The man fixes his gaze on the ground, eyes somewhere far away. "Did you happen to see a woman in a cloak? A red cloak?" He doesn't respond immediately. "Holding a scythe."

He looks back up at me, ending his staring match with the floor. "No."

He's lying. "You said you wanted the blinds up, right?" Sunlight shines over both of us as I pull them. The sunlight doesn't go through him, it casts over him, as it would if he were here in the flesh.

"Yes, I did." He moves towards the window. "I was wondering if those were waves I was hearing. Do you live here or is this a vacation for you, Green Eyes?"

"Jillian." I join him by the window, wishing I could find the peace the waves once brought me. "Jillian Williams." My dad's last name and that horrible name that they were going to give me until I came out with green eyes.

"Blaise Nicholo." He sticks out a hand, his face full of

brightness. I doubt that's his real name either. "Oh wait. Right, we can't . . . " I rifle through the clothes in my dresser for today's outfit. "You know, it's funny. When I'm asleep, I can do this." He thrusts his hand through the wall next to him. "But when I'm awake—"

"Do you sometimes walk into walls?" I give a halfhearted smile.

"Maybe." He smiles wryly. I try not to stare, but his smile is captivating. Annoyingly.

I grab my clothes and walk down the hall. He follows, not entirely of his own free will. I can hear him yelping in protest if I walk too fast. I turn to face him, my hand on the bathroom doorknob. "So. You can stay out here, right?"

"Should be more than six feet away from you. Yeah." He shrugs.

"Stay out here."

I change into my clothes for the day, tight fitting dark jeans and a loose teal V-neck. I'm about to put my hair into a bun like Mom used to wear, but I catch a glimpse of my mark. I can't, not when everyone in town knows everyone. I leave my hair down.

"Alright," I whisper to myself. "Brush teeth, wake the girls, breakfast, visit Father Rodriguez, work."

When I come out of the bathroom, Blaise is gone.

Chapter Eleven

Nurses are in and out of Father Rodriguez's room today. They let me come in, but only if I stay out of the way.

"All these tests," he sighs, holding out his arm to get more blood drawn.

"You were screaming bloody murder in your sleep last night, Father Rodriguez." The nurse holds his arm steady. "We were all good and worried."

We share a glance. I bite my lip. I have to figure out what's going on. He deserves to sleep peacefully. "Any idea why?" I ask.

"That's what we're trying to figure out." The man pulls the needle out.

"Did you dream about anything?" I scoot forwards in my chair.

"No." Father Rodriguez shakes his head.

"I'll be back with your test results soon. Jade can keep an eye on you for now. Call someone if anything goes wrong, okay?" I nod obediently and the nurse leaves.

"Jade, I'm fine. Must have been a nightmare." He smiles warmly at me, beads of sweat gathering on his forehead. "Don't worry. You should get to work."

"You were in my room last night." He furrows his brows in confusion. "You don't remember?"

"No. I don't."

"You were in my room, but it wasn't really you. Your eyes were glowing red. My hand went right through you. You were some sort of ghost." He runs a hand over his eyes. "Do you remember anything from when you were sleeping?"

"No." He clenches his eyes shut. "Just pain."

"Pain? What"—he shakes his head and falls back onto his pillows, breathing raggedly—"what's wrong?"

"I feel horrible. So dizzy." He shudders and closes his eyes. "It hurts to sleep." His eyes fly open again, wide eyed and delirious.

I put a hand to his forehead and yelp. "Holy mother of"—it burns red-hot—"help!" I shout down the hallway. The nurse comes running back.

"What happened?"

"Fever. Red-hot, barely felt like skin," I say. Father Rodriguez's eyelids flutter.

I look up at the nurse and instead meet Blaise's eyes. He's back.

"What's happening to him?" At this point, I don't know who I'm asking.

"Very high fever. I need to get a cold compress and the doctor, stay with him." The nurse sprints from the room.

"Fever?" Blaise inquires.

I nod vigorously, placing my hand in Father Rodriguez's. "It's going to be okay. I promise." I turn back to Blaise. He seems to know a lot about these Red Eyes. "What's happening to him?"

"Tortured in his sleep," Blaise whispers, horror casting a dark shadow across his face.

"Who are you talking to?" Father Rodriguez whispers groggily.

"Imaginary friend," I shoot back, not breaking eye contact with Blaise. "Can you help him? Please."

Blaise shrugs, staring at Father Rodriguez. The nurse comes back. A doctor follows closely at his heels. They both walk directly through Blaise.

They shove cold compresses on his neck, under his armpits. He shakes violently. I can hear his heart rate rising on the monitor.

"It hurts," he groans.

"Where?" The doctor stands over him, his brow creased with worry.

"To sleep. It hurts to sleep."

"Where does it hurt?"

Father Rodriguez sobs in response.

Panic rises in my chest. I've never seen him cry. Not once. "Help him!" I plead, surprising myself by making eye contact with Blaise instead of the doctor.

"We will." The nurse is readying a vial of something.

"Please." My voice comes out half whisper, half prayer. Blaise scans the situation carefully.

"I can help him if he sleeps," he says. "I think."

"Tony. You need to sleep. Okay?" I squeeze his hand. "You need to sleep."

The doctor spins around, eyebrows furrowed. He doesn't protest.

"Trust me," I whisper to Father Rodriguez. His brown eyes flutter shut almost immediately as he surrenders to sleep.

A red glow floods the room. No one else seems to notice. No one except Blaise, whose gaze is now fixed on the new figure in the room.

I turn my head towards Father Rodriguez's soul, mouth open, eyes glowing red. He whimpers in pain on the hospital bed. The ghostlike version of him rises into the air, limbs unmoving.

Blaise creeps towards the figure cautiously. His hands reach for Father Rodriguez and pull him down. There's a faint white glow around Blaise as he touches his forehead to his. Blaise's eyes are screwed up in concentration.

I reach a timid hand to Father Rodriguez's forehead. Only a slight fever now. "It's working." I laugh. "How are you doing that?"

"Shh," Blaise warns.

"We're not doing anything." The nurse's voice wavers.

I turn my gaze back to Father Rodriguez, the real one. His face relaxes. I grip his hand firmly. "It's going to be okay," I whisper.

The red glow diminishes slightly. Blaise exhales heavily and comes to stand next to me. All the air leaves my lungs as I gape at him in wonderment.

Blaise averts his gaze abashedly. I school my gaze back onto Father Rodriguez. "Room 14," Blaise whispers to me. I turn to him, but he's gone again.

"Vitals are stabilized." The doctor notes. "I'm gonna watch him. You go get his test results."

"Is he going to be alright?"

"For now, it seems so."

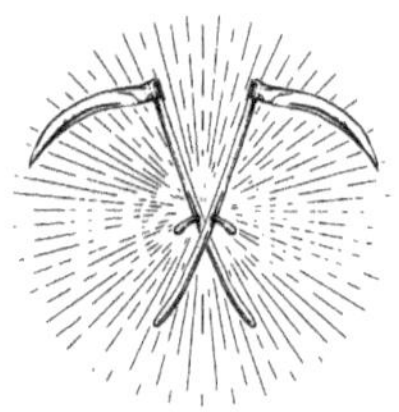

I wander the halls of the hospital instead of leaving immediately. His test results all came back normal. They're talking about transferring him to a hospital in the city instead of this one. They'll have more advanced facilities, a way to scan his brain for abnormalities.

"Room 14," I whisper to myself, turning a corner. There it is. I peer through the window of the room. Blaise is on the bed and turned away from me. He doesn't appear all that injured anymore, but I'm sure that there are plenty of internal problems for him to contend with. At least they cleaned up all the blood.

I rest my hand on the doorknob. I could go in, talk to him, figure out how he fixed Father Rodriguez, make him answer my questions.

Or I could stay as far away from real life him as possible. I withdraw my hand and turn away. I have to get to work, anyway.

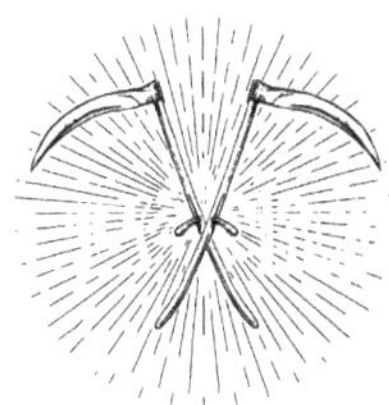

"You didn't visit me," he says by my shoulder. My writing stalls and I drop the pen. "I told you what room I was in, and you didn't visit me." I turn my head over my shoulder towards him.

"You're right." I nod, turning back to my list. "Peach roses, pansies, camellias . . . "

"Why didn't you?"

I sigh heavily and make my way back to the storeroom. Kate's wedding is less than a week away. We had to special order a few different kinds of flowers. Some haven't arrived yet and Amelia is only getting more stressed. I'm supposed to take inventory and tend the front of the shop while Amelia obsessively tends to the greenhouses. "Because I don't know you."

"Sure, you do, Green Eyes," he whispers. "Besides, you intrigue me. Really. I mean, I want to know more about you."

I glare inwardly at the slight flutter of my heart. "Yeah. About all the Reaper stuff and why I can see you. The point is that I don't know and I'm never going to know. You won't find answers through me."

"Who knows? Maybe you've got something in that head of yours that's important." He shrugs. "Why all the flowers, anyway?"

"I'm at work," I reply, plucking flowers for this afternoon's online order.

"Didn't take you for the pretty flowers type of person."

"Yeah, well, something's gotta pay the bills. Plus, it smells nice."

"I'll bet." He sighs.

"Why are you still asleep?" I head out to the front, confirming that no one is in the store before continuing. "It's practically two o'clock."

"I'm recovering," he says. When I snort, he darts in front of me, forcing me to meet his eyes. "Did you forget that I got hit by a car?"

I blanch. "No. But you were dead, and you randomly came back to life. Don't you have enhanced healing or something?"

"Nope." He shakes his head. "Good old-fashioned broken ribs being fixed by modern medicine."

The shop bell dings. I cringe inwardly at the sound. It's already annoying me. "Hi!" I say warmly over my shoulder. "I'll be with you in just a—"

Officer Meyer is marching up to the counter. "Officer Meyer." I smile tightly. "How are you?"

"Could ask you the same."

"Alright. Getting by." She has a hand wrapped around her holster. I tense. She's not in here for flowers. "What is it?"

"Oh, she's totally here to arrest you," Blaise whispers. My jaw tenses and I shoot him a glare out of the corner of my eye.

"I had some questions." Her voice is clipped.

"About?"

Blaise moves in front of me and behind Officer Meyer. He throws up two fingers behind her head as bunny ears. I fix my eyes on my paper, biting my lip.

"Father Rodriguez."

I snap my gaze to her. "How is he? Did something happen?"

"He's fine." She sounds disinterested. "You mentioned he said something about Vanessa." I nod.

"Who's Vanessa?" Blaise asks, making his way back to me and leaning against the counter.

"Yeah. He said he saw Mom." I give Blaise a pointed look out of the corner of my eye. "But he doesn't remember anything now." Officer Meyer sighs heavily and pinches her brow. "Officer Meyer, this confirms what I've been telling you. The cases are connected. Father Rodriguez, my mom, Aaron—"

"What connects them?" she practically barks.

"I—I don't know. I just—"

"Because we have *no* suspects. Not a single lead. And you refuse to tell me anything about your father. So don't try to tell me how to do my job if you won't give me basic information."

I tie a white ribbon tightly around the bouquet. A thorn that I neglected to shave off pierces my finger. I withdraw it before any blood can get on the ribbon. The water runs and drowns out my muttered curses.

"Jeez, I thought you were religious," Blaise mutters. I shush him.

"I've told you," I growl, turning to face her again. "I don't even remember what he looks like. I can give you a last name, Williams. That's all I have on that man." Her face is set in a stern expression. She doesn't believe me. God, can Amelia get back here already?

Blaise lets out a low whistle. "This bitch."

I write rigidly on the paper in front of me: *SHUT UP BLAISE*

"Are you sure that he holds nothing against your mom?" she asks, her eyes narrowed at me.

"I don't know." I focus on keeping my voice even, my body still, nothing else. "He left when I was a baby and Mom never told me why. So, he might, but probably not enough to kidnap her and Father Rodriguez and murder one of my friends."

She presses her lips together. "Then I'm afraid, if you're not going to be honest with me, we'll have to close the investigation."

"But Father Rodriguez just came back! You can't—"

"We have no leads." Her voice is monotone, almost bored. Has she even tried to find leads?

"And Aaron was murdered. Is that investigation still open? You can't—"

"We have no leads on that either."

"I've told you everything I know. I've been completely honest with you. You're just going to give up?"

"At this point, we have to assume that your mother is dead."

"But Father Rodriguez—"

"I'm sorry." She holds up a hand. "But your father was our only lead. And if you won't—"

"I don't know ANYTHING about him!" I shout.

She stares at me, mouth gaping. I snap my mouth shut and stammer out an apology, holding my hands tightly behind my back.

Blaise's hand is outstretched protectively in front of me, and he's glaring at Officer Meyer.

Amelia peers out from the back room. "Is everything alright?"

"Yes." Officer Meyer nods curtly and turns back to me. "I am very sorry, but that's just the way it is." And with that, she leaves the shop, bell dinging obnoxiously behind her.

I growl at the floor. Blaise is conspicuously silent. I look up to find him staring out at the entrance, his jaw clenched. I raise my eyebrows at him.

"I don't like her," he mutters in response.

My heart pounds violently, fingers curling around the side of the counter for support. She's giving up. Everyone is giving up.

I don't even know where Mom was taken from. Does she? Did she bother to check? Did she even bother to ask Mom's coworkers when they last saw her?

Amelia comes around the corner and lays a hand on my shoulder. Her eyes flit between me and the door, forehead creased in worry. I don't say anything. My blood is boiling over, and I don't want to lash out at her. I exhale slowly, hands shaking.

Finally, with an air of trying to distract me, she says, "Got the list of flowers we need?" I nod slowly, retrieving it from the counter up front. She studies it, furrowing her brows. "Who's Blaise?"

Blaise freezes behind her. "Imaginary friend," I blurt out.

Amelia laughs, the shattered laugh of someone entirely too stressed. "You are too funny. I'm glad I hired you. Never gonna be boring, is it?"

I sigh heavily. "No. Never going to be boring."

Chapter Twelve

A thick liquid covers me from head to toe. The waves are clashing violently, pummeling the sand. My hands hurt from putting pressure on something. Roses, dozens of them, surround me on the sand. They are blood red. A metallic smell fills my nostrils. Their thorns are embedded in my hands. It stings.

A red cloak whips across the corner of my vision. I follow it with my eyes, not daring to move. She takes down her hood and opens her hands to the waves. The misty rain forms dozens of ghostly figures.

I look down at my hands again. "Aaron," I whisper. The roses have become Aaron. My white dress is covered with blood. He gurgles at me. Then unintelligible words form. "What are you saying?" I lean towards him, hands on his throat.

"Jade." He grabs my neck violently. "Why didn't you come with me?"

"I'm sorry," I rasp.

Someone screams for me to run. The red cloak whips in the wind, following me wherever I turn. I keep running anyway, towards the flashing lights in the distance.

The red cloak envelops me, tenderly at first, then suffocating. It pushes me to the ground and only when I stay down does it let up. My body shakes with the effort to stand. The cloak is filled with a person again. A woman. I yank back on the hood, teeth bared.

A woman with blue eyes and blond hair, what once was a soft

smile, now a tight line. Her eyes are wide with fear. "Mom?" She lifts a hand to my head, running her fingers through my hair. Then something is at my throat and I'm on the ground again. She's crying.

Thunder rattles my window. I gasp, sitting bolt upright. My breath comes in short gasps, fingers raking at my throat.

"Are you alright?" It's a man's voice. A familiar man's voice. I jerk my head around. Where is it coming from?

Green covers. A bed. My childhood bed. The room is dark save for the occasional lightning. "Hey," the voice says again.

I hold my hands close to my chest, shivering. "Aaron," I whisper.

The voice speaks again, but I don't hear the words. I turn towards it.

A man, tall, with warm chocolate brown eyes and curly black hair. He's wearing sweatpants and no shirt. I blink several times, trying to decide whether I should be scared of this strange man in my room or not. "You're not awake yet," he says sagely, turning back towards the window.

It's too hot here. My feet carry me in a dead-on sprint for the bathroom. Everything is too bright and too loud. The man protests as he is dragged behind me. I slam the door shut and turn on the bath water.

I close my eyes, letting the freezing water run over my arms. My hands shake uncontrollably.

The man phases through the door and kneels down beside me. "Green Eyes," he whispers. "Jillian. It's me, Blaise."

"Blaise," I repeat slowly, blinking heavily. "I'm not afraid of you."

"Why—why would you be?"

I turn my gaze back towards the bath. The sound of water rushes towards my ears. I blink away the images of red cloaks and roses. The bathroom tile, cold and grey. The bath water runs over my shaking hands, shocking my nervous system back to life. The man kneeling beside me, not really here, but appearing perfectly solid.

I choke on air. "Aaron's dead." The words leave my mouth unwillingly. His gaze softens with pity. "My friend. That woman, in the red cloak." My heart seethes with rage. "She killed him."

His voice is remarkably steady compared to mine. "How do you know?"

"He showed me." I scrub at my hands, determined to wash away the memory of Aaron's blood beneath my fingernails. "I looked into his eyes, and he showed me. The Red Reaper." Blaise tenses.

There's a soft knock on the door. "Hey," Deanna whispers. I'd forgotten they were staying here.

I turn the bathwater off and open the door for her. Her eyes widen when she sees me. "Are you okay?" she asks, kneeling beside me.

She goes right through Blaise and shivers but doesn't seem to think anything of it. For Blaise's part, he sighs heavily and moves out of the way. I blink several times before responding. "Nightmare."

"I get them too," she confesses. "Sometimes, I think he's talking to me. Like he's visiting me in my dreams."

"He talks to me, too. He says it's my fault."

"No." Deanna's voice is soft, but her eyes are firm. "It's not. No one could have known Ja—"

"Father Rodriguez and Mom went missing, and I let him go outside by himself. It was a stupid decision. I wasn't thinking. I'm sorry Deanna. I'm so—"

"Stop that." My mouth clamps shut. "No more. Whoever it was that killed him. That's who I'm blaming." I inhale deeply. I should tell her. I should tell her about the Red Reaper. But when I open my mouth to speak, nothing comes with it. "You should go back to sleep. You've got a big day with the wedding set up tomorrow." I can't believe the week went by this quickly.

"Right," I mutter. "Right, yeah. Get some sleep." We hug

each other tightly. She leaves the bathroom and I return to my scrubbing.

Once my hands are so raw and dry that I can't remember what it feels like for anything to touch them, I stop. I take a second in front of the mirror to compose myself and shove the resurfacing emotions down, then return to my room. Blaise is conspicuously silent as he follows. I turn to make sure that his eyes haven't become glowing red without warning.

No, same warm chocolaty brown eyes. "You have something to say?" I ask. He shakes his head. "Alright." I shrug and make my way back into bed, before remembering that my shirt is completely soaked through. I turn to him. "Well turn around!"

He chuckles to himself. "What? Not even a peek?"

"No!" I half laugh. "Nothing for you. Turn around." He does. I yank the drenched shirt over my head and grab a blue pajama set from my closet. A thought occurs to me, but I don't ask it until I'm fully dressed. "Do you—Do you watch me while I sleep?"

"What?" He remains facing the other way.

"You can turn around now." He does. "Do you watch me while I sleep?"

"God no," he says. "That's disgusting. Why would I do that?" I shrug nonchalantly. "Do you think you're interesting to watch when you sleep or something? Let me tell you." He makes a list with his fingers. "You don't snore. Or talk in your sleep. You don't even breathe all that loudly."

I smirk at him and cross my arms. "So, you have watched me."

He splutters. "No. I mean. Well. No!" I raise my eyebrows. "Maybe. For like ten minutes. It's not like there's anything for me to do here. I can't mess with your stuff, or play chess, or read, or anything!" I take a step away from him as he walks towards me. My back hits the door. "Mostly I just stare at your posters and try to find meaning in them."

"And what have you found?" I ask.

"Nothing, Green Eyes!" He points to one of them. "Your posters mean nothing."

"That one's kind of inspirational." I laugh.

He takes a step towards me, rolling his eyes. "Oh yeah, 'Attitude is Everything.' I've stared at that poster for hours. Irrefutable logic. Not very meaningful."

"Hey! My Nani got me that. Have some respect." I snort. "And your posters are so great?" I challenge, taking a step towards him.

"You haven't seen my posters." He holds back the smile that's playing around his lips. "They're great."

"I'm sure. I see you're out of the hospital." I gesture to his clothing, trying not to linger too long on his bare chest. "So, what's in your room, 'Live, Laugh, Love'?"

He takes another step towards me, sending my heart racing. "I will have you know that I have no posters in my room."

I take half a step forwards, practically touching him. Warmth emanates from him. The air between us crackles with static electricity. I wonder . . . "What do you have?"

"Cement walls." His breath dances across my forehead. Strange. He seems so real, so solid. If I could just make myself—

"I have bare cement walls and the only thing hanging up is a calendar."

I meet his brown eyes to find my own curiosity mirrored back at me. "What kind of calendar?" I whisper. He blushes. "Go on, Blaise. What kind of calendar?"

"Flowers," he mutters. "February is violets."

"Sounds pretty." I smile. My hand reaches towards him of its own accord. He takes a step back and runs a hand through his hair. Both of us exhale as the tension dissipates. "Also, meaningless."

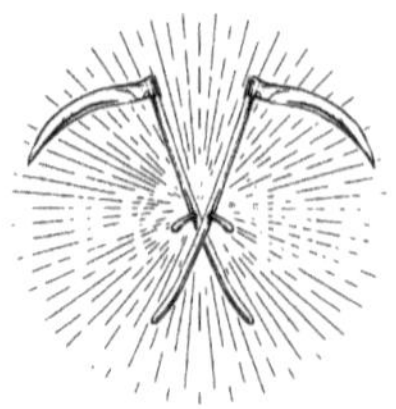

I knew I wasn't going to be able to get back to sleep, but Blaise in my peripheral vision isn't helping. What if I reached out and tested —

I shake my head and make my way down the hallway to Mom's room. I knock softly.

Deanna peeks her head through the door. "Sleepover?" I ask. She nods and follows me back to my room. We burrow into the single bed together and I wrap my arms around her.

She drifts into a fitful sleep. Blaise is determinedly staring only out the window. "It rains a lot here," he whispers.

"It's what happens when you live near a body of water." My voice is barely audible. "I'm guessing you don't?"

He shakes his head slightly. "It's nice. The rain."

"It is." Deanna stirs next to me. I run my fingers through her hair slowly until she settles back down. Blaise presses his lips together and turns back to the window. I bury my face into the top of Deanna's head, hoping to drown it all out.

Chapter Thirteen

We wake up to the shrill screams of my alarm clock. Deanna groans and burrows further into my arms. My left arm is numb and prickly. Blaise attempts to turn the alarm clock off to no avail.

I yawn heavily and extricate myself from beneath the covers, slamming the off button with all my might.

"Why is your alarm clock so loud?" Blaise asks.

I shrug and lie back on the pillow. I want nothing more than to go back to sleep. "Deanna?" I whisper. "Hey. It's time to wake up."

"Ugh. Nooooooo," she mumbles into the pillow. "More cuddles."

I chuckle. "This. This is why everyone at school thought we were dating." I'm saying this more for Blaise's benefit than hers.

"Fine. Fine." She rolls over, her black waves in disarray.

I rush downstairs to set up breakfast: oatmeal and chai. It's bagged tea, not nearly as good as Nani made, but it'll do.

Carl is the second one in the kitchen. Since Aaron died, there's hardly any life behind his eyes. This morning is no different. His brown eyes are glazed over, as though he's staring through everything, not at it.

"Big day today?" he asks in a monotone voice.

I nod. "Kate's wedding."

"They're hosting it at The Ridge?"

The Ridge, a circular building that rests on the edge of one of our many cliffs. They installed a fence around theirs though. We host everything in our town there. Deanna and I had prom at The Ridge. Mom was planning to get married at The Ridge. They were nice enough to give her the deposit back.

"Yup."

Deanna and Carl are taking the girls to school today since I have to be in early. I give each of the girls a quick squeeze goodbye and set out for the shop.

Blaise has finally woken up by the time I arrive.

Amelia is stressed as ever, flying around the shop to ensure we have every flower and arrangement we need in her truck bed before we go. She double, triple, checks before we finally set out.

"Calm down," I say. "We have a whole hour, it's okay."

A glint of red fabric whips in the corner of my vision. I gasp and crane my neck to search for it. I can see her through the rearview mirror, in the red cloak, standing in the middle of the road.

"Oh God." My heart sinks to my stomach. Just like with Aaron. And a week later he was dead. I pull my hair over my left shoulder. Maybe I can hide it. Maybe she doesn't know . . .

No. She does. I'll have to fight and lose. "Anything wrong?" Amelia asks.

"No." I shake my head. "Just realized that I forgot—"

"What did we forget?"

"—to make the girls' lunches." She sighs in relief. I can barely turn my attention away from the beating of my heart and the prickling of my neck.

Is today the day the Reaper gets me?

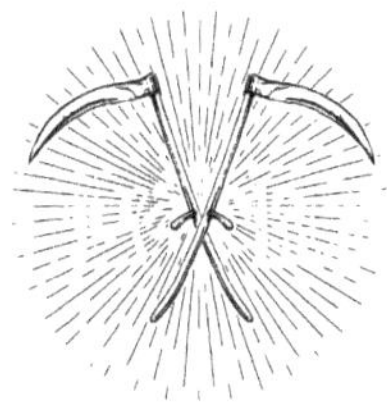

Amelia pulls into the parking lot. We transport flowers inside in batches. I bring them to Amelia, and she arranges each centerpiece and doorway to her liking. Sweat trickles down my neck, but not from physical exertion.

Where is she? Where is the Red Reaper?

"We've only got ten minutes left, Jade!" Amelia shouts as I make my way back to the truck for my final trip.

Blaise appears in the corner of my vision. "Green Eyes!" he shouts, his voice panicked. I turn to him, my arms full of flowers. "Behind—" His voice breaks off in a choked gurgle all too similar to Aaron's and he disappears. I turn towards the trees where his gaze was fixed.

The hair on my arms stands on end and my throat goes dry. A red cloak is glaring out at me through the trees. I'm alone. I'm all alone.

Nothing to stop her. We stare at each other. I can't see her face, but I can feel the danger radiating off her. She is oddly still.

I can see the reason for that. Amelia is beside me. I didn't notice her. "Are you alright?" she asks, following my gaze into the trees. The Red Reaper is gone. I make myself nod. "Come help me do the final arrangements then."

I follow her back inside, my legs shaking. I'm about to be murdered. The second I am alone, I'm going to be—

Jade?

The voice comes from my head, but it's male. And familiar. I've definitely heard him before. It's not Blaise. It's not Aaron.

Jade? it says again, hesitantly. As if he's not sure I'll answer. I'm not even sure if I should. *Jade. Please listen to me. I know this must be strange, someone talking in your head.*

I'm frozen where I stand. Amelia's eyes narrow with concern, but the more pressing matter to her is taking the flowers from my arms and finishing up our arrangements.

There's a voice in my head. He's talking to me. How is he doing that? Why do I recognize his voice?

I need to tell you. To warn you. They're going to kill you today.

I return my mind to that much more pressing matter. My oncoming demise. I have to stay calm, stay present, or I won't survive. *I'm aware.* I think at the voice. *I saw her.*

The only way for you to get to safety Jade is, well, it's best not to explain until you get there. But you need to go to the church on the cliff.

I stare at the centerpiece in front of me, frozen with indecision.

Jade. Are you hearing me? There's a way out at the church.

My eyes fixate on the table where Amelia has left the keys to her truck. "Okay," I say out loud this time. I snatch up the keys before I can think twice. Hearing voices in my head is just one more thing in a long list of weird things that have happened to me lately.

I sprint for the truck ignoring Amelia's questions.

I'm in the truck and out onto the road before I can fully process what I'm doing. The Red Reaper runs towards me but stops when she sees Amelia behind me.

The truck does not handle well on the curvy road back into town, but I go as fast as I can. There's a blue car that I can barely make out behind me. One with a suspiciously red hooded driver.

I barrel through town far past the reasonable speed limit and make a sharp left turn into the church parking lot. The blue car has followed.

"Okay." I run from the car. "Now what, guy in my head?"

Jump.

"Off the cliff?" I squeak as the blue car pulls in behind me.

Yes.

I curse. "Do you *want* me to die?"

Of course not. You're precious to me. But it's the only way.

I hear a car door open. My feet approach the edge of the cliff. I stare over the precipice. The crashing waves are so far down. "What will jumping off a cliff do?" I whisper hurriedly.

It will take you to Death.

"Well duh!" My heart pounds in my ears. Measured footsteps creep up behind me. I glimpse part of her red cloak in the corner of my vision.

No. I mean Death. The kingdom. You won't actually die.

"No. No. Absolutely not."

If you don't jump, she will kill you.

"I'm going to die either way!" I take several deep breaths as the footsteps get closer. I turn to face her, watching as she ambles forwards leisurely. The cloak fully obscures her face, but her scythe is out for blood.

You won't die. I promise.

She growls low and fierce, a growl of pure hatred. Her legs are gearing up for a sprint. Panic rises through my every limb. This is the craziest thing I've ever done. I look to the church.

A leap of faith.

The Red Reaper breaks into a sprint. I shut my eyes. "You'll catch me?"

Yes.

Her hand wraps around my shoulder, but she doesn't have enough resolve to plunge with me. Her grip slips.

The sound of the waves grows louder in my ears as the ground disappears beneath me.

Chapter Fourteen

My scream dies in my throat, my heart settling somewhere in my stomach. The wind rushes past me and I clench my eyes shut, preparing for a horrible impact and a saltwater grave.

The impact never comes. The fall never stops. I'm still falling, falling, falling . . .

I open my eyes hesitantly. I'm in the water, still falling through it like air. It becomes darker and darker until I can't see anything around me. Pitch black, and I'm still falling. I blink in confusion. Where am I?

Maybe I died on impact and my soul is taking a road trip instead of going directly to a Reaper. I don't feel dead though. Not in the slightest.

I can't tell if I'm falling or flying upwards anymore. Direction means nothing. I close my eyes again, trying to reorient myself.

My feet hit solid ground softly. Before I can open my eyes again, my legs give out underneath me, becoming jelly.

I don't dare open my eyes, still half convinced that I'm falling. Or that I've finally died. "Is she alright?" A woman's voice breaks through the silence.

Tears spill from my eyes and laughter from my mouth, both completely out of my control. Elation and horror mix within me until I'm hacking with coughs on my hands and knees. "Poor thing," another voice says, male this time.

The crazed laughter won't stop. I've never felt so alive, yet so convinced that I'm dead. I gasp shakily and force my eyes open.

An endless night sky stretches above me, twinkling with the lights of millions of stars. I blink slowly at it. No. Black stone makes up the ceiling, and countless jewels make up the stars. It stretches on forever, or at least for as far as I can see.

A young woman kneels beside me, her hands hovering by my shoulders. Her skin is covered in freckles and her auburn ringlets are pulled back into a short messy ponytail. She leans forwards nervously, hazel eyes peering at me in concern through large round glasses. "I'm sorry. We were warned in time to take the stairs." She turns her head, showing me her mark, two scythes crossed below her left ear.

"You're alive," a man's voice says from behind me. I spin towards him. Gangly and tall. Everything about him is pointy from his black hair to his bony elbows. He's somewhere in his midforties. He tilts his head to show me his matching mark, although his skin is darker, and it's more difficult to see. I pull my hair to the side to reveal mine.

"Where am I?" My voice is hoarse and thick, but at least both the laughing and the tears have stopped. "We're all Reapers? What's going on?"

"My name is Esley." The freckled woman speaks low and slow. It's soothing. "This is Palmer. And yes, we're both Reapers."

"I'm Jade." I rise shakily. My legs are barely able to support me, but I'm determined to stand.

"This is the land of Death," Esley explains, taking my forearms in her hands to steady me.

"And I can't stress this enough, you are *not* dead," Palmer says firmly.

"Only Reapers can come down here." Her freckled visage breaks across my line of sight again. "And live, I mean. Everyone comes down here, eventually."

I only now notice a piano playing in the distance. Parts of

the music are haunting, others bright and light. It's an odd combination, calming and unnerving at the same time. I spin around, searching for the source, but I can't find it anywhere. "You hear that too, right?"

"The pianos?" Esley asks. "Yes."

I exhale the tension from my shoulders, only for it to return as the piano music stops. Crisp and clear footsteps replace it. "We've alerted everyone that we can." This voice reaches through me into my very bones. It's ancient and young, stern and friendly, all at the same time. "I'm expecting a few more of . . ." The voice trails off as it reaches us.

A hooded figure stands before me. Inhumanely tall. Somewhere near seven or eight feet. The figure pulls down the hood to reveal . . .

I peer at the face in front of me. I can't quite pin down features yet. Part of me sees a man, part of me sees a woman. Part of me sees someone old, part of me sees someone my age. All I can tell is that they are taller than any person I've ever seen. I clench my eyes shut against the rapidly changing figure before me.

When I open them, the hood has become a blue veil embellished with white stars. A young cherubic face pears out from the veil with full pink lips and porcelain white skin. No . . . Dark skin, dark as charcoal. I close my eyes again and open them.

The figure alternates between full figured and incredibly lithe. I squeeze my eyes shut again, rubbing my eyes. Upon opening them, my brain has settled on somewhere in the middle. Many layers of white and red fabric drape them.

I glance back up at their face again. Dark wavy locks escape from the blue veil and there is a glowing halo around the top of their head. I exhale heavily as my brain finally settles on the Virgin Mary.

Although, something isn't quite human about this figure. The neck is a little too long. They are still insanely tall, and their eyes . . .

Their eyes never changed form. They are a bright unnerving shade of yellowish green that penetrates everything they look at, glowing like the jewels hanging above us.

It's a moment before I realize my mouth is hanging open and yet another moment before I think to shut it.

"Jade Zaveri." Their voice courses through my whole body, light and powerful. Their eyes are full of emotion, but much like the paintings I've seen of the Virgin Mary, the rest of them is immovable.

"Do I know you?" I can't tear my eyes away, determined to see through whatever illusion is being presented to me, but terrified to fully uncover it.

"No," they say, pulling the veil down to their shoulders. "But I know you." They approach me. I know I should be afraid, but I can't bring myself to be. "Do not be afraid," they say. "I am Death." The voice reverberates around the entire room. "But I would prefer that you call me Desdemon."

"Desdemon?"

"Yes. I've known many names to many people, but this is the one that I've chosen for myself."

"It's a pleasure to meet you, Desdemon." I nod cordially, hit with the sense that I am speaking to something more ancient than the world itself.

"May I ask?" Desdemon circles me. Esley and Palmer are equally transfixed. "What do you see me as?"

"Mary. I see you as the Virgin Mary." The words leave my mouth before I can think. "Or that's what my brain's settled on for now. Will you tell me what you really look like?"

Desdemon's laugh rings off the walls again. "Palmer, what do you see?"

"You're an old man, frail, wispy white hair." When I blink, for half a moment, I see what Palmer sees.

"And Esley darling?"

Esley takes a deep breath before speaking. "You are transparent. Like an anatomy model. I can see the different systems, skeletal, muscular, your organs. I can see your heart pumping, blood moving through your veins. Female and male reproductive organs, but no"—her voice cuts off suddenly. Desdemon nods, encouraging her to continue—"no womb."

"Interesting." Desdemon tilts their head at Esley, then turns to me. "I'm afraid you'll have to find out for yourself, Jade. I could tell you, but that doesn't mean you'll ever see it." Desdemon smiles at me in an entirely un-virgin Mary like manner. It's teasing and sad at the same time.

I open my mouth several times, trying to remember what brought me here. "Desdemon?" I finally blurt out. "How did you know where I was? Who is the Red Reaper?" They cock their head to the side. "And when can I go back home? My sisters, they're—"

"Slow down." Their voice is a command that I can do nothing but follow. "Red Reaper? What is this?"

"I haven't seen a Red Reaper." Esley adjusts her glasses.

"What is this Red Reaper?" Desdemon asks.

"A woman with a scythe. She always wears a red cloak. I've never seen her face. She"—my voice catches in my throat—"she killed my friend. And she's been following me." Desdemon's green eyes are filled with sorrow, but blank with confusion. "You're Death! You must know this already! Don't you know everything?"

They shake their head mournfully. "I knew about your friend. A terrible loss, truly. But Jade, that is the world of the living. I know only what touches the world of the dead." Their appearance flickers again, just for a moment. They no longer have porcelain white skin. Now they have skin only a shade or two lighter than mine.

"Then, how did you know to save me? Whose voice did I hear?"

"We received a message," Desdemon speaks slowly. "Anonymously, relayed through Elian—Life, that is, that the

Reapers were in danger. I was told that you were the next mark, and that Esley and Palmer were to be the next marks after you." They adjust their veil again. "I've only heard of three other marks, and they have been alerted to join us here."

"But my sisters, I have to go back. I need to make sure they're safe. I have to—"

"Your mother will take care of them. Do not worry," Desdemon whispers.

Their words force a feeling of comfort through me that lasts for only a second before logic breaks through the haze. "My mother is missing. I'm all they have left."

"Vanessa Zaveri is missing?" Worry exudes from Desdemon, infecting the surrounding air.

Despite it all, my heart fills with hope. "You didn't know? Thank God, that means she's alive!" I pace, searching for a way out of here. "I have to find her!"

"Wait!" Desdemon's voice echoes through my bones again. My limbs stop moving, even though I want to continue. "Let me look into this. It's not safe for you to return." I don't even get a chance to respond before Desdemon disappears through some portal that is only in existence for a second. The piano music starts back up, hurried and abrupt.

"Why does Death know about your mother?" Palmer asks.

"I don't know!" I shout back, my brain rifling through everything I know about Mom's disappearance. "Sorry. I didn't mean—It's just that she's—we're nobodies. Honestly. We're from a small town and we are nobodies." I pace back and forth, running my hands along the air in search of a portal. "How do they know our names, anyway?"

"They said that the Grim Reaper tells them the names of all the Reapers," Esley responds. "What are you looking for?"

I don't answer her. "Is this place a different dimension or very, *very* deep underground?"

"I'm not sure." Esley strides towards me. "Maybe both? We took the stairs, so there must be something underground about it."

"Stairs?" I whisper. "Show me."

"Right." Palmer straightens up. "They said three more were coming. We ought to see if they've arrived." He starts off in one direction, closes his eyes, and then turns around. "This way. I'm sure of it."

We follow him through endless darkness. Palmer occasionally makes a turn through what appears to be a nonexistent hallway until I take the turn a moment too soon and smack directly into an invisible wall. "Ow." I rub my nose as Esley giggles. "Oh, shut up."

"Like a bird into a screen door," she says, following Palmer's right-hand turn. "Ow!" she says, rubbing her shoulder. I laugh once loudly. "Point made." She smiles. "Palmer, could you slow down?"

"Nope!" he says, barreling forwards. "Or I will lose my sense of direction."

"Does he even know where he's going?" I whisper to her out of the corner of my mouth.

"I don't know." She rolls her eyes. "I only met him earlier today. He certainly acts like it."

Soft and urgent piano music follows us wherever we turn. Some notes float through me like air, others stick in me, like honey. There is a clash of notes that is ear splitting and jarring.

A flash of green takes over my vision.

Esley screams and ducks to the ground. I blink, shadows passing across my eyes even as the light clears. A bright green and glowing gemstone waits in front of us, pulsing.

"You see it too?" I ask Palmer.

He nods. "I don't like this," he says.

I think the whole place is fascinating. I reach out to touch the stone in front of us.

Chapter Fifteen

By the time I finish blinking, I'm in a new place entirely. Palmer is no longer in front of me. All the sparkling stones and lights have disappeared. "Hello?" I call out into the darkness.

A low voice rumbles through me. I feel the voice rather than hear it. "Jade Zaveri." The voice whispers my name as though it's a statement all on its own.

"Yes?" I answer. "Who are you?"

It tells me to come closer, not with words, but with something else, something much deeper than words. I can't help but obey.

"Where am I?" I ask the darkness. I should be more afraid. I can't even see what I'm speaking to. But I'm not. It answers by showing me.

I can see again. Thousands upon thousands of blue orbs wait before me, all encircling something or someone in the center. I can't quite see the center. I shift my attention to the orbs at my feet. The ones nearest me are the faintest blueish grey hue, but farther away I see bright glowing blue ones. I stoop down to inspect the orb at my feet. Someone's face, an old woman's, peers out at me. The ones next to it also have faces.

The orb grows fainter and fainter in my hand until it disappears entirely.

I'm bid to walk further, but I resist. These orbs are important. Shock that I have resisted washes over me from whatever is speaking to me. "What are these?" I ask.

"Windows to souls," it answers, out loud this time. "Those who have reached the outside are meant to die soon."

"That woman just died?" I ask. Did I speed it along by touching it?

It beckons me closer. My feet move of their own accord. "Please stop," I beg. My feet stop moving almost immediately.

I peer towards the center of the space again. I'm able to make out a monumental, hooded figure, with bone thin hands and a scythe as tall as a one-story building. The scythe extends out somberly and plucks a bright blue orb gently. The figure makes a gesture with their hands, almost like praying. The orb disappears.

"Are you who I think you are?"

He nods. "Come closer, sister Reaper." I will myself forwards, determined not to smash any of the orbs. "STOP!" he shouts suddenly. My feet freeze in an awkward tiptoe position. I have to use every ounce of every ballet lesson I've ever had not to topple over.

Deanna's round face peers up at me through the orb beneath my feet. She wears an expression of utter despair. I clap a hand over my mouth and flex the muscles of my calves to steady myself further.

The scythe extends out to meet me, the blade at the end large enough to be a platform. I step on gingerly and allow myself to be lifted towards the center with ease. "You will be pleased to know that her time will not come for many years, as long as nothing unforeseeable occurs."

"I . . . thanks?" He places me on a column next to a large book. "How did I get here?"

"I wanted you to," he says. "I have information about your mother, and I would prefer that my parents not find out."

I furrow my brows. "Was Aaron telling the truth? Are you the child of Life and Death?" He nods. "Literally or figuratively? And how? And—"

"Well, when two people love each other very much . . ." His tone is teasing. "They—"

"Oh." I laugh. "So literally." He bows his head. "Sorry. Um . . . "

The blue orbs around me glow brighter, allowing me to see more of our surroundings. We're surrounded by columns on all sides. They're all different styles and as tall as skyscrapers.

"My mom," I start. "How do you know and neither of your parents do?"

"They deal in lives. I deal in souls. And your mother's soul is," the Grim Reaper sighs, "screaming for help."

I wait anxiously, perched on the tips of my toes.

"I know who has your mother. It will be a perilous journey. It isn't your time to die, but"—his cloak changes to red for the briefest of moments and my heart responds in anguish—"these people don't care much for life."

"Just tell me how to find her."

"It is as you suspected. The people who killed Aaron are the same people that have your mother. And they will not hesitate to kill you." The Grim Reaper lowers his head mournfully. "As I said, it is not your time."

"If it's not my time, can't you just decide to let me live?"

He shakes his head. "I can only warn you away from Death. I have no power to stop it."

"If I do this, is it guaranteed I'll die?"

"Nothing is ever guaranteed," he says. "But the risk is certainly higher."

I let the words settle. My heart is jittery. Mom is in pain. She needs me. I take a deep steadying breath and come to my decision. "I'll do anything to bring her home."

Without any warning, Mom's face is in front of me, encased in a dark blue orb. Her blue eyes are bloodshot, her blond hair matted and dirty. Her normally immaculately clean face is covered in dirt and bruises. "What are they doing to her?" My voice trembles.

"The worst thing that can be done to a person." His voice shakes with barely restrained rage. "Denying her death."

I cock my head to the side, trying to puzzle out the meaning. "Torture?" A nod. "Why?"

"She has something that they want."

"Desdemon knew her name earlier. Why is Mom important to them?"

The Grim Reaper gives no response. "I believe they want Desdemon to come after her. Des would if they knew, and we can't have that. It's too dangerous."

I hesitate. Something too dangerous for Death and the Grim Reaper is sending me? Mom's face peers out at me from the dark blue orb again. "I won't tell Desdemon. What do I do?"

"This is a window into your mother's soul." He holds out the sphere with Mom's face. "It will lead you to your mother. But be careful with it. Breaking it releases the soul and when that person is already alive, that kills them."

I stare at the orb apprehensively. I've never considered myself to be a klutz, far from it actually. But this, this is too much to rest on that. "Do you have something I could carry it in?"

The orb floats towards me. I hold my breath as it passes through my peripheral vision and melds with my Reaper mark. Cold drips down my neck. My shoulders tense as I shiver. The coldness dissipates. "It will only break if you die."

"And if she dies?" I ask.

"So do you," he says solemnly.

I don't have time to let that settle. A strange sensation is urging me upwards. I stand. Up. I need to go up. Higher. It's an unpleasant sensation, like there's a string attached to my neck.

I'm seeing through someone else's eyes, pulling at shackles around my wrists. My daughters, all three of them, alone. Footsteps approach down a hall. Panic rises through my throat.

My surroundings change from that dark room to the one with

all the blue orbs. I step back on the metal part of the scythe and allow the Grim Reaper to lift me towards the outer edge of the circle.

"Good luck, Jade," he says.

I have to get to her.

The scene around me changes again. A bright light flashes in front of me. I'm back in the hallway, standing next to Palmer.

"Where did you go?" Palmer asks.

"I don't know," I say honestly. "Another room maybe?"

"Three Reapers passed by us. There's no point in going to the stairs anymore. We're all down here now," he says.

The tugging string urges me upwards. "But I need to get to the—"

"Desdemon might know something about your mom. C'mon." I follow them reluctantly back to the main area.

Desdemon is busy welcoming three bewildered Reapers in when we return but breaks off almost instantly to find me. Nothing. They have nothing on Mom, as I expected.

It settles in me like a ball of lead that I am Mom's only hope. And I have to get out of here. Desdemon's distress only shows in their bright green eyes.

The tugging sensation grows more and more insistent. "I know," I mutter. "Soon."

Chapter Sixteen

Desdemon leads the six of us through the incomprehensible twists and turns of this world until we enter a small room. A single chair waits at the head of a small table, but with a wave of Desdemon's hand, six more appear and the table lengthens.

At Desdemon's insistence, I take the seat closest to them. It's taking most of my concentration to keep my shoulders relaxed. That tugging sensation is hellbent on pulling every part of my body up. We must be underground in some sense then.

Forks clatter in strained silence before I even notice that food has appeared in front of me. Or how incredibly hungry I am.

My plate is laden with airy bread and a variety of spreads and sauces. The airy bread turns to naan in the blink of an eye before I even register the wish crossing my mind. Mulligatawny soup accompanies it.

I raise my spoon to my lips, intent on wolfing it all down. It smells incredible. I'm back home. Nothing is wrong. Aaron is making mulligatawny soup in the kitchen and the girls are running a bath upstairs.

A scream rattles through my brain.

My spoon clatters against the bowl, soup splashing everywhere. The trance is gone. And everyone is staring at me.

That same vision of a red hooded woman slitting my throat, Aaron's throat, flashes before me. My hands shake, remembering the feeling of Aaron's blood coating them.

The mulligatawny soup disappears, replaced by tomato soup instead. I can't decide if I want it back or if I'm glad for its absence.

"Are you alright?" Esley hisses.

I clench my eyes shut and shake the images from my mind. "Yes. I'm fine. Thank you."

I turn to Desdemon, their cat-like gaze fixed on me curiously. "How exactly does this food work?" I ask. "Are you doing it?"

"No," they say. Their appearance flickers before me again, no longer quite the same Virgin Mary as before. They have darker skin now and curly black hair that is coarse and dry beneath their veil. "It is a special room. It can sense your emotions and what would make you feel full."

"Is it real food, then?"

"Real enough to keep anyone who's ever been down here fed well."

I nod and return to my plate. Small talk resumes around me. Anyone who's ever been down here. Huh.

Deanna went through a period in middle school where she was obsessed with Greek myths. She wanted to be Persephone, half springtime, half death.

The queen of the underworld, trapped because she ate pomegranate seeds.

Neither of us had seen a pomegranate before. Carl bought them in the city, and we popped the seeds into our mouths one by one, counting out the months and laughing.

The food changes before me, replaced by twelve pomegranate seeds. I furrow my brows at them. Esley's eyes are on me, full of concern. I chance a glance at her plate, also full of pomegranate seeds. My eyes meet hers and she raises her eyebrows. I give the tiniest of nods. We're not supposed to eat.

The thought has barely entered my mind before both of our plates empty themselves.

My stomach rumbles from the long day, but still nothing

appears. Around us, Palmer and the other Reapers are discussing their lives and families. I swallow hard, building up my courage and waiting for a break in the conversation.

I seize my opportunity before I lose my nerve. "Have any of you seen the Red Reaper?"

They turn towards me with varying expressions of confusion. "The Red Reaper?" An old man wearing glasses and a white button-down shirt peers at me from next to Palmer.

"Yes. It's someone wearing a red hood and carrying a scythe? Have you seen one?"

"No. I've never heard of it," a middle-aged woman with black hair and a heavy accent that I can't place speaks. "Why?"

"She killed my friend. She's been killing Reapers." Everyone shares a worried glance with someone at the table and then turns their gaze to Desdemon for an explanation.

"We're looking into it." Desdemon's voice rattles my bones yet again. "We called you down here because you were the next targets. You'll stay here until it's handled and you're safe." Their voice has a calming effect on me. I will be safe. I will stay here.

It has a similar effect on the other occupants of our table. Shoulders relax and they return to their food.

The tugging sensation breaks through my sense of calm, drawing me up as though a string is attached to my spine.

A pair of eyes drills a hole into the side of my head. I turn to meet them. Desdemon is assessing me with worry and some other emotion that I can't quite identify. Perhaps pity. Their eyes flit to my empty plate and then back up at me. Desdemon resumes conversation with the blond Reaper across the table.

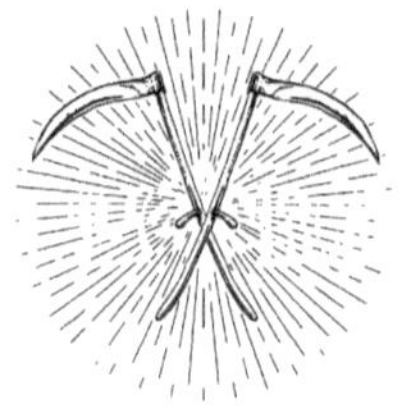

We're led to another room after dinner. It's full of little alcoves with incredibly comfy mattresses. Between my cheap bed at home and a few college dorm beds, I don't think I've ever slept in something this soft. Although, one guy did have a mattress pad. It doesn't compare to this.

I don't lie down for long. The incessant tugging in my head pulls me upward shortly after Desdemon leaves.

I need to go up, but I have no idea where the stairs are. I highly doubt I'll be able to find them on my own.

I pull myself to a seated position and search the pile of sleeping bodies for Esley's auburn curls.

She's in the alcove across from mine, pulling her hair up into a wild ponytail. We make eye contact, and she jerks her head. I follow her out of the room.

"When we get out of here, I'm gonna need food. Deal?" she whispers.

"Deal." I nod. "How did you know not to eat the food?"

She runs a hand along the space next to us until it hits a wall. "Unhealthy Greek myth obsession when I was younger. You?"

"You would love my friend Deanna," I mutter.

Our surroundings get even darker without warning. It startles us into silence. We follow the walls aimlessly.

Piano music drifts through the air, the chords dissonant and sweet. Something about it makes me want to turn around and go back to sleep. Esley yawns. "These stairs are gonna suck," she mumbles. "Maybe we can take a nap first?"

I rub my eyes. "I was thinking the same"—the tugging sensation returns—"no." I shake my head. "It's a trick, Esley. Or a lullaby. But we have to keep going."

Esley nods sleepily and readjusts her glasses.

A blinding green light flashes in front of us. A large emerald gemstone waits on the wall directly in front of us.

"This again?" Esley inspects it. "Why does it do that?"

"Just grab this one." She grabs it at the same time as me and in the blink of an eye, we're somewhere else.

An archway stands before us and beyond it, stairs and the dimmest of lights. We rush forwards, but Esley stops dead in her tracks.

I turn back to her, brows furrowed. "C'mon. I already told you. We can't nap." She still doesn't move. "If you want to stay here, that's fine, but I have to go." I turn towards the stairs again.

"Going somewhere?" she says in a strangely deadened voice.

"Up the stairs?" It's eerily quiet now. Too quiet. The piano music has stopped. It's as if all the air was sucked out of this hallway. Esley's eyes are glowing a bright yellowish green.

I shuffle backwards, looking for the source of the change in her. Was it that green gemstone?

"You can't leave," Esley hisses. Her voice is ominous and commanding.

"Esley?" I whisper.

"I am trying to protect you. You were the first mark."

Her voice is entirely unlike her own. It's more clipped and formal. "Ah." I fold my arms in front of my chest. The green glow in her eyes. "Desdemon." I shudder involuntarily. "Could you stop with the possession thing? I doubt Esley likes it."

Esley's eyes are hazel again. She shakes and almost collapses forwards. I rush to support her.

Decisive footsteps are coming down the hall towards us. "You can't leave," Desdemon repeats. Their voice courses through my body, cementing my feet to the floor.

It's a struggle, but I turn to face them. Their face is different again, more angular than the angelic cherubic face of the Virgin Mary that I'm used to.

"They will kill you." Their voice resounds in my chest, the certainty of it crashing down on me.

They will kill me. I won't escape.

I grit my teeth against the incredible persuasiveness of their words. "I have to finish this." Esley is a dead weight leaning against me, hell bent on becoming one with the floor. "It's my fight. They're after my family. I can't stay down here and hide until maybe you sort this out."

"They aren't after your family, Jade. They're after Reapers, which you are one of!"

I want nothing more than to sink into Desdemon's arms and let the world take care of itself instead.

I shake my head. "That didn't stop them from taking my mom, and it certainly won't stop them from taking my sisters."

"They're the ones who took your mother? They took Vanessa Zaveri?"

Crap. "No. I don't know. I mean"—I scramble for words—"I don't know where my mom is, but I have to find her. And I'll be damned if I don't make sure my sisters are safe, too." I take a step towards the stairs, helping a semi-conscious Esley along with me.

"You can't leave," Desdemon repeats forcefully, practically rooting my feet to the ground. Esley becomes much harder to will forwards.

"I can do whatever I damn well please!" I force another step out of myself.

"You cannot once you've eaten the food. Not unless I give my permission." I force another step. "You ate the food, didn't you?"

Finally, their voice is uncertain. I smirk. The archway is two steps away. I fling Esley through it. She finally gets her wits about her once she crosses the threshold of the archway.

I take the first of two steps towards her, but my feet aren't my own anymore.

Thoughts and memories from eras I've never lived in flood my mind. Hundreds of thousands of losses weigh on my heart. People are crying out in languages I've never even heard of before. A woman doing up someone else's corset, a man tending a garden, a ship sinking to the bottom of the sea, discovering fire.

The weight of it all brings me to my knees. My breath comes in heavy gasps as more memories from times long ago pass through me.

I push against them with everything I have, shoving out the thoughts and memories from before I was born. I push out everything that isn't mine. My eyes fly open. The space between us glows a sharp, bright green. I grit my teeth. "GET OUT!"

Desdemon's mouth is agape as I bring myself up to my feet. I turn away and hurl myself through the archway, almost colliding with Esley.

It's only when I meet Esley's awed gaze that I realize the greenish glow isn't coming from Desdemon. It's coming from me.

"Your eyes," Esley pants. "Why are they glowing?"

"Just go!"

She sprints up the stairs with me close on her heels. I glance up only briefly to see how far we have to go, but it's too far to even see the end of.

Why are my eyes glowing? I clench them shut in desperation, and trip over the next step. I yelp in surprise as my hands hit the stone step in front of me.

Esley is several steps ahead of me now. And Desdemon—

I turn my head, expecting them to be mere steps behind me. Nowhere to be seen. A shaky sigh of relief escapes my lips. I lean back against the steps. Every bone in my body is heavy and weak, weaker than I should be from simply running up a few stairs.

My eyelids flutter shut. I try to ignore the simultaneous pounding and tugging in my head. I swallow hard, forcing down a wave of nausea.

I need to get up. I need to save my sisters. Mom. Avenge Aaron.

Or I could sleep. I can barely fathom standing up.

"Jade." Esley's voice sounds incredibly far away, but her fingers are on my shoulder. "We have to go."

"I want to rest."

"And yet, we still have to go. Come on. You can stand."

I funnel every bit of willpower into my legs. "Are my eyes still glowing? What was that?"

"Not anymore. And somehow you got Death out of your head." She circles her arms under mine and helps me to my feet. "I'll consider myself lucky that I picked such a powerful ally to go up against these people."

My legs are still shaky, but at least my head is adjusting to the new position. My vision fades out for a few seconds and then refocuses. "That's your plan too?"

"Of course. Why else would I want to leave?"

I take a shaky step forwards. "I dunno. That place wasn't exactly comfortable."

"Ah yes. The land of Death isn't comfortable, so I'm going to go back up to the surface only to return when they inevitably kill me. Nah. I'm smarter than that."

Another step. "Then, I'm glad I've picked a smart ally." My limbs are rapidly regaining feeling. The tugging in my head pulls me upwards and upright. "I can take it from here. Thanks."

"You said you've seen the Red Reaper."

"Yes. Have you?" She shakes her head. "She wears a red cloak. That's all I know."

"Your friend?"

"She killed him."

"Did you see her kill him?"

"In a sense." I shake the vision from my mind. "Through his eyes. After he died." Esley nods somberly. "I saw her eyes. They were brown if that helps."

"Ah yes. The most common eye color on the planet."

I chuckle. "How long were these stairs when you came down them?"

"They took"—she cranes her neck up hopelessly—"*Forever*."

"Great."

We ascend step after step until our legs are jelly. I could collapse right here and now and be happy with it. I could fall asleep on these steps and not regret my decision of such an uncomfortable resting place one bit.

If only it weren't for that incessant tugging in my head. The higher we ascend, the more insistent it gets. I had hoped that getting closer to the surface would dull it, but I don't get any such relief.

"Are we almost there or not even close?" I speak through gasps. "Because at this rate, we're going to get killed immediately because of how tired we are."

"I really do think we're almost there," Esley huffs. She's pulled her auburn curls into a bun instead of a ponytail and has to keep pushing her glasses back up her nose because of the sweat. "I can sort of see something through that archway up there. Do you hear waves or am I just about to pass out?"

I close my eyes and listen. The familiar calm sounds of crashing waves and the occasional bird's squawk flood my ears. I smile slightly. "Yup. That's home."

"Great." Esley pushes forwards, taking the steps two at a time. "Hurry up!" I groan and force myself to go faster.

There is indeed an archway up ahead. I can see grass and whitewashed brick through it. Church.

"Wait!" I shout as Esley nears the archway. She stops reluctantly, turning back towards me. "When I came here, I had to jump off a cliff in order to escape the Red Reaper. It's going to spit us out right into her. We can't go through."

"What are you talking about? That isn't a cliff, it's a city!" She points through the archway.

"No. That's my church. It's where I had to jump off from."

"No." She cocks her head to the side. "That's an alleyway in Portland."

We stare at the archway, perplexed. "Did you enter from an alleyway in Portland?" She nods. "Oregon?" Another nod. "I entered from Marbhaven."

"Where?"

I sigh, exasperatedly. "Are you kidding me? We live in the same state!"

"Small town?" she asks. I nod. "So, what do we do now?"

"I guess we should go through?"

"It's gonna spit us out in separate places."

"Yeah . . . " I swallow down another wave of nausea. "Tell me about your alleyway and I'll meet you there."

Chapter Seventeen

I stare at the archway apprehensively. Esley went through about five minutes ago. I can't make myself move. What if I walk directly into the path of the Red Reaper? What if no time has passed at all?

The tugging sensation returns and urges me forwards. I clench my eyes shut and throw myself through the archway.

I'm immediately hit by heavy wind and the salty smell of the sea. All the fatigue from climbing the stairs has vanished. I suck in the air gratefully, searching for the Red Reaper. Nowhere in sight. No one in sight, in fact, except for . . .

"Thank God." Blaise is in the corner of my vision, hand to his heart. "I thought you were dead. I kept appearing at the edge of this cliff when I slept."

"Seriously, are you ever not sleeping?"

He smiles ruefully at me. "Never mind that. What happened?"

Amelia's car is no longer in the church parking lot. Her keys aren't in my pocket anymore, either. They must have fallen into the waves below me. I sigh heavily and begin the trek back home. Hopefully, I can use our car without being noticed.

"I had to walk up a *ton* of stairs to get back. But apparently, I'm not dead." My stomach growls. I guess I haven't eaten anything in a few days. "Although I am absolutely starving."

I pull my hood up as a car passes. If everyone does think that I'm dead, that will put me at a competitive advantage against the Red

Reaper.

"The stairs don't explain what happened at all." Blaise trails alongside me, trying to catch my eye.

"I was in the land of Death, the Underworld, whatever." I examine his face carefully. "What happened to you? When you warned me that she was behind me? You couldn't speak and then you were gone."

"You were in the land of Death, and you didn't die?" He raises his eyebrows.

"Blaise." I stop walking and cross my arms.

"Jillian." He mimics me. I glare into his eyes determinedly. "Okay. Fine. I don't know, okay?" he says. "I don't know why that happened. One moment I was talking, the next everything hurt."

"Do you think it has something to do with the Red Reaper?"

What is she? Does she have powers that normal Reapers don't have?

"Maybe." He shrugs. "It was kind of like what happened to your friend. In the hospital? Anyway." Blaise shakes his head. "You were saying, about Dead Land?"

"Right. Yeah. There was a voice, a man's voice, in my head. He told me that in order to get away from the Red Reaper, I had to jump off the cliff."

"And you just went, yeah. Alright. And jumped off a cliff." I nod. "Now hold on." He quickens his pace, getting in front of me. He holds my gaze. "So, when your mom asked if all your friends jumped off a cliff would you, your answer was yes?"

I shrug. "It wasn't fun, you know."

"What's it like?"

"Dark. And full of stars. Lots of piano music."

A car blows past us. My shoulders tense and I shrink further into my hood. When I turn back towards Blaise, he's gone. Again.

All the lights are out at home. My heart breaks for Raina and Anisha. Wherever they are right now. But it's probably best to stay away from them. Best to keep the Red Reaper away from them.

I find the spare key in the fifth planter pot to the left and turn the lock. I'll need food, some clothes. A first aid kit would be good. What else?

The living room furniture is exactly as I left it, pushed to the side to allow room for ballet practice. I bound up the stairs and grab a black backpack from my room. I shove two outfits into it: a purple sweater and a black tank top with a pair of jeans. Then I raid the bathroom for any supplies I think Esley or I might need.

Back downstairs and into the kitchen. I rifle through the cabinets for any food that will keep for a potentially very long road trip. I can't tell how far away the tugging is pulling from. Maybe it will only be a day, maybe a month.

Just as I'm sticking my hand into the thin gap between the stove and the fridge for our stash of emergency cash, the door creaks open. Every part of me goes completely still.

She's come for me. The Red Reaper knows.

"Alright, girls. Get what you need from upstairs." It's Deanna's voice, subdued and monotone. I want nothing more than to step out into the living room, to let her know I'm here. That I'm alive. The girls' footsteps creak up the stairs.

"I'll see if they left their books in the kitchen." Carl's voice draws closer to me. I look around, panicked, hoping to make a dash for the back door, but there isn't enough time. Carl steps through the archway.

I clutch my backpack to me. For a few agonizing moments, all we can do is stare at each other.

I shake my head violently at him and put a finger to my lips. "Please," I mouth.

"Jade?" he whispers, shakily.

"What?" Deanna sprints through the hallway. I brace myself, gritting my teeth. Deanna stands before me, her eyes wide. She drops her bag to the ground.

"Please don't be mad. I had to—"

Her arms are around me before I can get another word out. "I thought you were dead! Father Iraci told Officer Meyer that you jumped off a cliff!"

"Shh. Shh." I motion to her, panicked. Raina and Anisha, it's too much for them. "I did jump off a cliff, but I didn't die. I—"

"We could have gotten you therapy Jade. I know it's been hard, but—"

"No! It wasn't like that. I—Oh God. Deanna, I can't tell you. It's too dangerous. You have to take the girls and get out of here."

"Why?" She furrows her brows. "You can tell me. What is it?"

"I can't. I can't. You all need to get out of here. Drive in the opposite direction of me. Please. I can't explain. We have to—"

The sound of a car pulling into our driveway makes us all go silent. Deanna narrows her eyes and seems to come to a decision. She turns to Carl. "Dad, take the girls, drive to Grandpa's house. Jade, I'm coming with you. You can explain on the way."

"You can't come with me," I hiss. "You have no idea what we're dealing with. It's too dangerous for you."

"And not for you?" she challenges. I have nothing to say in response and the sound of someone walking towards our front door isn't helping. "Dad, upstairs, grab Raina and Anisha. I'll distract whoever it is. Jade, get in the car, I'll join you."

"You are not going to distract her. Absolutely not," I say. "She is dangerous. She killed Aaron."

There's a knock on the door. Both Deanna and Carl freeze where they stand. The veins in Carl's neck are popping out.

"You have to get the girls out of here, Dad," Deanna whispers.

"No." He shakes his head. "I'm not leaving you. Both of you need to come with me."

"She's after me," I hiss. The door handle jiggles. "We're running out of time, get the girls, let me distract her. And then get out of town."

"But—"

Before either of them can say another word, I dive out of the back door and shut it behind me.

I tiptoe around the side of the house, pushing past the shaking in my legs. Three cars are parked in front: Carl's truck, our old green car, and an uncomfortably familiar blue one.

A red cloak flutters in the corner of my vision. I turn to face it. My breath stops. "You," I whisper.

"You're not dead," she hisses. Her voice is low and laced with venom.

She stands between me and my car. I stand between her and the front door. I can't help but think of myself as a pawn in chess, pinned between the Queen and the Knight.

Only the bottom half of her face is visible, and her lips are quirked into a cruel smirk. "Who are you?" I ask.

She takes a step forwards, almost gently. The metal of her scythe glints above me. It's unnerving how calm and focused she is.

"Okay," I whisper. My eyes dart to our car, the key is in my pocket. I'll never make it past her.

I take a large step towards our car and quickly dive in the opposite direction as her scythe comes down. It misses my ankle by inches.

Something to fight with, I need something to fight with. I dive back towards our front door as she charges towards me. She moves so fast all I see are flashes of red and silver.

Her foot knocks into my chest, throwing me to the ground. All the air leaves my lungs at once. The scythe is at my neck, taunting me, a gruesome promise. I scramble backwards until a bush scrapes at my back.

She swings the scythe upwards, preparing for the final blow. She whispers, "May your sacrifice bring others life."

The blade seems to move in slow motion towards me.

My hands latch onto a shovel behind the bush. I throw it in front of me, just in time to block the scythe.

The sound of metal against metal reverberates in my ears. I struggle against her weight, trying to get back on my feet.

She topples backwards without warning. I scramble back up, searching for the culprit. The Red Reaper is on the ground and Deanna's hands are around her neck.

I meet Deanna's eyes and raise the shovel. Deanna nods at me, struggling to keep her still. The shovel comes down across the Red Reaper's head with a sickening thud.

I look down at my own hands, trembling.

Deanna pulls my arm, and we sprint for the car. I twist the key into the ignition. Another car starts behind us. I spin in my seat to see the Red Reaper in the driver's seat of the blue car.

"You did *not* hit her hard enough," Deanna says, buckling in hurriedly. There's no time to argue with her. She's coming with me.

"Shovels can kill people!" I shout, putting the car into reverse and backing onto the road inelegantly.

"That's the fucking point!" Deanna trains her gaze on the car behind us. "Drive!"

I slam my foot onto the gas pedal. The tires squeal for a split second and the engine whines in protest. "Come on. You can do it, Cartholomew," I whisper the car's nickname. The speedometer slowly climbs up far past the speed limit of our little residential road.

Deanna holds her breath in the seat beside me, her gaze firmly trained on the blue car behind us. "We're screwed," she whispers.

The blue car runs much smoother than ours and is mere inches away from us. I swerve to the right, barely missing a building on the corner. "Nice!" Deanna watches the blue car slam on the brakes and redirect.

I push my foot even harder onto the accelerator, my hands gripping the steering wheel until my knuckles hurt. I fix my eyes on the road to town up ahead. The engine protests heavily, but it's cooperating for the moment. The scent of years old cigarette smoke mingles with the smell of gasoline and tire rubber.

We barrel towards the central town statue of a sea lion.

"What are you doing?" Deanna's voice echoes through my concentration, but I don't respond. The car is mere inches behind us and isn't likely to fall for another swerve. I know that she can see the statue too.

At the last second, I brake and turn at the same time, barely allowing the statue to scrape the side of our car. People dive out of our way on the streets and Deanna screams. The blue car follows my every turn and moves to our outside, helming us to the inside between the shop fronts and them.

My eyes dart to the surrounding streets, trying to decide which route out of town I can take. "Brace yourself," I mutter. Deanna holds onto the side door automatically. I slam on the brakes and let the blue car pass us as I turn towards the street and punch the accelerator again.

We fly towards the cliffside road. Mountains on one side of us, cliff and ocean on the other.

The Red Reaper is close behind us again. "What's your plan?" Deanna speaks through gritted teeth.

"Remember Prom?" My hands are steady, but my heart is practically shaking inside of me.

Deanna makes the sign of the cross. "You sure?"

The blue car is a foot behind us now. The Red Reaper doesn't know the turns as well as I do, but she is still too close for comfort. "We're not gonna lose her any other way."

We come to the straightest part of the road. Trees line both sides, inhibiting the ocean view and the cliff side view.

The blue car speeds up even more and nicks the back of our car. The Red Reaper encroaches on our right, clearly planning to sideswipe us into the cliffside. I can sense her gaze on me. I meet it for only a split second.

Deanna makes to grab the hand grip. "Don't. She's watching." She puts her hands down in her lap in clenched fists.

I grip the wheel and move my left foot to hover over the brake. It's the only way I'm going to pull it off this fast.

Time slows down to heartbeats echoing in my ears. The trees continue, but the road doesn't.

I brake as hard as I can and turn the wheel all the way to the left. Everything in the car protests in anger. The wheel shakes as I guide it back towards equilibrium.

The Red Reaper isn't as lucky. I watch with bated breath through the rearview mirror as she brakes far too late, and her car topples over the edge.

My heart sinks. Deanna covers her mouth in horror.

It's an impressive optical illusion, one that mothers have been begging to have fixed ever since the incident. Prom night our senior year two boys got drunk and went for a drive. They were tricked the same way the Red Reaper was. The other side is in fact a completely separate road that comes from a campsite, not linked to this road at all, separated by a chasm of waterfall and ocean.

"Oh God," Deanna whispers.

I exhale heavily. "I wish there was another way to—"

"You bitch." A voice from the back seat. I scream.

Chapter Eighteen

"What?" Deanna whips her head around. She finds an empty back seat.

Only I can see her. The Red Reaper, or rather, her soul, is in the backseat of my car.

"I promise I'll explain everything, but we have to pull over for a second."

"And *then* where are we going?" I stop the car on the side of the road, hands clenched around the steering wheel.

The Red Reaper continues cursing me out beneath her hood. "Portland. I have to pick up a friend."

The misty air hits my lungs as I step out of the car. I wait for the calm that the mist usually brings me, but it never comes.

The Red Reaper is beside me, still cursing. "I'm sorry." I face away from the car so that Deanna can't see my lips moving. "I didn't want you to die." My voice catches in my throat. "I just wanted you to stop."

She scoffs derisively. "I'm not the first and I won't be the last. You will die."

"Why?" Even in death her face is obscured beneath the hood. "Why do you want me dead?"

She takes a step towards me. If she were alive, her breath would be casting a chill down my spine. "That."

The mark burns into my skin. Not in the present but rather the memory of it. The pain. My fingers soaked in Aaron's blood. "I didn't want this!" I turn on her. "I didn't want any of this. If I could give it up, I would!"

"Then give it up," she spits.

I gaze into the spot where her eyes would be beneath the hood desperately. There's a way out of this? "How?"

"Send me on and I can help you."

Before I can think, my hand is on my mark and I'm meeting her amber brown eyes. She grabs an orb without thinking. The soft orangey glow turns red sharply. "Wait!" I shout. She merely laughs and allows the red light to zip down her body in silence.

I stand there, frozen, staring at the spot where she stood. Deanna is beside me now. "What's wrong?" My head whips around, fixing on the edge of the cliff several hundred feet behind us. "Jade?"

A strangled cry pierces the foggy air. "We have to go. Now. Get back in the car."

"And then answers?"

I nod, slamming the driver's side door shut. We take off again.

Deanna allows me a whopping two minutes of silence to gather my thoughts. "So?"

"I—I don't know how to start this, Deanna."

"Just tell me already."

"The woman, in the red cloak." I clench my jaw. "She killed Aaron."

A pregnant pause fills the car. "How do you know?"

"She wants to kill Reapers." I pull my hair aside and turn to show her the mark.

Deanna studies it closely. "Aaron had that tattoo. She wants to kill people who like a band?" Her voice is filled with skepticism.

"No. Reapers, Grim Reapers. Except there's more than one. Aaron was a Reaper too. When he died, he transferred it to me. I didn't believe it at first either. I—um . . . I didn't believe that I could send people on, but I can. I—"

"Did you send Aaron on?" I can't tell if she's humoring me or believing me.

"Yes. He begged me to."

"And you don't think that you're just seeing things."

"No. I mean, at first that's what I thought, but then, Aaron's funeral. At the church. When you—"

She gasps. "I felt him." I nod. "You saw him? He touched my shoulder?"

"Yes," I say. "He also said that he loved you."

"How does it work? How did you send him on?"

I put my hand on my mark lightly, unsure if it carries other abilities that I don't know about. I think back to the stairway with Desdemon, my eyes glowing green. How much should I tell her? Should I even be telling her this? She's surely humoring me. Testing how far I'm willing to carry a lie. How much I'm going to make up.

"I put my fingers onto this and then I look them in the eye, their soul that is. And with Aaron only one showed up. One of the little orange balls. They float in the air around you. Aaron said they were afterlives. But then, there was this other man . . . "

I let my voice trail off. Blaise. His afterlives filled the air with light. That horrible red glow.

"This other man?" Deanna prompts.

"They grab their chosen afterlife, and it takes them there. That's how it's supposed to work. But with this man. And with Father Rodriguez. And now with the Red Reaper. They grab it . . . " I fix my gaze on the road in front of me. Deanna allows this for all of five seconds before clearing her throat. "They grab it. It turns red. And it sucks them back into life. Father Rodriguez said it was painful."

"Why did he die?" she asks. "I know he flatlined, but why? He was fine when you saw him that morning right?"

"They said there was something wrong with his heart."

"He's never had heart troubles a day in his life."

"I know. But we don't know what those people did to him."

"Why did it turn red for him?"

"My best guess is that they did CPR or something on him and he didn't end up dying? I don't know. Because with the other man, he said that he hasn't been able to die. That it doesn't stick for some reason. And now, with her. I don't know why. By all accounts that should have killed her. It did. But she's . . ."

"And you?" Deanna prompts.

"What about me?"

"Jumping off a cliff? You didn't stay dead?"

"I never died." Now she laughs. More of a snort than anything else. But it's disbelieving and pierces me right through my chest. "I didn't!"

"You didn't jump off a cliff."

"No. I did. I didn't die."

"That's impossible!" Her laugh continues.

"No, what happened is—"

"You can't jump off a cliff and survive without even a scratch on you. Even if you were pulled back—"

"I wasn't pulled back like that. I never died. I jumped and what happened was—"

"It's impossible! It didn't happen that way!"

"Why not?"

"BECAUSE IF YOU COULD SURVIVE THAT, WHY COULDN'T AARON SURVIVE TOO!"

My heart sinks into my stomach. All the way down. Deafening silence fills the car. I gaze at the road in front of us even though I can't focus on it. Aaron's death plays through my mind again. His choking gasps. The warm blood all over me. Deanna, happy and teasing only minutes before, her face crestfallen.

It's not fair. It's not fair. It's not fair.

I can feel her unspoken screaming of the same words over and over again. It's not fair. Why him and not me? Why didn't they save him, have him jump off the cliff and go to Desdemon? Why didn't they?

"Tell me." She speaks flatly.

I have no choice but to answer. "A voice in my head told me to jump so that I would be safe. I jumped and entered the land of Death. They told me I was the Red Reaper's next target and that I'd be safe there."

"Why didn't they save Aaron?"

"I—I don't think they knew about the Red Reaper then." I pause. Anger radiates off of her. "I'm sorry."

There is nothing but Deanna's silence for the rest of the freeway. Through all the twists and turns Deanna sits there, her arms crossed, staring out the window.

Finally, a whole hour later, she sighs heavily. "I know it's not your fault, Jade. I'm just—"

"I know." My voice is barely audible above the car's engine.

Another pause. She puts her hand on mine momentarily. "So, you're a Reaper who sends the souls of the dead onwards into the afterlife and someone's trying to kill you for it. What now?"

Her voice sounds almost joking. I smile slightly in her direction. It sounds ridiculous. "Now, we are going to pick up someone I met in the land of Death. Death has a name and goes by Desdemon by the way."

"Sure. Why not?"

"They look like the Virgin Mary to me."

"Death uses they/them pronouns and looks like what now?"

"I—never mind. I'll explain that later." I pull my shoulders down from next to my neck. "We'll pick up Esley, so that she doesn't die."

"As one does."

"And then"—as if on cue, the pounding in my head returns full force, pulling at the base of my skull—"then we find Mom."

"Alright, let me guess. Vanessa is with the Reaper hunters?" I nod. "Do we know where they are?"

"Sort of. I can explain that too."

She shrugs. "You brought supplies and money?" I nod. "Okay then."

"Seriously? You believe me?"

There's a mixture of seriousness and mirth in her eyes. "Listen Jade, the way I see it, you're either telling the truth or you've had some sort of psychotic break. So, either way, what kind of friend would I be if I didn't go with you?"

I allow the ghost of a smile to cross my face as we exit the freeway towards Portland. "Besides, I super-duper just committed some form of manslaughter with you, so . . ."

Chapter Nineteen

Esley described her alleyway as behind a church and covered in plants. From the look of this city, that could be anywhere. We're three hours away from Marbhaven and I've only been to Portland once in my life.

"Okay, she's got auburn hair, it's curly, and she wears glasses." She gave me a street name too, but I have no idea where it is. "Put Stark Street into your phone?"

We drive up and down the street. I slam on the brakes and turn whenever Deanna sees anything remotely resembling a church.

Thirty minutes later and I'm worried that Esley has already been found, and worse.

"Wait!" Deanna shouts, pointing to our left. I veer left, cutting off someone behind me and narrowly avoiding getting us rear-ended.

The church is covered in ivy and surrounded by dandelions. It more closely resembles a hiking trailhead than a church. A dilapidated sign in hardly legible peeling yellow greets us out front.

I peer down an alleyway as we drive further into this poor excuse for a parking lot.

"Look." I jerk my head at a woman in front of us. Her auburn hair is in a ponytail, and she's leaning against the wall of the church, limbs stiff.

I take the keys out of the ignition. We step out of the car. At the sound of the car doors shutting, Esley whips around, holding two silver daggers in her hands and on the defensive.

"Woah!" I shout, throwing my hands up in surrender.

"Oh." Esley sheathes her daggers. "It's you. Who's this?"

"I'm Deanna. Nice to meet you."

"Esley." Esley chuckles and pats Deanna on the shoulder. "Likewise. Ready?" She turns to me.

"What's with the daggers? Do you carry those with you everywhere?"

"Not everywhere." Esley follows us back to the car. "Only when voices in my head tell me I'm being followed."

Deanna almost laughs, shoving herself ahead of me into the driver's seat. "Jade?" She jerks her head towards me, and I clamber into the passenger seat. "Where to?"

I allow the pulling sensation in my head to come to the forefront again. It tugs to the right, pounding at the inside of my skull. "That way." I point.

"Okay, but where are we going?"

"So . . . Here's the thing."

"Another thing?" Deanna snorts. "Awesome."

"The Grim Reaper told me how to find Mom. But—"

"Hold on." Esley leans forwards in the back seat. "You got to talk to THE Grim Reaper? What was it like?"

"So weird. It's like, it's like the voice was coming from me, not the Grim Reaper. It was so weird. Anyway, the window to Mom's soul is kind of inside of me now? And if we follow that, we'll find her."

Deanna sighs again, pressing her fingers to her temples. "Okay. Sure. Yeah. Okay."

"Are you not a Reaper?" Esley asks. Deanna shakes her head. "Ah."

Deanna turns the keys in the ignition. Cartholomew stutters to life, and we're off.

It's not long after we get out of the city that Deanna makes me take the wheel. She's too confused by my directions, and too frustrated by the frequency with which I'm shouting, "Wrong way!"

I drive until the sun is long gone. Only when the exhaustion of the day hits me do I pull off the road and find a motel.

We park, talk to the front desk lady, and are ushered into Room 410 just before two in the morning. Deanna and Esley pass out almost immediately, but I can't ignore the pull of Mom's soul.

My voice hums of its own accord, trying to block out the incessant pounding in my head.

You need to keep moving. Why aren't you moving? Why did you stop? She's that way. Go that way.

I hum louder, blocking it out. I need to rest.

"Ugh. Fine. Fine. I won't sleep. Jesus," I mutter, clambering out of bed and towards the shower.

The steady flow of scalding hot water dulls my headache slightly. My head is ten pounds lighter. I allow my eyes to close. It's so tempting to just sleep in here and waste all the hotel's water.

A bright red glow pierces my eyelids.

My eyes snap open and I yelp, tumbling backwards. Not one, but two figures stand before me in the bathroom. One is Father Rodriguez, his expression lifeless.

The other is a woman that I don't recognize. Her jaw is square and severe, as is the widow's peak of her hairline. Light brown hair hangs in a ponytail down her back and her skin is almost as pale as Deanna's. A thin nose, the very picture of a pixie if it weren't for her height.

"The Red Reaper," I whisper to myself, staring at her through the glass. Her features are tight, twisted in pain.

I'm staring at the lifeless soul of Aaron's murderer.

I exit the shower, glaring at her. "Are you kidding me?" I growl, pulling my green hoodie over my head.

I'm never going to be free of her again.

I briefly consider putting my jeans back on, but I didn't pack much else to wear. And I have no idea how long we'll be on this journey. I pull the hoodie down low enough so that no one can tell as I exit the bathroom and kneel beside Esley's bed.

"Esley?" I hiss. "Esley, I have to ask you something."

"What?" She rolls over, bleary-eyed, but awake. She is a much lighter sleeper than I'm used to.

"Do you see anyone behind me? With glowing red eyes?" She sits bolt upright and peers behind me. "They're not dangerous; they're souls."

"No. I don't see anyone."

"Have you ever had someone die and then get pulled back by this weird red light?" She nods. "Have you ever seen any of them again at night?"

"No?"

"Okay. Thanks. Just curious." She lies back down and falls asleep almost immediately. I wonder if she really heard anything I said.

"See? Told you no one else could see us." I jump at the sound of Blaise's voice. "Just me." He puts his hands up, as though in surrender.

"You scared me." I narrow my eyes at him and make my way back towards the bathroom.

"I'm sorry. I never know what you're doing when I fall asleep. You are quite the night owl you know." He catches sight of the Red Reaper and freezes. "What is she doing here?"

"You are scared of her," I whisper, locking the bathroom door behind me. Father Rodriguez and the Red Reaper are at the end of their tethers outside the bathroom. Inside, it's only Blaise and me.

He either hasn't heard me or doesn't want to acknowledge what I've said. "This is different." He appraises the room. "We're in a hotel?"

"Yeah, I'm officially on the run." My legs shake violently. I sink to the floor, the day finally catching up with me.

"What happened?" he asks.

I cross my arms tightly in front of me, trying to hide the trembling.

"You can tell me."

I do want to tell him. I want to tell someone everything that's happened today. How much I miss my sisters already. How damn worried I am about if they are truly safe with Carl or if someone else is after them too. But all that comes out is, "I'm starving."

"It's been like eleven hours since we last talked. You haven't eaten?" I shake my head. "Jillian!"

"What? I've had a busy day." He opens his mouth to protest. "Aww, are you worried about me?"

"Yes!" he shouts, flinging his hands up. "I mean—Not really, I just—"

"Someone's flustered!" I make to playfully shove him but stop before my hand reaches his shoulder. My face falls. I don't know why I'm so disappointed.

"I'm not flustered! You're just being so"—he pauses—"what's wrong?"

"Nothing." I shrug. "Just um—the fact that my mom is missing. I'm being chased by a woman in red that is like you and can't die. I've roped my best friend into it, and she could die. So, you know, nothing."

"Yeah." His gaze is so insistent that I have to raise my eyes to meet him. "Nothing." I roll my eyes and make to turn away. "Jillian."

"Hmm?"

"What do you mean she's like me?"

I open my mouth, but no words come out.

"What did you do?"

CHAPTER TWENTY

THE SUN GLARES THROUGH a tiny gap in the curtains. I untangle myself from Deanna and blink into the light. Blaise is already gone. I guess neither of us got good sleep last night. My tangled hair falls in front of my face as I roll over to see if Esley is still asleep.

She's up and lacing her boots.

"Food?" She raises her eyebrows. "Did you pack cash?"

I nod, my head pounding from the pull towards Mom. Would pain killers even fix this?

Esley nods her head towards the still sleeping Deanna. "Friend or . . . ?"

"Friend." The soreness in my abs makes it difficult to sit up quickly. "Childhood friends. With some serious trauma. Hence cuddling."

She snorts. "Worse trauma than recently?"

I shake my head and reach into my bag for my jeans. Black tangles fall into my face again. "You didn't happen to pack a comb, did you?"

"Pack?" Esley puts her hands on her hips. "Dude, when?"

"Sorry." I raise my hands in surrender. "Sassy in the morning, aren't we?" I poke Deanna awake. "Sassy, meet clingy." Deanna rolls over as if on cue, searching for something to hold. "Deanna. We gotta go. Food is a thing that my imaginary friend said I need. I kinda agree with him."

Esley shoots me an inquisitive look but shrugs off the comment as a bad joke. Which I'm grateful for. I don't want to explain Blaise. Not to her, not to Deanna. Maybe not to anyone.

Food is every pastry and fruit that the hotel has to offer with their breakfast. I pile them on, shoveling down anything edible. Muffins, an apple, a bowl of cereal, two cups of coffee. Deanna is still half-asleep at the table, picking at her own muffin. Esley sneakily stuffs food into my bag.

"Oh good. You're eating." I jump halfway out of my seat. Blaise has appeared next to me and is talking before I can make the mistake of speaking. His eyes are deadened, devoid of emotion. "And to answer your question, no. I am never awake."

I roll my eyes and turn back to Deanna and Esley.

"So, what's our next move?" Esley leans forwards, dropping an apple into my open bag as she does.

"Follow this stupid pounding in my head until I find Mom."

"And when we get there?" I shrug. I haven't thought much past finding Mom. "Fighting experience? Either of you?" Deanna shakes her head mournfully, finally taking a full bite of her muffin. "The three of us are gonna waltz into a pack of clearly skilled red hooded people and just like . . . " She mimes her throat being slit.

I wince. Deanna puts her muffin down, turning green. Images of Aaron flash through my mind, slick blood on my fingers, that horrible gurgle, his eyes fading away.

"What?"

"Let's go." I stand from the table abruptly, grabbing my bag as I head for the door. The other two scramble to gather their things.

"You okay?" Blaise reaches for my hand.

I pull away at the last second. "Fine." Something burns deep in the pit of my stomach, and I grit my teeth. I force myself to take a calming breath before turning to him. His gaze is distant. "Are you okay?"

"I'm good." His shoulders tense.

"Hey." Esley taps my shoulder. "Ummm . . . Deanna and I, we're wondering if you're ever planning on telling us who the hell you're talking to?"

Deanna has her head cocked to the side, squinting at the spot where Blaise stands.

"Just a soul. That's all."

"Rather you than me." Esley grimaces. "Send 'em on quick? We gotta move."

"Yeah, of course." I place my fingers over my mark and meet Blaise's eyes. Esley returns to explain to Deanna. Still, Blaise's eyes are empty. We stare at each other for a few moments, then Blaise shakes his head, and disappears.

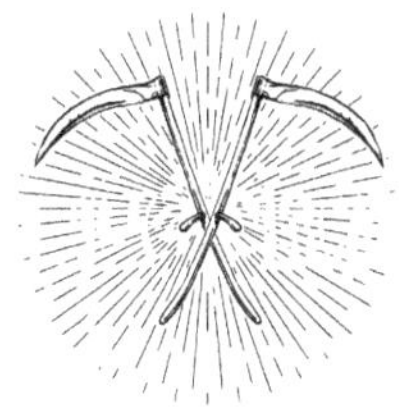

We're about fifty miles down the road and the pounding in my head hasn't stopped at all. Nor has the tug changed direction. Deanna and Esley are chatting away. I haven't been following their conversation very closely, still preoccupied by the events of yesterday.

The Red Reaper's car careening over the cliffside. That horrendous scream echoing through the air. She's still alive. How am I going to fight her again? Much less possibly tens or hundreds of them.

"Oh. And then my boss tried to get me to work the day after!" Deanna cackles. "That was my last day."

"*After* he stole your lunch?" Esley says.

I shake myself out of my thoughts. "You telling the lobster mac and cheese story?" Deanna nods, shaking with laughter. "Gotta love when someone steals your wages via your mac and cheese."

"I once got fired for the Reaper thing, actually!" Esley leans forwards, meeting Deanna's eyes. "I had to pretend that it was a smoke break every time a soul showed up. But I live in a big city, lots of souls. He fired me for taking too many breaks."

"Oh, that sucks." Deanna grimaces. "Do you smoke, though?"

"Nah, had to make up something." A look of relief passes over Deanna's face, although I can't think why. "Someone in this car does, though," Esley continues, sniffing the air. Deanna shakes her head and Esley's eyes turn to me.

"That would be my dad." I raise my hand. "Last time I saw him, I was like a literal infant? Don't smoke, kids. The smell never goes away."

Deanna snickers. "Unless of course, it's Vanessa."

I snort. "Yeah, sounds like Mom, for sure." A tug to the right. "Oh finally!" I exclaim, veering over two lanes to take the exit.

"Woo!" Esley cheers. "The town of Fruitland, Idaho. Exciting."

We stop for gas in Idaho, then continue onwards. The day continues without so much as another direction change. The tugging pulls us forwards, and forwards, and forwards, forwards, forwards, forwards—

"You need to sleep." I jolt up and veer back into my lane. Deanna and Esley have dosed off. Blaise is halfway phased into Deanna.

"I hate when you do that."

"What? Make you take care of yourself?" Before I can retort, he shouts, "Pull off the damn road, Jillian!"

The next exit is for Cheyenne. I glare at Blaise, taking the exit begrudgingly. Within the next half hour, we're in a small motel room and Deanna and Esley have crawled into bed, asleep again already.

I can feel Blaise's rage from the exact six-foot tether he has. "What?" I cross my arms.

He grits his teeth and turns away. As I walk towards him, he is able to walk farther away. And then, he's on the other side of the door. "Blaise!" I grab my room key and follow him. All the way outside and onto a railed balcony that overlooks the parking lot. "What's wrong?"

"Nothing's wrong!" He shouts. I quirk an eyebrow at him. "You-you—"

"Spit it out." I pull my arms closer to my chest.

"What's the point of killing someone if you're just going to kill yourself falling asleep behind the wheel?" He explodes.

"Killing someone?"

"The Red Reaper. You killed her."

"I didn't kill her. She drove herself off a cliff." I pause. "And she's still alive, unfortunately."

"Unfortunately?" Blaise growls. My heart skips a beat. "It's unfortunate that someone is still alive?"

"That's not what I meant." I shake my head. "How do you know anyway?"

"You told me." He turns away from me. "Last night. You were like half-asleep and crying in the bathroom."

"I didn't—" Did I?

"I don't understand you." Blaise grips the railing, turning his knuckles white. "One moment, I think you're one thing, the next—" He sighs heavily.

"What are you talking about?"

"I thought you killed in self-defense, and then you say something like 'unfortunately'!"

"I didn't kill her at all." I grit my teeth. "She was chasing me, she wasn't paying enough attention, and she drove herself off a cliff."

"She, she, she." He whirls around, his face contorted into something monstrous, murderous almost. "What about what *you* did Jillian?" My heart hammers in my chest. My feet are rooted to the wooden planks beneath me. "Look me in the eyes and tell me that you really think you played no part in her death. That you didn't lead her straight off a cliff."

"She's still alive, Blaise."

"You didn't know she would live though, did you?" I seal my lips shut. "Did you?"

"No," I admit, turning my gaze to my feet.

"So, you wanted her dead."

"Of course not!" Air rips through my lungs. "I wanted her to leave my family alone!" I charge towards him, stopping just shy of slamming into him. "First, she took Father Rodriguez, then my mom. Then it was Aaron. The Red Reaper wasn't going to stop. She would have killed Deanna too if it came down to it. What was I supposed to do?"

"You still—"

"What would you have me do, Blaise?" My voice comes out as a low snarl. "What if she did go after Deanna next? Or God forbid my sisters. What then?"

"I-I don't—" He snaps his mouth shut.

"You don't know what you'd do, do you?" It's several moments before he shakes his head. "Then what are you so upset about? What do you think I am?"

It's his turn to look at the floor. "I hoped you were—"

"Hoped I was what?" I ask. "Perfect? I'm not. I never have been."

Finally, he looks at me. "I'm not perfect either, Jillian. I just want you"—His brown eyes are starting to thaw. He holds my gaze for several seconds before continuing—"to be safe. You did what you did. It's got to mean something, doesn't it?"

"I'll sleep," I say. "If it makes you happy, I'll sleep."

Chapter Twenty-one

I jerk up in bed. The hair on the back of my neck stands on end. My hands shake. I could have sworn I heard something.

The only light in the room comes from Father Rodriguez and his glowing red eyes. Deanna is fast asleep next to me, and Esley's snores fill the room. Blaise is gone already.

My phone reads 5 a.m. The only notification is a text from Carl.

> "Girls are safe. Not in Marbhaven. Deanna?"

I shoot back,

> "Safe. Not in Marbhaven."

The tugging resumes almost immediately after my body becomes aware of being conscious. I clench my eyes shut and massage my temples, desperately trying to ignore it.

"Help!" Mom's voice comes from inside my head.

Before I can stop it, my feet carry me from bed all the way across the room. My nose is practically pressed against the wall, and still, I feel the pull towards Mom. I have to go forwards. I have to.

I turn my head towards Deanna and Esley, sleeping soundly. Esley may not be able to escape this, but Deanna could. Esley is right. We're heading straight into a massacre, and I shouldn't bring Deanna along with me.

As quietly as I can, I tip toe over to grab my bag and pull my jeans on. I grab the car keys.

Esley's snoring breaks through the silence. I freeze where I stand. I should wake her, bring her along with me. But risk waking Deanna? I shake my head and continue out the door, pulling it shut carefully behind me.

The balcony creaks with every step forwards I take. Step. Creak. Step. Creak. Step.

Two creaks.

I whirl around. A curtain of bright red fabric hangs over the shape of a woman. Father Rodriguez is next to her, pulled unwillingly on the six-foot tether. His glowing red eyes are even more prominent in the darkness of early morning.

"Thought you'd never go to sleep," I whisper at her, my teeth grating against each other.

Maybe she's like Blaise was weeks ago. In the hospital, in and out of consciousness, and in immense pain. If there was any room to pity her, I would.

The sun is peeking out along the horizon, lightening the sky to a hazy indigo. There's not a sound in the parking lot, not a soul, but me.

I think this is the first time since Mom went missing that I've been truly alone.

Creak.

I move on instinct alone, dropping as low as I can. A light breeze passes above me with a low whistle.

My knees shake as I turn and stand, face to face with the Red Reaper again. Who is very much not a red eye and very much *here*. Rage radiates off her, burning the air around us.

"How did you—"

Metal cuts through the air next to my shoulder, although I

don't remember moving out of the way. I look around wildly for something, anything, to defend myself with.

She slices across, barely missing my stomach as I manage to dodge out of the way again. I scramble backwards, my heels dangling over the edge of the top step.

Red fabric whirls around and her scythe slashes out for my neck again. My foot catches me on the next step.

My heart beats in my throat, my knees knocking together. I give our surroundings one last desperate look for something I can use.

Nothing. I dodge again. I can practically taste the blood she almost spilled.

I've got to get close, away from that blade. I rush towards her, using the top step as a launching pad. My hands wrap around the wooden handle of the scythe. I pull it towards me.

She grapples with it for a second, almost succeeding in twisting it from my grasp.

I panic and pull so hard my center of balance moves too far backwards. There's no saving it. I fall to the ground and she's standing over me, still grappling for the scythe.

My right foot lands against her hip and I push, hoping it will get her off me.

Red cloth and my own black hair cloud my vision as she catapults over me. I wince at the sound of several limbs hitting the ground over and over again, down the steps.

I wrap my hands tightly around the scythe, shocked to find myself holding it as I scramble to my feet. It's a lot heavier than I expected. That blade is no joke.

She's sprinting towards me again, feet thudding against the wooden steps. I lift the scythe over my head and launch it forwards, nearly taking my whole body with it. I expected to hit her shoulder, but it misses her entirely, landing instead against the wooden balcony. It cuts one of the boards almost clean in half.

I wrestle with the scythe, trying to pull it out.

She cackles mercilessly, back on even ground with me. "A Reaper who doesn't know what to do with a scythe?" She circles me.

That voice is different, high-pitched like a cruel melody. "You're not her." I yank the scythe back into my grasp, gripping as tight as I can.

She lunges forwards. Red fabric whips around me. She grabs the scythe. Her foot is against my leg.

Then I'm flat on my back, the wind knocked out of me. She raises the scythe and slices towards my neck.

My left arm moves in front of me of its own accord.

I smell something metallic. The scythe moves away from my arm, gearing up for another attack.

Blood is everywhere, all over me, red all around. I'm bleeding.

Pain erupts across my shoulder. I cry out. The sharpness of the scythe moves through my upper arm again and again. Pounding, agonizing sharpness.

I'm covered in blood, and he's dying beneath me again.

Someone's arms are on me. Someone is screaming. I'm going to die. This is it. She's going to kill me. Deanna's going to wake up and find my body just like Aaron's.

The red cloak whips through the air and she's gone. Several voices are talking, screaming. People are peering out of their doors out onto the deck.

I'm screaming, I realize. They've heard me.

Someone is on their knees next to me. Frizzy auburn hair and freckles. I try to focus on her. Esley's eyebrows are knit in concentration, but otherwise, she barely looks fazed. She barks orders at someone behind me. Footsteps sprint and then return almost immediately with a bed sheet.

Esley wraps the sheet as tightly as she can and pulls me to my feet. Parts of the sheet are soaked through almost immediately, but her hands remain steadfast and tight around my arm. They pull me back into the room.

Esley forces me to lie down and holds my arm high in the air, her hazel eyes never wavering from my wound.

"Deanna. A pocket in my pants. There's a needle and thread." I inhale sharply, completely failing at pushing down my panicked breaths. "Look at me," Esley says. I do. "Don't think about it."

Deanna returns with the needle, thread, and two small bottles of vodka from the hotel mini fridge.

"Open them quickly." Esley's voice is even-keeled. Deanna's fingers are shaking, but she manages to get them open. Esley takes them in her blood-stained hand and holds one out to me. "Drink it." Her voice darkens. "You're gonna need it."

I down the whole thing, barely noticing the burn in my throat. The hotel room spins.

"It's a pretty clean cut. That should be good," Esley whispers to Deanna.

"You sure you know what you're doing?" Deanna asks.

"Positive." Esley nods. "I'm an EMT, studying to be a doctor."

Deanna lets out a shaky breath and pours the vodka over the needle and thread.

A scream escapes my lips, but I don't register why until I notice the steady trickle of alcohol down my forearm.

Deanna shoves a wad of cloth into my mouth, and I bite down on it.

Something sharp pierces my skin all the way through. I bite down even harder, pouring all of my concentration into keeping my arm still. Then slick, slimy thread drags through me. The pain of the initial puncture fades slightly, then my skin is pierced again.

The cloth falls from my mouth and a steady stream of curse words fall from my lips. Thread slithers through. Puncture. Thread.

Black spots dart across my vision. I try to examine my arm, but the mere sight of the wound sends the world into a tailspin around me. My whole arm is being lit on fire over and over and over again.

"Okay." Esley exhales heavily.

I blink blearily. My arm is throbbing and sore and I have no idea how much time has passed in the slightest.

Deanna sinks to her knees beside me, squeezing the hand on my good arm. The sink runs in the bathroom.

Esley emerges with clean, unstained hands, and a cup of soapy water that she dips a washcloth into and gently scrubs over the stitched-up wound. Despite her gentle hands, I wince. I glance over at my arm and count twenty stitches in total, each of them stained red. I have no idea what color the thread was originally.

"We have to get out of here," Deanna whispers. "There were people. They probably called someone. We can't afford to stay here when we know the Red Reapers are here, too."

Esley nods, tying clean strips of the bedsheet around my arm. "Can you stand?" I inhale deeply and nod, pushing off with my uninjured arm. My legs wobble and I tilt forwards.

Deanna catches me and guides me back to the bed. "How were you so calm?" Deanna directs her voice to Esley.

Esley shrugs. "Couldn't afford to freak out. What happened?"

It takes me a moment to break through the fog and realize she asked me a question. "I thought that she wasn't there," I whisper, making to hold my arm. The cut is almost a foot long and still throbbing. In time with my heartbeat or in time with the pounding in my head, I can't tell.

"Why?" Deanna frowns.

"I thought she was a red eye."

"A what?" Deanna's eyes move between me and Esley. Esley furrows her brows in confusion. She doesn't remember our half-asleep conversation.

"It's—there are these people. They die." I focus my gaze on my knee. I don't want to tell them. I can't help but feel like Blaise is mine, my little secret. But after this, not telling them, they could be in danger. "And they come to me. I try to send them on. And they get pulled back. Father Rodriguez said it was awful."

"Father Rodriguez is one?" Deanna shoots me a sharp glance.

I nod, black spots dart across my vision from the movement. "When he sleeps, his soul comes to me, but it's not really him. He can't speak. He has glowing red eyes." I exhale heavily. "And it hurts him."

Esley furrows her brows. "I thought they died, but then got resuscitated. I've never seen them after."

"I don't know why I can see them," I mutter. "But when the Red Reaper drove off that cliff, she didn't die. Her soul has been here these past two nights."

"Can she see us?" Deanna bites her lip.

"I didn't think so. But now . . ." I furrow my brows. "Maybe she can."

Esley chances a glance out of our window. "I don't see any flashing lights yet. We should make a run for it now."

Deanna turns to me, dark hair falling over her shoulder. I nod. She grabs my backpack, her eyes set in steely determination. "I'm driving, let's go."

Chapter Twenty-two

They situate me in the back seat, lying down on my back. Esley instructs me to keep my arm elevated. "And pray, if you're into that sort of thing."

"Why does she need to pray?" Deanna buckles her seatbelt, her voice high. "The bleeding stopped."

"Well, there's two things we need to watch out for. One"—Esley holds up one thick finger—"if it opens up again. And two"—another finger goes up—"infection is a bitch."

I snort. "Comforting."

I hate being this far down and away from the windows. I can't see anything that's coming our way. There's no hint of red in the corner of my vision, but then again, nothing else is either.

We pass the day with Esley and Deanna taking turns at the helm. They're only briefly interrupted by me shouting out instructions when a strong enough pull breaks through the throbbing pain in my arm.

The sky turns a deep orange hue as the sun settles down for the night. My eyes flutter several times before I decide, finally, to succumb to the fatigue.

Screams, horrible screams fill the air. They're Mom's. I recognize them from when I was little. The sobbing screams from when Raina and Anisha's dad left. The terrified screams from when I walked directly into traffic as a five-year-old. All compounding on themselves into something worse. Screams of pain and fear.

Tangled blond waves fill my vision. "Mom?" I cry into the darkness, the air ripping at my vocal cords.

The screams die out for the length of three panicked breaths and then come back with full force. "What's happening? What are they doing to you?"

I'm thrashing on a table, my wrists strapped down. I can't see anything. Fingers are pressed over my eyes.

I jolt awake. The sky around us is pitch black and I think we're surrounded by trees. "You said the turn is in how many miles?" Deanna's voice hisses through the air.

"Three, and it's a left." Esley's voice is on edge. "Is she still asleep?" I close my eyes as she turns. "How do you think they found us?"

"Found Jade, not us," Deanna whispers. "I'm more concerned about why she was alone. They could have found us, and Jade wouldn't have gotten hurt if she was with us."

"Ha." A humorous snort comes from the passenger seat. "You think they give a damn about if we're in a group or not? We've got two daggers between the three of us."

"She knows better than to go off alone." I peer through my eyelids. Deanna's eyes are fixed on the road ahead, her shoulders tense.

Esley exhales heavily. Her voice is gentle and calm as she turns to face Deanna. "Can I ask you something?"

"What?"

"You and Jade, yesterday morning. You both got all weird when I made the slit throat gesture. And now, that cut on Jade's arm. I don't believe it was the arm that Red Reaper was going for. How did you know?"

Deanna shudders. It's a long time before she speaks. I can't imagine what she saw after the EMT took me away. "My brother. Aaron."

"Was he, did the Red Reaper—"

"Yes." Her voice breaks. "He was a Reaper. And he went off for a walk on his own." She takes a deep shaky breath. "And they slit his throat." Those words are in a tone I've never heard her use before. It's bone chilling, full of revenge.

"I'm sorry." Esley reaches out, grasping her shoulder. "How long ago?"

"Three weeks ago."

"Jesus."

A thick silence passes through the car. I debate going back to sleep as the twists and turns of the road rock me back and forth. Deanna makes a left turn at Esley's prompting. "Jade said that she became a Reaper because Aaron transferred his ability to her. Umm, if you don't mind my asking, who . . . "

"No one," Esley cuts her off. "There was no one. I was chosen. At random."

"What? Ow!" I jolt up, pain radiating from my arm.

Esley whips around to face me, worry creasing her thick eyebrows. Her eyes move rapidly, doing a point-by-point check of my makeshift bandages. "Lie back down," she concludes.

"How long have you been awake?" Deanna asks.

"Not long." I lean back gingerly onto the hotel pillows we stole. "What's this about you being chosen randomly?"

"You sure you haven't been awake long?" Deanna says skeptically. "Sounds like you were eavesdropping."

Esley snorts. "I didn't realize you could become a Reaper because another Reaper gave it to you. Like the worst disease ever." She pauses. "I was seventeen, finished finals. This voice was in my head, telling me to follow what it said. And of course, I'm not an idiot. So, I didn't. I had an existential crisis instead. But it wouldn't shut up. And eventually, someone showed up. Guy named Jeremiah. By that point, the tattoo had already appeared, and I was starting to see people. He explained how to send them on. I was skeptical, but I tried it and what he said worked. So, I knew he had to be right. That I was a Reaper now."

"But why did this Jeremiah pick you?" Deanna asks.

"He didn't." Esley shakes her head, auburn curls bouncing. "The Grim Reaper did. And I've never met the Grim Reaper." She sighs. "Right in one mile, Deanna."

"No!" I shout, a great tug ripping through my skull. "You need to go left!"

Deanna grips the steering wheel tightly. "We need to sleep. And regroup. And pray that we weren't followed. It's dark out. We're tired."

Esley turns to face me. "And honestly. It doesn't matter how fast we get there if you can't fight. You. Need. To. Rest."

"But—" Deanna moves her fingers together in an indication for me to shut up. My mouth snaps shut. I frown.

We arrive at a large hotel with a covered driveway that Deanna pulls into. I'm instructed to stay in the car with Esley while she gets the room keys. Tables and chairs line an outdoor courtyard dimly lit by two streetlamps. A long building suggests a covered pool.

My suspicions are confirmed by the smell of chlorine that permeates my nostrils as Esley helps me out of the backseat.

Deanna walks directly in front of my injured arm, shielding it from view the whole way through the lobby. We avoid the gaze of the desk clerk and shuffle into an elevator.

The second-floor lobby opens up to a fireplace surrounded by three couches. The TV is on to a news channel, which is reporting an incoming snowstorm.

Our room, Room 208, has two beds, a couch, and a small kitchenette complete with two worn wooden chairs and an equally old table.

"How much was this place?" I ask suspiciously.

Esley props up some pillows for my bed. "Weirdly cheap. Only like $240 for this."

"For one night!" I exclaim. "What are you doing? We don't

know how long we're gonna be on the road."

"Three nights, Jade." Deanna runs her fingers through my hair. "Calm down."

"Three nights?"

"I repeat." Esley shoves me back into the pillows. "You. *Need.* To. Rest."

"And we need a plan." Deanna nods her head. "As evidenced by this morning, we can't go storming into a whole place of those people and expect to make it to Vanessa, much less out alive."

"But—"

"Rest."

"Just because I'm not at 100 percent doesn't mean I don't get a say." My voice raises a hair above my normal speaking voice, laced with indignance.

"Jade." Deanna puts her hands on her hips, her black hair matted so much it doesn't do its usual flip. "If you had your say right now, you'd go out there and get yourself killed. Esley says we need to watch that arm and I intend to watch it. Your mom wouldn't want you killing yourself to get to her. Lie down. Let Esley change your bandages. And we'll make a plan—*together*—in the morning."

I glare at her. She glares right back, grey eyes challenging me to tell her she's wrong. Even when I know she's not.

And I'm exhausted. Heaviness takes over my eyelids as Esley leads me to the bathroom to wash my cut and retie strips of bedsheet where needed. I barely focus on any of my surroundings. I can't take in any more information than the pounding in my head that beats in tandem to the pounding in my arm. As soon as Esley eases me back onto my pillows, the world fades out around me.

Chapter Twenty-three

I WAKE UP SEVERAL times in the middle of the night. First to Father Rodriguez standing above me, his face hollowed and gaunt and his eyes glowing. Then to the Red Reaper, my terror only calmed by Deanna and Esley assuring me that they couldn't see her.

Her glowing red eyes are a comfort. An assurance that she isn't really here.

I never wake up to Blaise. I wonder if he too is having a restless night, and we keep missing each other.

The final time I wake, it's late morning. Esley is lounged across the couch, reading the provided Bible with a glazed over expression and a half open mouth. I turn my head towards the bed next to me to find it empty.

"Deanna in the bathroom?" I mumble, easing myself up onto the pillows.

Esley shakes her head. "Went out for supplies."

"What?" I turn my gaze sharply to her.

"We discussed it. And she agreed that it would be best for the non-Reaper to go out. Least risk."

"I—what were you"—I splutter out—"my mom wasn't safe, and she isn't a Reaper and—"

"That you know of," Esley interjects lightly.

"That's not the point!" I make to stand up. "She's in danger! Where did you send her? We need to go."

"We're staying here."

"No! We need to—"

"SIT YOUR ASS BACK DOWN!" Esley shouts. Her hazel eyes are alight with fire. I freeze where I am, half sitting, half standing. "After the shit you pulled yesterday? Deanna was a goddamn mess. Do you understand that?" I press my lips together. "She's already out. The decision has been made. If you want to go out and be a dumbass again and get yourself killed, I will fucking tackle you."

"She's not safe."

"Neither are we. None of us are. We're all on this hell trip together. You're gonna have to accept that Deanna is also going to be in danger every once in a while." She collapses resignedly to the couch, her limbs turning to jelly. "Trust me, I don't like it any more than you do."

I stare at her for a long time. My mind battles between going out anyway and sitting back down and accepting that she has a point. Sitting down wins out by default as pain rips through my arm.

"Here." She tosses the Bible at me. "Only reading material in this place. I can finally turn the TV on now that you're awake."

We watch a full episode of *Blues Clues* in complete silence before Esley comes over to check my bandages. She carefully peels off the strips of fabric and investigates. The wound is a bright red. She pokes it lightly. "Ow!" I exclaim.

"That's probably good."

A clear substance is leaking out from underneath the stitches. "Why? Doesn't pus mean infected?"

"Well normally I would say yes, but this isn't that. The pus is leaking out, not staying in there. In a deep wound like this, this is stage two. Inflammatory. So! It's healing!" She does a little dance in her seat.

"Oh. Good."

"At least act excited." She rips new strips of fabric from our stolen bed sheet. "It could have been a whole lot worse. You could still be bleeding."

A beep at our door lets us know that someone is entering. Esley turns abruptly, whipping out her dagger from the bedside table. Deanna walks in, her black hair tangled and windblown and her nose and cheeks bright red. She's carrying four bags that she sets down on the floor as she shuts the door and bolts it into place.

I scramble up from my bed and run towards her, wrapping my good arm around her in a crushing bear hug. "What were you thinking! You could have gotten hurt!"

"Oh, you mean like you did yesterday?" Her voice is full of bite. I stagger back. "Why would you go off alone? When you knew what happened to Aaron, why would you do that? What were you thinking?"

"I thought that—"

"That by leaving we'd all be safer. Is that right?" I open and close my mouth, crumpling under Deanna's unfamiliar anger. "Is that right!"

"Yes!" I find my voice again. "Yes, you'd be safer. Neither of you have to be in this with me. Especially not you, Deanna! You should be with your dad, where it's safe."

"You think I could sit at home while my sister is facing certain death? Do you honestly think I could do that? Could you? Do you really think that little of me?"

"This whole thing with my mom, it has nothing to do with you!"

She narrows her eyes at me. "Nothing," she half spits out. "You think that Vanessa means nothing to me." She storms past me, grabbing the bags as she goes.

"That's not what I said, and you know it!"

"Then what did you mean?" Before I can say anything, she erupts, "Because the way I see it, and I know it's different, but I am just as worried about your mom as you are. I have every right to want revenge on the bastards who killed my brother. So let me help you!"

I've never seen this side of her before. The side that has fiery eyes and bared teeth. Or at least, I've never seen it staring me directly in the face. Maybe she will be alright. "Okay."

She nods shortly at me. "How's your arm?"

"Esley said the pus is good?"

"It's not pus, it's drainage." Esley rubs her temples. "She's doing good. We'll clean it and rewrap it." She goes back to ripping her strips of fabric. "What all did you get?"

"First things first." Deanna empties out the bags onto her bed and picks up a tan roll. "Actual bandages." Esley tosses her fabric strips aside instantly in relief. "And some antibiotic ointment."

"Genesis brand? Is that all the store had?" she asks. Deanna nods. "Oh well, they'll do." She sets to work on my arm.

"Got something against them?" I ask.

"I think they're cheap. They take shortcuts." She dabs the ointment on my arm.

I survey the contents strewn about the bed. Medical supplies, food that keeps, three winter coats, and two metal tubes. "What are those?" I point at the tubes.

Deanna picks one up, holds it away from us, and presses a button on its side. It expands into a long silver staff. Deanna gives it a twirl in her hand. "Woah." Esley looks on in admiration.

"Yeah, I got it at Walmart," Deanna says. "I'd heard you could buy anything there, and that turned out to be true. Told the cashier I was camping."

"You got to see a Walmart?" I exclaim.

"You guys have never seen one before?" Esley raises an eyebrow.

"Not all of us live in the giant city of Portland." Deanna smirks playfully. "Some of us live in reasonably sized towns."

"Hick," Esley mutters.

"City slicker," Deanna shoots back, a teasing smile playing across her lips. Deanna returns to sorting through the pile, eyes drifting up every once in a while to Esley.

Esley's eyes keep flickering over to her while she changes my bandages. It takes everything in me not to laugh.

"I hate to ask this." I inspect the staffs. "Why not just get a gun?" The idea makes my skin crawl, but I don't let it show. "In the interest of survival, I mean."

"Turns out." Deanna collapses into a chair. "That if you want to buy one in the state of Colorado, you need a Colorado ID. Which we don't have. So." She gestures at the staffs. "Next best thing."

My stomach rumbles. "Food?" I ask.

"Here." Deanna tosses me a green box.

I turn it over in my hand. "Oh, Nani Anisha would kill you." I laugh. "Frozen potato and pea samosas? She's rolling in her grave."

"Oh, shut up." Deanna laughs. "She's gonna have to kill the girl who had them in her dorm freezer first."

Esley snorts.

"Want some?" I gesture, opening up the microwave. They nod.

We sit around the provided table, samosas on makeshift paper towel plates. Esley wraps the bandages around my arm slowly, being careful not to tie them too tightly this time. The pounding in my head has yet to cease. My phone pings from my pocket.

I reach for it.

"Girls watching home videos,"

captions a picture of Raina and Anisha sitting in front of a TV. On the TV, tiny versions of Deanna, Aaron, and I are playing in the sand in our bathing suits. The next text from Carl reads,

I shoot back quickly.

"Hey, Deanna." I hold the phone up for her. She smiles softly. "Esley, these are my sisters."

Esley furrows her eyebrows. "Oh, they're blond?"

I nod. "Mom's blond too."

"And Nani Anisha?" Esley cocks her head to the side.

"Mom's mom." I shrug.

"She was Indian. Vanessa, Jade's mom, was adopted," Deanna explains helpfully. "Hence, Nani Anisha hating the frozen samosas."

"Ah." She nods, finishing up the bandages. A single bite of her own samosa later and she opens her mouth. "Oh!" She reaches for my phone. "Your sisters, have you been in contact with them this whole time?"

"Yeah. Why?"

"That's how they found you! It must have been."

I did text Carl mere minutes before that Red Reaper showed up, didn't I? I grip my phone, hopelessness creeping up on me. I need to know that they're safe. A picture of them here and there, the knowledge that no one has taken them, how could I possibly give that up? Deanna meets my eyes.

How could I possibly put her in more danger than she's already in? "Are you sure?" I ask.

"Look, we don't know what equipment they have. Or who these people are. But how else?" Deanna says.

I rack my brain. "If they were tracking our car, they wouldn't have waited for the second night in a hotel."

"They wouldn't have," she says.

"I should text Carl one last time, so he doesn't worry." I go to pick up the phone.

Deanna reaches out and takes it. She gazes longingly at the photo on the screen. "No." She shakes her head, eyes watering. "We need to keep them safe too." She turns the phone off, whispering, "Stay safe, Dad."

"We need to chuck that thing and move," Esley says. Then at my groan of annoyance, she says, "If I'm wrong then the worst thing is that we move. If I'm right, then we could, you know, not die?"

Deanna throws everything but the coats back into the plastic bags. She tosses a rolled up black coat at me. "It's snowing outside," she offers.

After leaving our phones in a couple of bushes outside of the hotel, we leave.

A few towns over we find a new hotel. This one is fairly nice too, with an indoor lobby and everything. I make a mental note to check how much cash we have left in my backpack later.

We're each able to have our own bed tonight. Our room has two queens, and a twin tucked into an alcove underneath the TV mounted to the wall. Deanna settles me into the twin bed, knowing that I like curling up in corners, anyway.

Again, I drift off to sleep in broad daylight, my head pounding out directions to Mom.

I wake up from my remarkably dreamless sleep at three in the morning. Father Rodriguez's faint red glow doesn't shock me anymore. The Red Reaper is here too, mere feet from me. Her eyes are glowing redder than ever and when I reach out to touch her, my hand goes straight through. I exhale in relief, allowing my shoulders to fall forwards.

My feet trudge towards the bathroom. I work water from the shower and shampoo through my hair, carefully keeping my body and bandages dry. Then I scrub the soap over my body and rinse before getting back into my hoodie and underwear.

Blaise pops into the corner of my vision. I smile. My heart is lighter seeing him. I was starting to worry that something had happened to him.

As I turn to face him, he shakes his head aggressively. "No!" He slaps himself across the face and he's gone.

Is he trying to avoid me? Is it because of our argument? Still? My face sours and I turn back towards my bed. The sound of Esley's snores permeates the room.

Why do I care what he thinks, anyway? I know who I am.

I know who I am. I know what I had to do. How can he expect moral perfectionism out of me? When these people are trying to kill me and worse, the people I love. How can he possibly—

I growl, loud enough to get the frustration out, but not loud enough to wake either of them up.

I stew in my anger, thinking through every interaction we've had together. And wondering what point it was that I started caring this much. Because I don't. I don't need to care. I've never even met him in person properly. I don't need him to think I'm doing the right thing.

A small voice speaks up inside of me. I do care. I care so much that the weight of the disapproval has me playing the argument over and over again in my head. And Deanna's pain-stricken face as she yelled at me this morning. And how badly I lost against the Red Reaper. How little I know of fighting.

How scared I am for when we finally get there. Wherever there is.

"Shit." Blaise is back again at the foot of the bed.

I cross my arms. "Are you avoiding me?"

He doesn't answer, simply shakes his head repeatedly. "Wake up!" He slaps himself twice, and he's gone.

"What the hell?" I whisper to myself.

I wait for hours, but he doesn't show up again. And eventually, my own sleep-deprived state wins out.

Chapter Twenty-four

We're in a forested area behind our hotel. The snow that covered the ground two days ago is already melting. The few people we've come into contact with have blamed the finicky Colorado weather.

After ages and ages of cleaning, constant surveillance, and rewrapping, Esley finally declared my arm healed enough to practice with them.

Deanna hands me a metal staff and shows me how to hold it away from myself first. Then I press the button on the top.

The whole thing expands in one swift metallic sounding movement. I blink back my astonishment and face Esley. She's holding her own staff, auburn hair up in a ponytail. I watch her survey my arm.

"If you go for my arm I will kill you," I call across the feet that separate us.

"So will I," Deanna says.

"I've put a lot of work into that arm." Esley rolls her hazel eyes, twirling the staff in her fingers. "I'm just trying to memorize where it is, so I don't accidentally hit it. Calm down."

"Okay." Deanna raises her eyebrows doubtfully.

"Alright." Esley nods. "Show me what you know."

"On your marks!" Deanna calls. "Two, three, go!"

Esley charges across the clearing, her staff raised in the air. As she swings down, I hold up my staff with both hands to block. I struggle against her for all of two seconds.

In a flash of metal, she flicks her staff out and hits my shins. I curse loudly but try to ignore the throbbing pain. I have to get used to getting hit and maintaining focus.

I swing the staff through the air and graze her ribs. She grunts in pain but is otherwise unaffected.

Esley lashes out again for my stomach.

I clumsily whirl the staff around, almost losing my grip on it. I block entirely by accident with the tip of it.

"Imagine that I'm one of them," she says. "You have to beat me, or you die. Come on!"

I'm able to dodge her next blow.

She's swinging again before I have time to recover, hitting me square in the stomach. I grunt. The world spins around me.

I refocus on her, determination breaking through the pain.

I block her next hit.

She just as quickly changes course and slams the staff into my thigh. I'm still reeling from that when she knocks the staff out of my hands.

I scramble to pick it up and Esley prepares for another strike.

"That's enough!" Deanna calls out.

But Esley doesn't stop. Her staff swings and I barely dodge it. "They won't stop," she calls back. I trip and fall backwards.

She swings again.

For a moment, I see the Red Reaper in front of me, not Esley. I throw my hands up to block, biting back a scream.

The blow never comes. I lower my arms, turning my head towards her.

Esley is frozen in place. Her eyes are glazed over with a bright green glow.

"Esley?" Deanna calls.

I push myself to my feet, inspecting her.

Drop the staff.

Esley's staff clatters to the ground.

"Jade. Stop." Deanna's voice comes from somewhere miles off.

I shake my head. The green glow dissipates. Esley unfreezes, staring at me. "Why did you do that?"

"I didn't mean to I—"

"You were in my head!" she growls, picking up her staff and running back towards the hotel.

Deanna shuffles between us for a moment, eyebrows furrowed. She ultimately follows Esley inside.

I lower myself to the ground next to my staff in shame and confusion. What is happening to me?

I'm not alone for long.

"Green Eyes." His voice is resigned.

I turn to meet his gaze. "Brown Eyes." I smile hesitantly at him. He's in jeans and a button-down shirt rolled up to the elbows. His hands are clenched into fists protectively around his thumbs. His eyebrows are knit closely together, and his breath is shaky and quiet. "What's wrong?" I survey our surroundings.

"Nothing." He sits beside me, screwing up his face in much more concentration than he usually needs. He exhales shakily. "What's with the snow?"

"Blaise, what's going on? You haven't been sleeping. Why?"

He inhales, clenching his eyes shut. "Jillian, I really hate the snow." There's something pointed in the way he says it.

"Why?"

"It's so cold. I'm not used to it where I live." He yelps in pain. "Evergreen trees," he whispers shakily, listing off other things he sees. It's like some strange sort of grounding technique.

"If you tell me what's wrong, I can help you." I reach a hand out for his but withdraw it at the last second. It's not helpful in the slightest to have someone remind you of your non-existence. "You're in pain. Who's hurting you?"

His eyes burst open, and he turns his gaze to mine. His beautiful brown eyes are warped, deadened, full of fear. Blaise exhales shakily, a loose curl twirling as a result.

"Green Eyes," he speaks with urgency. I lean forwards, hanging on his every word. "I have to tell you something." I nod quickly, urging him to continue. His eyes don't leave mine for even a second. "There's a reason that I'm not like the other Red Eyes. Why I am aware of you. It's because"—he stops speaking as abruptly as he started. His features screw up in anguish. He grits his teeth and squeezes his hands into tighter fists—"because I'm—"

A terrible shrill scream escapes his lips.

"Blaise!" I find myself on my knees in front of him, desperately searching for the source of his pain. The scream is never ending, it goes on and on and on and—"BLAISE!" I scream even louder to make myself heard. He writhes in place, curling in on himself.

The screaming stops. His eyes fly open. He's gasping for air. "What's happening to you?"

He opens his mouth to speak, once, twice, then shuts it again. "Evergreen trees. Snow. Cold air. Mountains," he whispers, hands over his eyes. "I'm trying to tell you that"—he gasps and his entire body tenses up—"that I know—"

Another scream escapes him, louder and more horrible this time. It rattles around my very soul. He presses down on his eyes with his fists as though trying to gouge them out.

I reach out for his hands and pull them away from his face. "Blaise!" His eyes snap open even amidst his pain as he stares at our joined hands. Shock floods my system, but I push it aside. "Blaise, can you fight it?"

He answers me with another scream as he jumps to his feet, bringing me with him. He stumbles around jerkily as though searching for a way out.

I cling to his hand for dear life, trying to convince myself that this is not a nightmare. That I am actually touching Blaise's hand.

And maybe if I can do that impossible thing, I can help him.

We collide with the trunk of a tree, my back scraping against the bark. I pull him to me by his hands and whisper his name. His eyes snap open again and I gasp in horror.

His eyes, his beautiful brown eyes, gone, replaced by red, not quite glowing yet. "I'm here," I whisper frantically. "It's me, Jade. That's my real name, not Jillian." He gasps shakily, his hands moving to my forearms and squeezing, surely leaving nail marks.

I wrench one hand from his grasp and reach up steadily to cup his face in my hand. "Blaise," I whisper. "You can fight this. I know you can. Breathe." My hand absently moves towards his dark curls.

It's what Mom always did to calm us down, ran her hands through our hair and sang a song. I sing the tune's notes instead of the words. My voice shakes too much. Every few seconds he jerks or gasps in pain.

At least he's not screaming. I keep singing the tune to him, carefully, gently, running my hand through his hair. "Blaise, it's alright. You're not alone."

He lowers his forehead to rest against mine and whimpers like a wounded animal. We're taking in the same air. I watch his closed eyes desperately. It's still him in there, it has to be. He doesn't move, doesn't say a word.

"Your eyes," I manage to say. "If you're still in there, show me your eyes." His eyes flutter open. There's only a fleck of red left in his warm brown gaze. I silently thank God.

His chin tilts forwards and before I can fully register what I'm doing, so does mine.

Our lips touch in the lightest and most gentle of ways. Despite its innocence, the kiss sends shivers down my entire spine. A quiet moan escapes his lips.

I dive back in, devouring his lips in mine. His hand is in my hair and pulling me closer to him with each passing second. I'm pressed up against his chest, his shirt bunched up in my fists.

I need him close to me. He needs to be closer.

We collide with the tree again, coming up for air. My body is warm despite the frost in the air.

His eyes meet mine. They are filled with a hunger that leaves me breathless. His lips claim another kiss from mine then he breaks away, leaving a soft trail of kisses up my neck and next to my ear. "I heard"—he whispers between kisses, his lips hardly moving as he speaks—"Jillian, not your name?"

"Jade," I gasp out. "My name is Jade Zaveri."

He grins and returns for a soft kiss that we press to each other's lips. "I like that much better."

I smile into his lips. He shudders violently.

"Sorry!" I gasp, pulling away. "God, are you okay? Sit down!"

His legs practically crumple beneath him. I help him lean against the tree. His mouth hangs open as he brushes a finger over his lips.

"We can touch," I whisper. He nods, his mouth still agape. "Why?"

He opens his mouth to respond, but promptly shuts it and shrugs instead.

"It's whenever you talk that you're hurt, isn't it?" Another nod. "Do you know what's going on?" A grimace. "Blaise, please. Just tell me how to help you. I'll do it."

Blaise clenches his eyes shut and turns away from me with clenched fists. A small squeak escapes his lips.

"I want to help you, Blaise. Tell me how."

"I need to find you." His voice cracks. "To tell you"—he shudders again, burying his face in his hands. I can't see his face, but judging by his voice, he's in incredible pain still—"I need help."

"What do you need?"

"Where you are." He exhales heavily. "Please." And that last break of his voice on the word please breaks me.

"I'm in Montrose, Colorado."

"Montrose," he repeats shakily. "Thank you, Green Eyes." Blaise squeezes my hand once, and he's gone.

Chapter Twenty-five

I stay in our snow dusted corner of shade, my back against the tree, completely dumbfounded. My hand shakily reaches up to touch my lips.

I didn't mean to kiss him. That should have been the furthest thing from my mind with how much pain he was in.

The strangest part is that it didn't feel any different from kissing Mark, or Daniel, or even Mary. People who were physically there with me, in dark corners at night. Blaise wasn't here. And still, I can't forget the feeling of his lips all over me. As though he was physically here with me too. As if he wasn't . . .

Whatever he is. Why was he hurting? Something is wrong with him. I need to find out. I need to—

Focus, Jade. Focus. I'm on a mission.

But what is wrong with Blaise?

"Jade?" Deanna's voice is growing nearer. She's going to find me soon.

I can't tell her about the kiss. I'd have to explain Blaise. How I've seen him every single night for the past few weeks. How I've never told her about him, even though it would have made perfect sense to.

Blaise isn't even what she'll want to talk about. She'll want to talk about why my eyes glowed green earlier and froze Esley in place.

"There you are." Her voice is a mixture of gentle concern and confusion.

"I don't have an answer for you," I mutter, staring at a spot of snow between my knees. Blaise stood there. No footprints.

"Your eyes were green."

"They're always green."

"*Glowing* green." She plops down beside me.

"I know." I bury my face in my hands. "The first time was in the Underworld. Desdemon, they tried to stop us. And I don't know what happened, but I pushed them out of my head. And my eyes glowed. I don't know why, and I don't know how and"—I finally turn my head towards her. She's grinning widely—"what?"

"Jade." She laughs. "Jade, don't you understand? You stopped Esley from moving." I nod. "You! You did that. With whatever weird glowy eye powers you picked up in the Underworld."

"So?"

"Don't you know what this means? We could actually stand a chance! If you can figure this out. How many do you think you could freeze at a time?"

"Wait, wait. You're happy?"

"Of course! Esley's still a little shaken, but she knows how big of an advantage this is. I don't care how you got it, or where it came from. It's going to help you not die. It's good."

I fling my arms around her in relief. A rush of emotions I didn't even know I was carrying wash away with her acceptance. Her arms snake around me tightly. "Thank you," I whisper, blinking back tears.

Check out is at 11 a.m., but I'm hesitant to get back on the road. What about Blaise? The pounding in my skull has barely subsided over the past few days. I should want to get on the road. And I do. But what did he need to tell me?

Is he safe?

Esley gives my arm a final once over before she decides we're ready. "Yup, stitches can come out. Superglue for you now."

"Thank God." Deanna sighs. "By the way, when this is all over, you and I are getting some freaking therapy." She points at me.

"Please start with an actual doctor's visit for this arm." Esley pats my shoulder lightly and gets to work removing the stitches. It takes everything in me not to squirm away from the sensation of thread dragging through my skin.

She dabs copious amounts of superglue over the wound and waits for it to dry before covering the wound with bandages again. It's a light brownish red now, apparently a good sign, the 'polifation stage' or whatever Esley said. Regrettably, it will scar, badly, judging by the much darker skin surrounding it.

Esley helps me pull my hoodie on without disturbing the bandages too much, then turns to Deanna. "Okay. Everything we need in the car?" Deanna nods in response. Esley claps her hands together. "In the words of my dad, let's get this show on the road."

I snort. "Ah, the ultimate dad joke. Or so I'm told."

Blaise is in the back of my mind as we walk down the stairs. Is it possible that something has gone terribly wrong, and he's turning into a red eye himself? Does he need my help? I can help him, I think. Even if that method might be kissing him, or his soul, rather. Why did it seem so real?

"Jade, you good?" Deanna asks.

"Yeah," I mutter. "Yeah, just thinking." I search through my backpack in the trunk and count the bills that are left. $178. "Thinking that we need to stop at an ATM."

"Already?" Esley remarks.

I nod curtly. "We'll go on our way out of town. So hopefully we should be good. But I don't want to trust that we're gonna make it gas wise and run out somewhere on the side of the road."

"That would be worse."

Minutes later, I stand in front of an ATM outside of a convenience store. The wind blows, making what was a sunny day completely frigid. Deanna and Esley are in the car, mere feet away from me.

They're talking to each other animatedly. Deanna tosses her head back in laughter, her black hair pooling out over the hood of her jacket.

The urge to run away and never let them get involved in this again courses through me.

I approach the car window and knock lightly. Deanna rolls it down, manually, which makes Esley crack up more. "Yeah?"

"So, I may have just remembered that I'm supposed to be dead."

"You can't access your bank account, can you?" Deanna raises an eyebrow.

"I cannot access my bank account."

"I got it." She opens the car door while Esley curses. "What?"

Esley reaches into the back for the two staffs and secures her daggers to her thigh. "That's bound to send one hell of a flag through the system." Deanna takes the staff that's offered to her, and I take mine. "If we're lucky, we won't need any of these, and Jade can just do her thing."

I turn my head away and press my lips together. If we're really, *really* lucky, we can leave before they show up at all.

"How much?" Deanna asks.

"How much is your ATM limit?" I hate myself for having to ask it.

"$1,000." Her finger hovers over the buttons. Esley and I wince. "We need all of it don't we?"

Esley exhales heavily and nods. "Strategically? Yeah."

"Well." Deanna shrugs and presses some buttons. "If we survive this, another few years in my dad's house, it is."

"I'll pay you back."

"You will do no such thing." The machine spits the money into Deanna's waiting hand.

The surrounding air thickens.

I whip around, searching the tree line. Snow crunches to my

right.

They're like three foxes in the snow, three red creatures prowling just out of reach.

Deanna follows my gaze and inhales sharply. She shoves all the cash into my backpack and flings it towards Esley. She catches it, tosses it in the passenger seat, and sprints back towards us in one swift movement.

They jump into action, three Red Reapers barrel towards us, scythes at the ready.

Deanna expands her staff to its full length. Esley draws her daggers.

I examine them carefully, trying to focus on what they might be thinking. Maybe I can get in there. Get in their heads.

The leader of the pack is stocky and gruff this time. Two more flank him, each nimble and tiny. We've never encountered any of them before.

The two nimble ones break off and head for Deanna and Esley.

The man makes a beeline straight for me. I duck out of the way at the last second, hurriedly expanding my own staff.

I block his incoming strike. "You're new." My breaths come fast and heavy. Maybe I can get him talking and then I'll be able to control him?

"How's your arm?" he taunts, swinging his scythe back to strike it.

I sidestep, grateful for the warning. He misses reopening the wound by inches. "Good!" I swipe at his arm and miss. "Yours?"

No more talking.

I bring the staff across towards his head.

He steps back effortlessly, completely out of range.

The scythe is longer. I barely manage to block his incoming strike.

I watch his feet shuffle, off kilter from the force of impact.

My brain is alight, as if on fire. The world comes into sharp focus around me.

Stocky, gruff, and off center. He's clearly well trained, but not one person bothered him about footwork. I shift to the balls of my feet.

I thrust my foot up in a quick jab to his chest. Both of my feet are back on the ground before he's done stumbling.

Before he can rebalance himself, I shove the metal staff into his jaw. He grunts in pain.

I switch arm positions, readying the staff diagonally in front of me. I duck out of the way of his next strike, then slam the staff into his stomach. He doubles over.

This I know. How to put on a show, a show of being skilled enough to beat him.

With every hit I get, he gets more and more off balance, more and more susceptible. One good knock on the head and he'll be down for the count.

Deanna cries out in pain.

I whip my head towards the sound. Her red hooded foe has Deanna cornered against the ATM. Blood trickles down Deanna's cheek from a small cut.

My feet shuffle towards her uncertainly, but her Red Reaper has abandoned her and is instead heading towards Esley, daggers out and swinging in a whirlwind of metal.

I hear a scythe cutting through the air behind me and stumble backwards before I've fully turned my head. My lapse in concentration has cost me dearly. The scythe misses my chest by centimeters.

I turn my attention back to the man in front of me, trying again to reach into his head. If I could freeze him in place, even for a second. Just one second and I'm sure I could knock him out.

Esley grunts. I turn briefly, but attack after attack comes for me. He's relentless. Half of my attention is on blocking, half on trying to get inside his head.

"NO!" Deanna screams. I chance a glance backwards.

Deanna is on the ground, scrambling for her staff, several feet away from Esley.

Esley's daggers are on the ground. She's reaching for them.

Two scythes are coming down towards her.

I change course instantly, sprinting for them.

I jump onto one of the Red Reapers, sending them to the ground. I reach out for the other one as we fall.

Esley manages to dodge out of the way of that one's slice.

My neck hairs stand on end. Metal slices through the air behind me.

I squeeze my eyes shut, bracing for the snowfall in front of me to be the last I ever see.

The blow never comes.

Instead, I hear a low grunt and the sound of something large falling to the ground.

I turn and see a man in a black leather jacket standing over the unconscious figure of the man I was fighting. He's holding a large broadsword. Next, the man runs for the one fighting Esley.

The one I'm on top of pushes me off her, reaching for her scythe.

I grab my staff from the ground and whack her across the back of the head as hard as I can before she can stand. She topples forward, groaning.

I stand, ready to aid Esley, but her opponent is also on the ground, the strange man standing over her.

All three are passed out.

Not dead. One of us would see them if they were dead.

The man walks towards us, peering at my target on the ground.

His skin is a deep brown that stands in stark contrast to the snow. His hair is as black as mine, but not smooth, curly and in shoulder length braids that he has tied in a low ponytail. He's the type of man I would expect to see a frown on at all times, but instead he wears a pensive expression. He's strangely calm for having just knocked two people out.

"Jeremiah!" Esley shouts, running towards him.

He opens his arms and embraces her. "Esley! Good to see you're well."

That voice. "You," I whisper. His eyebrows knit together, and he releases Esley. "You're the one who told me to jump off a cliff."

His expression gives way to a small laugh. "Yes. That was me. Jade . . . Right?" I nod. "Jeremiah. I guard the Reapers." His head turns to the Red Reaper I hit as she stirs. "And we need to go. Follow me."

Esley doubles back for the backpack. We sprint after him into the woods. We're barely out of sight of the Red Reapers when he stops in his tracks. He doubles back a couple of steps and nods, pulling his sleeves up to reveal metal cuffs on his arms. "Here. Grab the metal."

Deanna and I share a look with each other, but Esley grabs on unquestioningly. "Jade," she says. We both grab onto the same arm uncertainly.

"Do not let go until I say."

He clenches his eyes shut and a black cloud envelops us all.

Chapter Twenty-six

The cloud clears. Small grey mounds of stone surround us. We're in a graveyard. There's a stone angel beside me. We're at the grave of Joseph Andrews, who died in the year 1982.

"You can let go now," Jeremiah mutters.

I relinquish my hold on the metal cuff.

"What just happened?" Deanna asks.

"I can travel between graveyards."

"We didn't come from a graveyard." I raise an eyebrow suspiciously.

"You're right." He surveys our surroundings, for people or for Red Reapers, I don't know. "But a body was buried there."

"Like, illegally?" Deanna asks.

"Maybe? Or an old body, I don't know." Jeremiah unties and reties his braids. "Jade, I heard that you know where Vanessa is?" His tone is entirely businesslike, none of the warmth that he has with Esley.

"Sort of. I know what direction she's in."

"Do you think I moved you farther away from where she is or closer?"

I close my eyes, tuning in to the tugging sensation. It pulls me to the left, hard. Harder than usual? I can't tell. "I feel tugging that way." I point to the left. "But I can't tell how far away."

"Here. Hold on." He turns to face me. His eyes are filled with some emotion that I can't quite identify, but he's not pensive anymore. "Esley?" he says without breaking my gaze.

"Hmm?"

"I need you to try something."

Esley stands in front of me, her glasses slightly askew. She straightens them.

"You're a Reaper," he says quietly. "There are two souls in there. One of them is Vanessa's. I need you to try to find her."

"I can't do that," Esley says. "Jade's the one who can get into other people's heads."

His eyes widen in surprise for a moment, but he doesn't comment on it. "I need you to try. Please." Esley nods once. "Put one hand on your mark and the other on Jade's."

Her fingers are freezing. She stares into my eyes long and hard, concentrating. "Nothing's happening," she concedes after a whole minute.

"You're looking for Vanessa's soul. Find someone stubborn and tough," he says. I furrow my eyebrows. "But gentle too."

"I've never felt a soul be a certain way." Esley presses her lips together.

"Okay, then. Memories. She loved playing the flute. She wore a green saree to her cousin's wedding and spilled curry all over it. When she first moved to the beach, the ocean terrified her."

"Her favorite animal is the dolphin," I say. "Sunday dinners. She loves cooking for everyone on Sundays."

"The first book she ever read was *Charlotte's Web*. When she was ten, she broke a bowl her dad made and blamed it on the cat."

"If you scrape your knee, she'll ask if we should amputate it."

Jeremiah snorts. I can hear him continuing to talk, but inside my head, Esley has made her way in. All the memories we've been talking about play through my mind. Mom in her green saree, the words of *Charlotte's Web*, the high-pitched notes of a flute, Sunday dinners.

The pounding in my head gets louder and louder. My body is

pulled by a rope towards her. Pulling, pulling, the rope snaps. The tugging gets duller.

"We're farther away now, aren't we?" I whisper, blinking heavily. Esley's eyes are glowing green. I shake my head rapidly until her eyes return to their usual hazel.

Esley nods. "Not too much farther, though."

Jeremiah sighs and nods, walking away from us. We follow him through the row. His head hangs down. "Jeremiah?" I jog to catch up to him. "How do you know my mom? How does Desdemon know my mom, for that matter?"

He falters in his step. "Vanessa Zaveri is . . . " He considers his words carefully, running a hand through his hair. "Important to Desdemon."

I turn back to Deanna and Esley, who both shrug. "But why?"

He sighs deeply, thinks about it, then says, "She helped me when I had nowhere else to go. Desdemon wouldn't forget that."

"Is that why they took her? Because she's important to Desdemon?"

"I have no idea." Jeremiah points ahead at a black car with a large trunk. "That's mine. Let's go."

"Why else would they have taken her?" I jog faster to keep up.

"If they took her because she's important to Desdemon, then they know way more than I thought and we're in trouble." He sighs. "Let's hope it's something else."

He proceeds with large strides to the car. The conversation is clearly over by his standards. I turn back to Deanna and Esley. "He's the one who told you that you were a Reaper?"

"Yeah," Esley says. "He was a lot more cheerful when that happened, though." She cocks her head curiously at him.

"They already returned Father Rodriguez," Deanna mutters. "There must be a reason they haven't given her back yet." She grabs the backpack from Esley and tosses it in the trunk along with our staffs and Jeremiah's sword. "We're farther away now?" I nod dismally. "We're just going to have to move faster. And not use anything trackable. I don't understand—"

"How they found us that quickly," Esley finishes. "That was inhumanly fast. Do you think they can travel through graveyards too?"

"No," Jeremiah says shortly. "C'mon." He gestures for me to take the passenger seat.

"But how do you know they can't?" I buckle my seat belt. "I mean, how much do we know about them, anyway?"

"Not much. I'll be honest. But unless one of them was given this power by Desdemon, then there's no way they can travel through graveyards." He pauses. "Although, I have no idea how they found you three so fast."

"We had to use an ATM," Esley pipes up from the seat behind me.

"And Jade's supposed to be dead," Deanna says, leaning forwards. Her black hair is frizzy and tangled from the fight. "When she put her info in . . . "

He knits his eyebrows together and turns the ignition. "Why are you supposed to be dead?"

"You." I cross my arms. "You made me jump off a cliff."

"And you were seen?"

"Of course I was."

"Amateur." His lip quirks up in the briefest of smiles.

"Well, I'm sorry I can't travel through literal graves to get away from things."

He opens his mouth to say something and then shakes his head. "Which way?" I point for him and we're off.

"Where are we now?" Deanna asks, peering at the signs we pass. "There's no more snow."

"Sedona, Arizona," he answers. "The Grim Reaper let me know that something was going wrong—"

A sudden hard tug pulls me almost physically to the right. "Turn right!" I blurt out. He turns the steering wheel deftly with hardly a break in his words.

"—I got as close as I could as fast as I could," he finishes. "Highway?"

"I think so." I nod.

We go the rest of the day with Jeremiah driving far over the speed limit. He asks Esley what she's been up to, and Deanna how she got roped into all of this. And hardly any questions of me, except for directions.

We pass four 'Repent to Jesus' billboards, two billboards advertising Genesis' new medicine, and one bright and garish billboard advertising a casino in six exits.

It's at least three in the morning before Jeremiah shows any sign of slowing down. Deanna and Esley are both passed out in the back seat. I force my eyes to stay open, knowing that I'm needed.

He stares determinedly at the road, his hands gripping the wheel in a vise grip.

"You care about her a lot, don't you?" I whisper, too tired to care if he doesn't want to talk about it. He nods wordlessly. "That's enough for me." I shrug. After a few moments, his grip loosens. "I mean, really." I laugh. "That's enough for me. I'm exhausted."

"I've noticed," he says. "There's a place to camp up the road. We'll stop there."

"You got tents in this enormous car of yours?"

He shakes his head. "We'll figure something out." A pause. "How is your arm?"

"How did you—?"

"You're carrying that arm differently." I wince. "I can't help it heal faster. That's not my area of expertise. If I tried, I'd pretty much only succeed in making any infected tissue die. Which isn't without merit, but not what you're looking for." He takes the next exit. "You're gonna have to figure out how to hide it or they will use it against you."

"How do your powers work, exactly?" I cock my head, bringing my legs up to sit crisscross in my seat.

"I got them from Desdemon. So, largely death based." Gravel smacks against the side of the car. "I travel between graveyards." He pauses for a long time and then continues in a whisper, "I could kill people by touching them, but I don't."

"So could anyone else."

"Not with a touch." He sighs.

"You got those from Desdemon?" He nods. "I-I have a—Desdemon was in my head."

He furrows his brows. "Why?"

"I wanted to leave the Underworld."

He furrows his eyebrows. "How are you here now?"

"I pushed them out?"

He stops the car and puts on the parking brake but doesn't move beyond that. "How?"

"They were in my head, and I could remember all kinds of things that happened thousands of years before I was born. So, I just . . . " I shrug. "Pushed all of that stuff out."

His mouth hangs open. And his eyes shine with shock. And pride, I think? "You are nineteen years old." I nod. "And you shoved a billion-year-old being out of your head?" I nod sheepishly. "Jade." He blinks, stunned. "Even I can't do that."

"Well of course not," I say. He looks taken aback. "If Desdemon gave them to you, of course they wouldn't want you to have the power to push them out."

"Desdemon gave you"—he stops, swallows hard, and then continues—"Desdemon didn't give you your powers?"

"I don't know where I got them." I stare at my hands. "Although now that you mention it, I never had them until the Grim Reaper put Mom's soul window thing in my body."

"That would make sense," Deanna whispers groggily, rubbing her eyes and leaning forwards. "The Grim Reaper probably gave it to you to help you get out.”

"Huh." I furrow my eyebrows.

Deanna turns to Jeremiah. "You're telling me, that she can push literal Death out of her head, but can't get someone to freeze on command?"

"They're different!" I say. "Pushing something out and forcing my way in are two entirely different things!"

Deanna opens her mouth to speak, but Jeremiah holds up one calloused hand. "And that's why we're going to work on that tomorrow."

Chapter Twenty-seven

I wake up to a sharp knock on the car window. Jeremiah holds up a staff with a raised brow. His green eyes are sharp, determined.

I remove my feet from the dashboard, put my boots on, and tie them. All of my joints scream as they unfold. Deanna and Esley have already practiced, judging by the state of their hair and how ravenously they are eating around a fire.

"Breakfast?" I ask, stepping out of the car.

"Not yet." Jeremiah shakes his head, leading me to a clearing next to a lake. I gaze longingly at the oatmeal they are wolfing down. Deanna waves at me with a full mouth as we pass. "From what your friend tells me"—he turns to face me—"you've had the best results under high stress circumstances."

"Oh." I sigh. My arm hurts from sleeping in that incredibly convoluted position. I remember Jeremiah deciding to sleep in the hatchback trunk with all the weapons.

"So." His tone is entirely businesslike. "Lesson number one. We can't trust our powers." He throws a staff onto the ground in front of me. I cock my head to the side and pick it up. "To be there for us I mean. You have to be able to fight without them." He pulls out Esley's staff.

"Oh, thank God you're going non-lethal."

He twirls it, getting a feel for the weight. I'm sure it's lighter than the sword. "If you're already having trouble getting this power to work for you on command, I don't feel good about sending you into a room of trained fighters without a basic understanding of how to defend yourself."

"Fair," I mutter, extending my own staff. "They move fast."

"Almost inhumanely so. I've noticed." He sighs. "But they do have some weaknesses. Which I saw that you already spotted a few of." His eyes are shiny again, but the expression disappears. Maybe I imagined it. "The cloaks for one, lousy footwork, and a long weapon."

I flourish the staff. "Whereas this one is short."

He rolls his eyes. "Their aim is to kill. They are trying to use the end of the weapon. Our aim—"

"Is to get Mom."

"And thus, we can hit with any part of the weapon," he finishes. "Alright Jade, show me what you're made of."

I barely have a chance to blink before he swings at me. I duck out of the way, getting a firmer grip on my own staff. He swings again. I throw up the staff to block.

He easily forces past it, tapping me lightly on the side with the staff.

I exhale in relief. I'm tired of getting hit.

"Hmmm." He surveys me. "Aware of your surroundings. Not very strong, but there are ways to work around that."

"Not very strong?" I put my hands on my hips.

"No need to get offended. I'm only stating facts."

I smirk.

"Facts that you already know." A small smile crosses his face. "Okay, this time when you block me, make your next move as fast as possible. If you pause in a block, they are trained, and they will win out in strength."

I've barely finished nodding before he strikes. This time, he hits me square in my good arm. I wince. He doesn't stop.

I block and struggle against him. He shakes his head. Instead, I sidestep and swing the staff out at his legs.

Our fight is a calculated dance of the same three moves over and over again until every block lasts milliseconds.

This time, after my sidestep, he throws in a jab. I spin out of the way, my feet turning in those familiar tiny steps, staff held out in front of me. My head whips back to that same spot I chose, the staff, and I cast my foot back to balance myself.

He blinks rapidly.

I jab at his stomach.

He barely blocks it.

We trade blows and blocks, Jeremiah dropping tips and words of advice, until finally, he's satisfied.

Thank God. I'm starving.

"That was ballet earlier, wasn't it?" he asks.

"It was." I nod. "Mom started taking me when I was three."

"Ah." He nods. "Why?"

I smile. "She needed somewhere to put me after school and before she was out of work. And I liked spinning."

"Do you still do it?"

"Nah." I shake my head fervently. "It gets expensive. I dropped out after Mom had the twins."

His eyes widen. "Twins?"

"Raina and Anisha. My sisters." I smile. "Little demons they are sometimes, but God, I miss them."

Pity passes over his face, and just as quickly disappears. "We should see if Deanna and Esley left you anything to eat."

Deanna stands up from her place next to the fire. "How is training? Can she—?"

Jeremiah holds up a hand. "Food," he says pointing a thumb at me.

Deanna offers up a granola bar. "There are still some eggs in the cooler."

"I'll cook," Esley offers. Halfway through cracking an egg over the frying pan, she turns. "How did we get eggs?"

"*When* did we get eggs is what I'm concerned about." Deanna picks up the now empty box which reads 'Greta's Farm' in thick black sharpie.

"Someone buried an animal over there." Jeremiah points towards the shore of the lake. "And there was a graveyard near a farm and a lovely woman with some eggs."

"Huh," Deanna says. "Could you go anywhere in the world if you wanted?"

Jeremiah nudges Esley out of the way playfully and takes over. "Technically yes. But it's not easy." We wait for him to elaborate, but his gaze is fixed pensively on the eggs. He smiles and mutters something I can't hear over the crackling flames. "The more people I take with me," he continues. "Or the farther I go, the more tiring and difficult it gets."

With a spatula, he smashes the egg into an amalgamation of yellow and white. The sizzling makes my stomach rumble.

"For example, I can't take us to Vanessa, because we have no concept of a graveyard map in Jade's head. If we spend all day going back and forth, guessing which graveyard is closest, with the four of us, I'd risk leaving half of Deanna here." Deanna's eyes widen. "Nearly impossible when I'm well rested by the way, but anyway. Yes, if I wanted to, I could pop over to Germany for the day."

"Why Germany?" Deanna asks.

"Because I love small German towns." He turns to me with a plate. "Egg."

I take the plate gratefully and try not to scarf down every single morsel too quickly. I could eat five, maybe more. Well salted, mixed up with an equal combination of white and yellow throughout, the perfect fried egg. It tastes like home.

Jeremiah puts another egg on the pan. "Eat up. You're all gonna help me with the next part."

Chapter Twenty-eight

We stand in a circle by the lake, staring out at the placid surface. It's strange, being near a body of water that doesn't make noise. The waves I'm used to are replaced by the soft lapping of ripples against pebbles.

"So." Jeremiah claps his hands together. "Who wants to go first?" Neither Deanna nor Esley responds. "Alright. I'll go first." He takes half a step forwards, hands shaking.

Is he afraid?

"I don't know how," I say. "I don't know how to get into your head or anyone else's. I've never been good at that."

"You aren't trying to get into their heads," he says. "You're trying to get into their souls."

"That's worse." I remember how it worked with Esley earlier, talking about Mom's memories. "Tell me some of your memories, let's see if—" I walk towards him with my hand outstretched.

He practically jumps out of the way, eyes wide. Yup, definitely afraid of me. My heart sinks into my stomach.

"You need to be able to do this without touching," he says, righting himself. "Try."

His bright green eyes bore into mine. I furrow my brows. Nothing happens except for the two of us staring at each other.

I shake my head. "I can't."

"Memories," he says. "Let's see. The first time I visited my favorite place, Passau, Germany, I got there accidentally. I was walking on a trail when I stepped over a place where someone was buried. And then I was in the middle of an old graveyard."

I try to imagine what it would feel like to end up in a different country accidentally. To be too tired to get yourself out of it.

Images flash through my mind in rapid succession. An old town, a tall red brick church, a dilapidated graveyard, a river.

I stumble backwards, jerking myself out of Jeremiah's soul from sheer surprise.

Jeremiah is massaging his temples.

"Does it hurt?" I ask.

"Not exactly. Sort of a dull headache." He shakes his head. "Try again. Do it on purpose."

I meet his eyes again, trying to peer back into that old town. I screw my face up in concentration, but it's not working.

"Deep breath," Jeremiah says.

I obey, filling my lungs and letting it all out.

Flashing lights. Hands pressing down on someone's chest. People speak urgently. The sound of ribs cracking.

I whip around to find Esley's eyes glowing green. I lose my hold almost immediately.

I turn back to Jeremiah.

Crumbling stone, ribs cracking, a red brick church, flashing lights. Everything cycles through my mind in rapid fire succession. Much more than I can process. I'm at peace. I'm stressed. I'm learning. I'm confused. I'm terrified. I don't know where I am.

None of it is me. All of this is them.

My legs give out beneath me and my hold on them snaps again. Screams echo in my mind, distant and far away, but gut wrenching.

"Mom?" I whimper. Black tendrils of hair cloud my vision as Deanna kneels in front of me.

My headache is back in full force, tugging desperately towards the right, as though trying to pull my brain out of my skull.

"Jade?" she whispers, pushing my hair back from my forehead.

I readjust to the sensation. "It's fine. I'm fine." I shake my head, pushing myself back up to my feet.

My gaze turns to Esley, wringing out her hands and shaking any remnants of me out of her head. Her auburn curls shake down from her ponytail. I notice Deanna's gaze lingering on her hair. How badly she must want to braid it. A short giggle escapes my mouth.

"What? You think being in my head is funny?" Esley snaps.

"No! I was laughing at something else." I bring myself to my feet and shake out my hands. "I'm sorry."

"She needs to practice. Would you calm down?" Deanna says. They stare at each other, locked in a stalemate that Deanna eventually wins when Esley turns away. "Maybe we should try me next?" She raises her hand.

"Yes." Jeremiah nods. "You know her best. Jade, try to get her to do something this time. No matter how small."

I stare into Deanna's piercing blue eyes.

She presses her lips together, bracing herself. But the expression on her face is anything but prepared. The way her face is scrunched up and all, it almost looks like . . .

I burst out laughing. I have to turn away. "Your face!" I cackle.

"Yours too." Deanna snickers.

"Will you two focus!" Jeremiah snaps. It startles us both into silence. "Sorry." He shuts his eyes and runs a hand across his face.

I turn back to Deanna, squaring my shoulders. We both almost immediately break. The sheer ridiculousness of it all. Of me trying to get into her head, to control her actions. As if anyone could control Deanna's actions but herself. I still my body and reach out to place a hand on her shoulder.

I meet her eyes. "Deanna, tell me what you're thinking right now."

"I'm thinking that this is the strangest thing I've ever done." I nod at her to continue, trying to focus on only her thoughts. "That maybe we're going about this all wrong. You've said it yourself before. You're not the language arts type where you can get in everyone's heads. You've always been more analytical."

"What do you think we should do?" I ask, placing my hands on either side of her temples.

"Maybe it's not important whose head or soul or whatever you can get into. Maybe all you need to do is add one more."

When my eyes open, it's like coming home. A green glow takes over Deanna's eyes.

Something is baking in the kitchen. Esley's hair. Esley's freckles. Weaving between metal staffs. Standing over Jade, me, heart clenched at the sight of blood.

Aaron's lifeless body on the beach, covered in blood.

Emptiness. Despair.

Tears soak my cheeks. I blink.

Deanna isn't in front of me anymore. She's on the ground. Esley's arms are around her. Deanna is sobbing from a pair of glowing green eyes. My hands hang empty in the air, and still she cries.

A faint green glow is in the air. I shake my head rapidly. More images of blood coating Aaron, a hospital room. Lauren Cherishé wearing a weak smile and an even weaker outstretched hand.

"No," I whisper. Deanna whispers it in unison. "Stop," we say.

I turn to Jeremiah for help.

He walks towards us, but then his gaze turns blank and glowing green.

Thoughts of countries I've never visited flood my brain. Uneven cobblestone, a single backpack, campfires. A stroll through old, abandoned graveyards. Waterfalls, old churches, and the smell of incense.

I turn back to Esley. Her curls shield Deanna's sobbing face from view. But as Esley meets my gaze, instead of hatred or anger, I see confusion. And then she too is crying. Green mist seeps from my fingertips.

It's me. It's all me. All four of us are me. I pace around, trying to push their thoughts out of my head. All three of them stand up and follow.

I see it now. When I do this, that person becomes an extension of me. Frozen only because I haven't known what to do with it. How many people could I take on?

What will I do with them? How will I get them out?

I turn to Deanna, touching her hair lightly and thinking only of wonderful food and marionberry pie. She smiles, her eyes still glassy.

I turn to Esley, imagining her in a white doctor's jacket, a stethoscope hanging from her shoulders. Her hair is tied up in a bun and her hands are in her pockets.

The confidence radiates out from her, and she stands up straighter.

And Jeremiah. What to fill his head with?

All I can think of is Mom, her blond hair tied up in a handkerchief as we paint my room together. Her cheap video camera capturing my every turn around the living room in a thrifted tutu. Sitting next to her in church, hands dutifully in my lap and her steady focus as Father Rodriguez reads the homily.

The tenseness dissipates from his shoulders and legs.

I'm satisfied that I haven't left them any worse for wear.

But they are still under my control. And I have no idea how to stop this. I clench my eyes shut, concentrating on pushing out what isn't mine.

"No!" A deep and familiar voice shouts. I turn around and meet Blaise's brown-eyed gaze. He raises a hand to slap himself.

"Wait!" I shout, running for him.

"No. NO." He shakes his head. "I don't want to be sleeping. This isn't what I want, Green Eyes. I want to wake up." With one final slap to his face, he disappears.

All three of them, Deanna, Esley, and Jeremiah are staring at the spot where he disappeared. The green glow recedes into me.

Not one of them says a word. The dull ache pulling me to the right returns slowly now, instead of with full force.

Deanna's mouth hangs open. "Who was that man and where did he go?"

"You could see him?" I ask.

"No." Jeremiah shakes his head slowly. "But you can."

I never thought that this was an exchange, one where I was a part of them just as much as they were a part of me.

"Who is he?" Esley's voice is softer than I expected it to be.

I start to stammer out an explanation.

Pain shoots down my neck, radiating through my whole body. It's not pulling me to the right anymore. It's not pulling me in any direction.

I fall to the ground, Mom's screams reverberating in my ears.

I can only see dark; fingertips press against my eyes. My bones are on fire.

"Jade!" Deanna is the first to get to me, propping my head up on her knee.

I clench my eyes shut, holding the scream inside of me. "This." I struggle to form the words. "This. Pain. Isn't. Mine." And then everything goes black.

Chapter Twenty-nine

"Right!" a voice shouts. I'm vaguely aware of the world moving around me. Someone has their fingertips on my neck.

A sharp tug to my left breaks through the haze. "Left now!" My mouth moves. I hear my own voice and Esley's speak in tandem.

I blink heavily. My eyelids are weighed down by anvils.

"How is she doing back there?" Deanna's voice.

There's no response for several moments, then something snaps inside of me. Esley's presence slips out of my control.

"I think she might be aware now." Esley's voice responds to Deanna in the driver's seat. Flyaway wisps of my hair are soaked through. "Jade. If you can hear and process my voice, tell me how many fingers I'm holding up."

I force my eyes open. Three spindly fingers greet me with a small wave.

"Three," I groan.

"Great!" Esley smiles wide.

"Thank God," Deanna says.

"You've been in and out of consciousness for hours," Jeremiah says. "Whenever you came to, you were speaking absolute gibberish."

"I was only able to rule out actual medical problems because of what I was able to find in there." Esley lightly taps my head.

"What happened?" Silence. I make to sit up, but Esley pushes me back down. "Tell me. Please."

"You let me in," Esley says. "I touched your mark like earlier, and you let me in."

"But what happened with—"

"Something is going on with Vanessa." Only now do I notice that Jeremiah's hands are shaking. "Esley thinks we're almost there, but I don't know if she's—"

"Still alive?" I ask. He nods. "She is. I'd be dead if she wasn't."

"No," Jeremiah whispers softly, immediately understanding. His eyes are wide, and his mouth is a thin line, allowing only small amounts of air through. "Why would you do that?"

"I had to."

"That's dumber than jumping off a cliff. Why would you—"

"What did she do?" Deanna asks.

Oh, she is absolutely going to kill me after this is all over. "Having Mom's soul thing in me came with advantages. Knowing which direction to go to find her. But there was a tradeoff."

"If she dies, you die?" Deanna finishes with a resigned sigh. And then she explodes. "YOU ARE NOT ALLOWED TO DIE JADE ZAVERI. DO YOU UNDERSTAND ME?"

Jeremiah and Esley both lean back, but I merely prop myself up on my elbows, meet her eyes in the rearview mirror and nod. "Yes ma'am."

"I need it in writing. And also, I need you to make a will. And put in there that if you do die, all of your money is going to pay for my therapy." I almost laugh, but I know she's partly serious. "Any more sudden turns ahead?"

Inside my head is nothing but a tugging sensation pulling me forwards. Forwards, and forwards, and forwards, down Highway 277. "No."

We pass an exit that reads Christoval. My blood runs cold. That tug got much stronger, more insistent.

"We're more than close, aren't we?" I whisper to Esley. "Closer than close. We're almost there."

Esley exchanges a look with Deanna in the front seat. "I almost want to tell you to go slower," Esley hisses.

"We can't," Deanna responds. "Not when she's this close."

"They almost killed her this morning." My voice comes out in a hoarse whisper.

"You're not ready," Esley says. "Your arm, collapsing, barely able to use whatever it is you have, Jade—"

"Does it matter?" I shake my head lightly. "If they almost killed her this morning, does it really matter if I'm ready?"

Because why else would we be in a moving car, Esley yelling off instructions from halfway being possessed, if it didn't matter how I was doing? Even Deanna knows it. She's driving. Mom must be in worse trouble than ever before in order for her to do that.

"We should at least pull off for food for you."

The thought of food adds nausea to my ongoing list of symptoms. "I couldn't eat if I tried, Esley." I sit up all the way, buckling myself in. "What were they doing to her?" Jeremiah is stone faced. He doesn't respond.

"What did they do to Father Rodriguez?" Deanna asks.

"Fever, heart issues. Soul appearing in front of me when he sleeps."

"Yes, but what did they *do* to him? Did he remember?"

I remember the blank expression on his face when I asked about Mom, how confused he was. "No."

We spend the entire rest of the drive in our own worlds. Deanna taps out a nervous melody on the steering wheel. Esley twirls her dagger between her fingers and inspects my arm and head. Jeremiah is taking stock of the weapons in the trunk far more times than necessary.

Mom's gone silent. Her soul is still pulling me constantly forwards, but something inside of her isn't alive anymore. They've broken some part of her, and I can't hear it anymore. Something I didn't notice until it was gone.

My mind is crowded with nerves, too many thoughts, and not enough at the same time. Apparently, I can control people easier than I ever thought possible. The look in Deanna's eyes as she sobbed, horrible memories brought to the surface.

And Blaise. Those words. *"This isn't what I want."* Have I entirely misinterpreted that kiss? Did I imagine him leaning forwards too? Was it me, assuming he wanted to kiss me, taking over in a moment of weakness on his part? I'm not entirely sure why I'm thinking of kissing at a time like this, but everyone else in the car has their own distractions.

Flashes of the kiss play through my mind. Our bodies colliding with the trunk of that tree, how real and present he was, a trail of soft kisses on my neck.

Did I imagine all of that? Did he want that?

I'm brought to my senses by a sign. A sign that reads, "Now entering Eldorado, Texas," in faded text. Another sign tells me that the population is a mere 1,897 souls, only a few less than Marbhaven.

"Turn left, Deanna." My voice cracks.

She does, turning past a building with a caved in roof.

Off in the distance is a strange yellow building. Taller than any other building in the area by at least four stories, not quite in the shape of a pyramid, but almost one.

"That's it?" Jeremiah whispers. I nod wordlessly.

We reach a worn-out metal gate, only about waist high. Deanna stops the car and takes the keys out, handing them wordlessly to Jeremiah. An unspoken agreement passes between us, to go the rest of the way on foot.

Jeremiah passes out staffs to me and Deanna, taking his sword and sheathing it. Esley checks the position of her daggers.

We approach the gate, a worn-out seal in blue, red, and yellow rests in the center. Faded words read, "They shall not pass." A rather large spider crawls around the center of the seal, blocking the lock. We weren't about to try breaking the lock anyway.

I take a deep breath, allowing the air to pass all the way to the bottom of my lungs and back out. Then I take a step forwards, hoisting one leg over the gate.

We enter.

Chapter Thirty

The sun sets behind the strange golden pyramid as we walk along the potholed road. I'm half expecting a Red Reaper to jump out from behind every tree.

The road continues in circles, up and up the hill. It's clear that the tugging is pulling towards this building. It stays a constant course to the center.

It hits me how blind we are going into this. I don't know if there will be Red Reapers, or if there will be no one except whoever is torturing Mom. I don't know where they will be, where in this building Mom will be. I know nothing, except that she is in that building and that I have to get her out.

We come up on the final circle. Jeremiah and I drop to the ground at the sight of a person standing near the building. Esley and Deanna follow, peering out at the man from behind the bushes. My first thought is that he's standing guard, but the smell reaches my nose as he lifts a lit cigarette to his lips.

"Smells like your car," Deanna whispers to me. I grin at her, grateful for someone to break the minutes' long silence.

Jeremiah shoots a sharp glance in my direction. Leave it to him to ruin the fun of infiltrating a building full of murderers. "I'm going to try to make him close his eyes so we can get past," I whisper.

"We don't know what's beyond those doors." Jeremiah shakes his head. "We should find another way in."

"Do you see another way in?" Esley hisses. "This building has no windows."

"It looks like an airplane hangar." Deanna cocks her head at the road beyond the bushes. She's right. The white markings on the ground are unmistakable, no matter how faded. "We'll want to go into the building behind it," she continues.

"The what?" I ask.

She points and I shuffle silently to the left, peering over her shoulder. I can just make out the outline of another building, this one red and made of brick.

I nod, staring at the man enjoying his cigarette. I'll get into his head. I have to. I try to imagine the sound of his voice.

It's not working in the slightest. I'm reminded of that stupid game my ex, Ava, wanted me to play in college. The game where you try to imagine other people's lives at a coffee shop. With zero accuracy. Just guesses, and stereotypes. How would we know?

Deanna nods encouragingly at me. Addition.

I close my eyes and reach out for voices in the area. Deanna's voice is easy and close by. She's part of my thoughts before I can stop it. A green glow takes over her eyes. I shake my head and force her back out. She blinks heavily.

I set my thoughts out again, male voice. Not Jeremiah, though. I'm searching for something else. Thoughts that I imagine to be calm.

Ah, there he is. His thoughts are quiet. I don't know if that's because of my presence in his head or on account of the cigarette.

Close your eyes. I think.

He does. The cigarette smoke around him seems to turn a faint green.

I urge the others onward. They sprint through the bushes. I continue my walk towards the man by road, intentionally keeping my footing and thoughts calm.

He's craving comfort, warmth, a bed.

I'm tired too. I respond. *Don't you just want to sleep?*

He nods lightly.

No one would blame you.

He sits down, his back against the wall of the hanger. His head falls back against the yellow wall and he's snoring.

I keep my gaze on him as I pace up the road to join the others. The only thoughts I'm getting from him are eye twitches behind the lids, but I keep him under my control, anyway. Just in case.

Jeremiah and Esley have their eyes fixed on the building ahead. Deanna watches me walk leisurely towards them. I'm sure if any stress comes to the surface, this man will wake up, best to walk slowly. I don't meet her eyes, afraid she'll become a part of me again by accident.

The red brick building is wide and has several windows reaching up four stories high. It reminds me of a dorm building. No one is outside of this building either. Did they really entrust their entire security to one man smoking a cigarette?

"Which window are we picking?" I whisper.

Esley and Jeremiah point to an open window on the first floor, two windows to the right of the front door. The lights are off, but it's still light enough outside to see that no one is in there.

Another glance around confirms that no one is out and about, and we run for it.

They each leap through the window seamlessly.

My concentration on keeping that man calm stops me from making it as far through the window as the rest of them. I land haphazardly on a desk. The napping man's thoughts leave me on impact.

"Ow," I groan.

"Shhh." Deanna turns around, finger to her lips.

My feet pad softly across the roughly carpeted floor. The door is cracked open slightly, revealing a limited view of the hallway when I approach it. A middle-aged woman with hooded eyes and blond hair is lounging at a desk.

Behind her, a long metal scythe leans against the wall.

How are we meant to get out? Everyone is watching me. Right. I'm supposed to do this.

I reach out for that woman's soul. Something moves past my feet. I freeze. It slithers around my ankle and moves through the door.

Footsteps come down the hallway. Probably the owner of this dormitory. "Oh Jesus. Olivia, it's one of these again," a deep male voice groans.

The snake on the other side of the door rattles. Deanna's eyes widen. Great, we'll have to watch out for rattlesnakes along with Red Reapers.

The woman at the desk, Olivia, stands up. I hear her scythe scrape lightly against the wall as she picks it up. "You know you don't have to worry about these hurting you anymore, right?"

"No," the man corrects. My heart pounds at how close his voice is to us. I'm certain he can hear me breathing. "I don't have to worry about them killing me anymore. Their bites are still gonna hurt like hell." Olivia laughs. The snake rattles again. "Stop poking it!" The man's voice gets farther away.

"Don't be such a wimp!" she says. I've decided that I don't much like Olivia.

Another rattle, angrier this time. Another laugh from Olivia. The man screams. Someone clatters over a chair. Olivia cries out in pain.

"Oh God, it bit you. Oh no. What do we do?" Olivia, for her part, curses quite fluently. I hear the scythe lash out at the snake. It rattles again. I watch the snake jump again through a gap in the door hinges. Olivia screeches.

"Give me that." The man lashes out with the scythe. The snake falls silent. "Are you okay, should we—Those are huge!"

Olivia's voice is short and snappy. "Take me to my room already."

"We should get her too."

"Don't bother," she snaps.

She whimpers in pain as the man picks her up and carries her down the hallway. I peer out of the door cautiously. His back is to us as they go down the hall and around a corner.

"What on Earth?" Esley whispers.

"Why don't they care about getting bit by a rattlesnake?" Jeremiah hisses, eyes fixed on the beheaded rattlesnake. Poor thing.

I share a look with Deanna. Flashes of the Red Reaper careening over a cliff play through my mind. "Because they can't die," I mutter back.

Before they can speak again, I sprint down the hallway on my toes. The relentless tug in my head pulls me upwards. The stairwell is halfway along the hallway. I can still hear Olivia and the man's uneven footsteps.

I hold out an arm to stop Deanna before she barrels too far forwards.

Olivia is still cursing. A good sign for her, at least. They clear the stairs. A door opens and closes. I nod wordlessly at Jeremiah. He ascends the stairs first, closely followed by Esley and then Deanna. I check behind us for any open doors before heading up too. Thankfully, there are none.

The stairs only go up one floor. I'm still being pulled upwards. She's not on this floor. Where are the other stairs? This floor is filled with dorms too. Laughter echoes down the hall from an open door to our right.

God, it makes me miss college. Those nights that didn't feel quite real as we laughed to death at 4 a.m., driven crazy by homework and sleep deprivation. These people took it from me. I almost want to storm down the hall and shut them up.

I shake the thought from my mind and continue straight after the others, down a third hallway.

A door opens behind us. Jeremiah, Esley, and Deanna all dive around a corner at the end of the hallway. I plunge into a room to my right, praying no one is in here. I catch Deanna's gaze. "Go!" I mouth at her, pointing up.

Footsteps continue down the hall towards them. They bolt towards a staircase behind them. The man from before passes me as I peer through the cracked door. Thankfully, he only knocks on a door in front of where they were. I exhale in relief as he stammers out an explanation about the rattlesnake.

I turn away from the door and towards a wall of laundry machines. Someone's in here, a young girl, still turned away from me. She can't be any older than fourteen. I stare at her in alarm as she continues to load clothes into the machine.

The man is still talking in the hallway. I'm frozen in indecision.

The girl turns around. She's not at all alarmed to see me. Her eyes are almost as green as mine.

Except, it's not her eyes that are green. It's a glow around them. I furrow my eyebrows at her. She follows suit.

I didn't do this on purpose.

"I know," she whispers in a sweet voice.

How do I get to the top floor?

"You wait," she says. "They will pass."

I step forwards hesitantly, and finish putting her laundry into the machine. She is standing stock still, peering out of the door for me.

Two sets of hurried steps go back down the hallway. She turns back to me, eyes glowing still.

Images of the hallway ahead of us flash through my mind, but we both stay rooted to the spot.

Up one flight of stairs. Now on the fourth floor. The fourth floor? Other bits and pieces of the building flash through my mind, but I can't make heads or tails of it.

I'm seeing what she's seen.

You'll forget about this. I command.

She turns back to her laundry. I relinquish control of her as I duck back out of the room. God, I hope that works.

The hallways are thankfully empty as I sprint on light toes to the right. The opposite direction from Deanna and the others. I hope they're okay. I wonder which floor that flight of stairs takes them to.

At the top of the stairs, the tugging pulls me down a hallway. It opens up into a large area filled with punching bags hanging from the ceiling. Gym flooring covers the ground. A man with ear buds faces away from me, punching one of the bags with all his might.

My heart beats in my throat. I follow the tugging along the wall behind him, praying that he doesn't turn around. The tug is so insistent that it's impossible not to follow. I couldn't stop my feet if I tried, even if he did turn around. I'm so close to her. I can feel it.

Around the corner, three doors down. The tugging pulls to the left. Towards one specific door. My hand hovers over it. I should prepare myself for anything else that might be in there other than her.

I open the door.

The room is dark. There are no windows. I shut the door behind me and scan the room.

Her blond curls are tangled together in one lump next to her head. Her face has none of the youthful glow I've grown to recognize and love in the presence of Raina and Anisha. She's gaunt, tired, and so fragile.

"Mom?" I whisper, making my way to her side.

Her eyes flutter open, blinking and peering through what little light there is in the room. She tries to move her hand but fails. Shackles hold her hands down. "Jade?"

Chapter Thirty-one

I drop to my knees by her side. Her cheekbones are even more apparent now than they were the last time I saw her. And up close, she doesn't smell like her usual self either. No hint of floral shampoo, only sweat and fear. "Oh, what have they done to you?"

She is silent on that matter. Instead, her voice comes out in a hoarse whisper as she speaks her own question. "How did you find me?"

"It's a long, *long* story, Mom." My throat is tight. I can hardly believe she's here. That she's alive. I grasp her hand in mine. "But I can tell you another time. Right now, we have to get you out of here. Can you stand?"

She laughs shortly. "No." Her face is full of bitterness, hatred even. "I haven't stood in weeks."

I clench her hand even tighter, my other hand balling up into a fist. My veins are filled with venom, my heart with fire. And then the worst realization of all.

"I can't carry you." My voice shakes. "My arm. I-I'm not strong enough."

"Your arm? What about your arm?"

"It's not important, Mom." I shake my head. I could certainly try to carry her, but not with any semblance of speed. We'd only die together.

"How did you find me?" she whispers.

"The Grim Reaper gave me the window to your soul so I could

find you."

Her head falls back against the table. "You know," she whispers.

"Know what?"

"About them. About Desdemon, about—"

"How do you know Desdemon? They were worried about you, but they wouldn't tell me why."

Mom sighs heavily. She opens her mouth to respond. Footsteps are coming down the hallway towards us. I jerk up, alarmed. "We have to—"

"Jade. Listen to me closely. At the back of this room, there is a closet. Get inside, say nothing. Do you understand?"

I nod wordlessly, my feet automatically obeying. The closet is filled with red hooded cloaks. My skin crawls at their touch. I close the door at the same time as the other door opens.

"Hello, Vanessa," an even and pleasant female voice says. Mom doesn't say a word. "I'm sorry we were so rudely interrupted. Are you ready to talk?"

"I would rather die," Mom spits.

The woman laughs. "We're all fighting to *live*. I'm trying to give that to you."

"I don't want it."

"And yet you shall have it. It is my gift to you." I can hear Mom struggling against her bonds. "And maybe." The woman hesitates. "Maybe then you'll be more willing to give us what you stole. Since you'll have a rather personal interest in its success."

It's Mom's turn to laugh. "You'll never find it. I made sure of that." My eyes widen. Mom stole from them. How did she even know about them?

"Did you know there's a group of Reapers making their way here? To save you?" Mom doesn't respond. I hear the woman's heavy footsteps circling the room, coming disturbingly close to the closet. "They won't get far. But if you were to tell me where it is, I might be willing to show them mercy."

I peer through the door hinges. The room is too dark to see much. I see the outline of the woman hunched over Mom, hands braced on both sides of her. Mom's voice rings clearly through the room. "No. You won't."

"Believe what you will," the woman says. "But we will begin."

Realization of what is about to happen overtakes me. It will affect me too. I will be discovered. Mom will never leave this place. I grab a loose scrap of red fabric from one of the cloaks and tie it tightly around my mouth, praying that it will be enough. I don't know if I was screaming earlier. They didn't tell me. I lie down so that she won't hear the thud of my body hitting the floor.

The door of the room outside bursts open. "You have to come quick." A man's voice is rushed, and nervous.

"Again? Tell Olivia to wait. Can't you see that I am busy, Alex?"

"There's a car parked at the end of the drive. It's empty."

"They're here?" The woman's voice is filled with alarm. Her footsteps follow his, and the door shuts behind them. Mom sighs in relief. I stay hidden for one, two, three minutes. She's not coming back.

I step slowly out of the closet, untying the gag. "Mom, we have to get you out of here."

"Jade, just go."

"No. I'm not alone. I have to find the others. I'll be back for you. I promise, Mom." My voice breaks as I clasp her hand. "I'll be back for you. I promise. I'll be back for you."

"I know you will." She weakly squeezes my hand back. "Be careful."

There are people outside. I can hear the commotion, people opening and closing doors, running around, clamoring about. Their voices are on edge and maybe even excited. Am I imagining how hungry they are for my blood?

I turn back to the closet. There is no other option. I pull on a red cloak, securing the ties. The material grates against my skin. I might break out in hives at the mere touch of it.

I turn back for one last look at Mom. She nods encouragingly. I pull up the hood until it obscures my face.

My fingers are sweating against the doorknob, and I plunge into the hallway. I'm not the only one in a red hood. Three people march past me, all pulling their hoods up as they pass.

I follow them, trying to mimic their purposeful walk. My hands clenching and unclenching.

Someone is bound to notice that I'm not one of them. I follow the red sea down an entirely different set of stairs than before. This path is darker than the others. It's a back way, secretive. I wonder if these are the same stairs that Jeremiah, Deanna, and Esley went up. Where could they be?

What if they're already discovered?

I reach the bottom of the stairs, weaving through the hallways with the rest of them. The red sea is headed towards the entrance. I follow them down the spiraling road, all the way to Jeremiah's parked car.

I fall in line at the back of their formation. I'm hyperaware of all of their movements, watching for any strange ritual I will need to blend in.

"They're here." That woman's voice cuts through the crowd. I can't see her face, but I know that she is quite the presence. Everyone around me straightens. I follow suit, drawing myself up to my full height. "Find them!" the woman shouts.

The Red Reapers scatter, breaking off into groups. I make it look like I'm joining one group of four, but instead stay on the outskirts, hoping they don't notice me.

This group of four strides back into the building, whispering to each other. They aren't the only group going back in, thankfully. I'm able to hover between two groups, appearing to be a part of both and part of neither at the same time.

She said to find 'them.' That must mean the others haven't been discovered. I have to find them first.

I should have thought to bring extra cloaks. This group heads back up a staircase that lets them off in a different corner of the fourth floor. At least, I think this is the fourth floor. Unless the third floor is the same as the fourth floor with its central open gym.

That door ahead, it's Mom's door. If I go back in there, I'll be able to find more cloaks for when I do find them. I wait for the group to continue down the hallway and duck through the doorway.

The room is similarly dark, but it's not the same room. Because that is not Mom lying down on a bed, weak and fragile.

Dark black curls obscure his face. Only his hooked nose peaks out. He's breathing evenly, but he can't be asleep.

Because I know those curls, that nose, his bare chest, covered in deep scratch marks. I lower my hood. "Blaise?"

Chapter Thirty-two

He looks up at me sharply, clearly put off by the red cloak ensemble. His eyes dart up and down my body, full of shock and something softer. "Jade. I'm not asleep, am I?"

I shake my head.

Before I can say anything, his lips are on mine, warm and desperate. My arms snake up his chest, holding onto his shoulders in a vise grip. His hands are in my hair and he's pulling me closer to him with every second. I shudder as his hand follows my jaw line and pulls at my chin, keeping my mouth on his.

If I thought he felt real before, I was wrong. He's more present now. His skin has depth and imperfections. Chills form on his arms.

We collide with the side of his bed. He breaks away as suddenly as he started. I search his eyes. My brain is foggy and at peace for a moment.

"What are you doing here?" he asks, coming to his senses and grabbing a red shirt from its resting place on the bedpost.

"What are you doing here?" I shoot back. I catch glimpses of the scratch marks on his chest, and around the eyes. My mouth hangs open in horror. "They're holding you here too. Oh, Blaise. I'm so sorry. Why didn't you tell me?"

He hurriedly pulls the shirt over his head. "Green Eyes, I—"

"What have they done to you?" I trail a finger along a deep scratch mark that runs from his eye all the way down to his chin.

"Was it Montrose? Did they find you there? I shouldn't have left, I—"

"Never mind that." He shakes his head, grabbing my hand and holding it near his lips. "You can't be here. You can't—" He plants a soft kiss on my palm.

His eyes are wide and innocent. "Of course. You're right." I turn to leave. "Come with me."

His hand slides from my grasp. "I can't. I can't."

"Because they'll know?" He doesn't move a muscle, but his eyes are all the confirmation I need. "Blaise, I have to get my mom, but I will come back for you. I promise. We'll leave here together. You'll be safe." I press myself against him and kiss him, hard. "I'll be back." He opens his mouth to speak. "I promise."

I pull the hood up and duck back out of the room. Too many things to do. How am I ever going to find the rest of them, and get Mom, and go back for Blaise? How is that possible when everyone is looking for us?

My mind is racing with every solution I can think of, from conservative to outlandish. I race up a flight of stairs and into the room that holds Mom. She's already out cold, her head lolling to the side. I brush the sweat from her brow hurriedly and grab four more cloaks to stuff under my own.

How will I find them? Where would they go? I don't even know this building, none of us do. It would be impossible to do a systematic sweep without someone getting suspicious.

In the end it's Mom's voice in my head, coaching me on what to do before we went into my first mall ever. *Go to the place where we last saw each other, Jade, and we'll find each other.*

I know exactly where to go. Down a flight of stairs, around a corner, where I can still hear curses from that Olivia woman inside her room. I duck into the laundry room.

There's a sword at my throat. I throw my hands up, too nervous to move and take down the hood. I've seen how fast Jeremiah can move. "Put down your scythe," he says.

"Don't have one Jeremiah," I whisper. The blade drops to his side almost immediately. I close the door behind me and pull the hood down.

"Did you find her?" Jeremiah asks.

"Are you okay?" Deanna rushes forwards.

"I'm fine. Yes, I found her. She's on the fourth floor."

"Why isn't she with you?" Esley hisses, coming out from the shadow of a washing machine.

"Because she can't stand." My voice breaks slightly. I clear my throat. "And I can't carry her."

"I can." Jeremiah nods. "What's going on out there? Tell me what I need to know, and I'll go get her."

"No." I shake my head fervently, holding out the stack of cloaks to him. "They travel in groups, we'll have to too." Jeremiah grabs one and pulls it on, passing the stack to Esley. "They know that we're here. I don't know if they know how many of us there are. They're all looking for us. We have to get Mom and find a way out as quickly as possible. Jeremiah, do you know if there is anything buried in the area?"

He shakes his head. "We'd have to make a run that way." He points to his right. "In order to get to the city's graveyard. Nothing is buried around here."

"Okay. The car is out of the question so—"

"Who's the fourth cloak for?" Deanna whispers, tying her own cloak on.

I don't even know how to start explaining this to her, never mind with any sense of speed. Her eyes are questioning as I meet them. "That man," I say desperately. "From earlier today. He's here."

"But who is he Jade?" Esley approaches me, her eyebrows furrowed.

"He's . . ." I don't know how to tell them. How he was dead, but he can't die. How he isn't like the other Red Eyes, but I don't know why. And I don't know why I can see him or why he can see me, much less touch, much less kiss me.

"He's important to you?" Deanna's voice cuts through my thoughts.

"Yes." The words exit my mouth without me having to think about them.

"Then he's important to me, we'll get him too."

"Thank you." I turn to Esley and Jeremiah. "Ready?" They nod. We pull up our hoods. "Let's go."

Chapter Thirty-three

THE JOURNEY UP TO Mom is thankfully uneventful. No one looks twice at a group of four Red Reapers. We have to loop around the fourth floor twice before going in to avoid another group patrolling the hallway.

Mom stirs only slightly at the sound of the door opening. "Mom," I whisper, pulling down the hood. I shake her lightly. "Mom." Her eyes flutter open halfway, and then they open wide. "What?" She sputters something about red. "Mom. Mom, it's me. It's Jade. This is a disguise, it's okay."

She exhales heavily, trying to lift her hands. The cuffs don't allow her to. "Jade. Thank God, I thought you were . . ." Her eyes dart around the room. "Who else is here?"

Deanna rushes up beside me, pulling her own hood down. "Hi, Vanessa." A weak smile passes over Deanna's face.

"Deanna!" Mom is more shocked by her presence than she was by mine.

Esley waves awkwardly, her auburn curls frizzier than before she wore the hood. "This is our friend Esley. We met her along the way," I whisper.

Mom nods politely at her. She turns her gaze to Jeremiah. He hasn't pulled his hood down yet and is hanging out towards the back. Deanna stiffens beside me and narrows her eyes. He takes a few hesitant steps forwards, pulling down the hood. Mom tilts her head to the side. "Jerry?"

"God, you know I hate it when you call me that Nessa." He laughs shortly.

Thousands of words seem to pass unspoken between them. Deanna clears her throat. "Esley, do you know how to pick locks?"

Esley shoots Deanna a glance. "How did you know?"

"You seem to have all the skills we need when we need them. I just kind of figured." Deanna shrugs. "What do you need to do it?"

"Something straight and metal." Esley pats the wall for a light switch. A dim lamp goes on in the far corner.

"Bobby pins?" Deanna pulls two pins from her hair.

"Of course, you have bobby pins," I snort, dropping to Mom's side.

"Do you have more?" Jeremiah asks. "I can take the other side." Deanna shakes her head.

Esley begins on the opposite side, fiddling around with the bobby pins. She methodically bends one to a right angle and is having trouble with the other. She curses out the offending bobby pin in hushed tones.

"What's the problem?" Deanna drops down next to her.

"The stupid plastic won't come off," Esley says.

"Oh." Deanna takes the bobby pin from her, shimmies it back and forth between her fingers, and hands it back to Esley.

"Thanks."

Several minutes later, there is a final audible click from Esley's side. The shackle opens and Mom lifts her hand, wringing it out in blissful relief. Esley comes to my side and resumes her work.

Mom's hand finds its way to my cheek. I have trouble meeting her soft blue eyes. "The girls?" she asks.

"Fine." I nod encouragingly. "They're with a friend." She smiles knowingly. The lock beneath me clicks. Esley rotates the lock a quarter turn. I turn to Jeremiah. "There's a closet at the back of the room. Could you grab one of these?" I gesture to my own red hood. "For Mom."

He pauses. "I'm going to have to carry her, anyway. I don't know what the point would be. They'd know something was off."

Esley's tongue is sticking out of her mouth as she fiddles with the bobby pins. She has her eyes closed, as though she's listening to the metal itself. Another click, another turn. "One more," she whispers.

We hear footsteps patrolling down the hall, purposefully. Deanna's eyes widen and she pulls up her hood. Jeremiah follows suit. I sprint for the light switch and turn it off.

"Esley, stop. We need to hide," Deanna hisses at her.

My heart pounds as Esley continues to pick the lock. What if they saw the light go off? The footsteps near the door, three sets of them. Jeremiah slowly unsheathes his sword. They stop. Another door opens across the hall.

An unfamiliar voice shouts out, "Anything?"

"No one here," another voice responds. I narrow my gaze at the door. The footsteps proceed back the way they came.

Another click. Esley exhales. Jeremiah wastes no time sheathing his sword and scooping Mom into his arms.

I resume my position of point and open the door a crack, peering out at the hallway. One of the Red Reapers turns towards me.

"Anything in there?" he calls out.

I shake my head slowly, hyperaware of the fabric moving around my face. He shrugs and continues around the corner. My eyes close and my shoulders fall.

We practically sprint for the next set of stairs. The ones that I'm fairly certain lead to the third floor. Blaise.

I turn to face Deanna in the echoing stairwell. She meets my eyes and again, it's easy to find my way in.

You three need to take Mom and go. I'll catch up once I have Blaise.
She shakes her head fervently.

I turn to Jeremiah for support and repeat my thoughts to him.

He also shakes his head. Fine. I relinquish my hold on them and continue down the stairs.

The stairwell opens up into a hallway that is an exact mirror of the one above it. I see a red cloak disappearing around a corner and make a silent run for Blaise's door. The five of us shuffle in. I pull down my hood.

Blaise is sitting on the edge of his bed, head in his hands. "Blaise," I whisper.

"Oh God, you came back," he whispers in horror. "Listen to me, they're patrolling the hallways for you. You need to leave."

"I'm not leaving without you. Look what they've done to you!" I gesture to the scratch marks still visible on his arms. His eyes are especially gaunt.

His gaze fixes on Mom in Jeremiah's arms. First, he's quizzical, then his eyes widen in dawning horror. "You need to get her out of here. She's trying to do the ritual on your mom."

"The what?"

"It doesn't matter. I'll explain later. You need to—"

"Shit," Esley says. I turn to her, a questioning glance. "Olivia, the woman with the rattlesnake bites?" I nod. Esley stares at a point in front of herself. "She just died."

"Send her on and do it quick. I don't want us followed," I mutter, knowing that we don't need to take time for her. That whatever afterlife she picks will only put her back, alive, in her bed.

Esley puts her fingers to her mark. Barely two seconds pass before she says, "Done."

Blaise's mouth hangs open, a half-formed sentence on his lips. "What?"

"She saw you. Where you are," he says.

I curse. "Come on. We have to move." I grab his hand and pull. He doesn't move. I turn back to him. He shuffles forwards a couple of steps. "Oh, you're right. Put this on quick." I shove the remaining red cloak at him.

"Jade," he whispers.

"What?" Doesn't he know that time is of the essence here?

"You need to go."

"We are. Hurry up."

I meet his eyes pleadingly. God, he's so scared. His eyes dart around the room and then he throws on the cloak, following us out.

We're halfway down the hallway when I hear hurried footsteps coming towards us. We turn back to go the other way, but there are people there too. We're trapped. They see Jeremiah carrying Mom. There is nowhere to go.

I try to reach out for their souls, but there are too many of them.

Deanna and Esley have their hands on their weapons, watching me for our next move. I don't know what to do. Blaise stiffens beside me at the sight of the crowd in front of us. There is no getting out of this.

Chapter Thirty-four

A woman, tall, with strong and graceful steps marches towards me. She's wearing combat boots and a long-sleeved red top. Her wavy brown hair is up in a high ponytail that swings as she walks. "Jillian Williams, right?" She yanks back my hood.

My blood runs cold. I turn to Blaise. He pulls down his hood too, his eyes painted in guilt. At a mere beckoning of this woman's fingers, he moves beside her. "Blaise?" He doesn't speak. His gaze is fixed on the floor. "You were with *them*?"

"Honey," the woman simpers. "Of course, he was." I stand before them, open-mouthed and useless. She lays a hand on Blaise's shoulder.

"Why would you—"

Blaise's face changes, no longer filled with guilt. The lines on his forehead run deep, his hands clench into fists. "Because you're a murderer." His voice is quiet and full of venom. "Did you think I'd forget? Did you think I'd forgive you? Katia's my friend and you killed her. You led her right off a cliff." I open my mouth to speak. He glares at me. "I couldn't care less about you."

The woman pats his shoulder and crosses her arms. "Blaise's charms really are known for this, Jillian. I wouldn't feel too bad. Although he didn't have to use them on that other Reaper. Aaron?"

Deanna screams, rushing towards him. I'm too stunned to stop her. Her staff is out, and she gets a few good whacks in before another Red Reaper wrestles the staff from her grip and holds her captive. Tears pour from her eyes as she stares down Blaise in utter hatred.

"That wasn't you." I shake my head. "Tell me that wasn't you, Blaise."

"I—Green Eyes—"

"DON'T CALL ME THAT!" He can't even meet my eyes. For all his talk of murder. "Tell me it wasn't you."

He meets my eyes for the briefest of seconds, defensive and caged. "I didn't deal the blow." His voice is directed at the ground now. "But yes, it was me."

Those images of Aaron on the beach, spluttering for air, choking on his own blood. His dying fingers brushing against me. My Reaper mark burns.

I scream, a loud guttural scream. It's echoed by thirty or so of the surrounding Red Reapers. Green snakes across the floor, infecting more of them. My head is filled with screams.

Deanna is free, by my side again. She's trying to unsheathe Jeremiah's sword for herself, glaring at Blaise murderously.

Jeremiah shoves Mom against my side, pointing towards a stairwell. I hardly register his words. He pushes Deanna and Esley behind him and holds the sword in his right hand with his left outstretched as the Red Reapers scramble to fight back.

Mom leans heavily against me. All I can think of is Aaron, lying there on the sand, unable to do anything for him but watch him die.

I shake my head, looping Mom's arm over my shoulder.

She weighs on me. The whole day weighs on me. It threatens to bring me to the ground, but I force myself to stand straight.

No matter how bad the shooting pain in my arm is, no matter how bad the sting of betrayal, how sour those kisses have become, I continue.

My hold snaps on the Red Reapers above when we reach the

bottom of the stairs.

There are only so many corners, so many hiding places before they run out and I have to face them. Mom mumbles something that sounds an awful lot like, "Left." Her head lolls to one side.

Should I trust her? She's practically half dead. The footsteps are rounding the corner, too close. I plow into the room on the left, slamming the door behind us. It only has a lock from the outside.

Gently, I lay Mom on her side and barricade the door with anything I can find and lift. It isn't much when I'm done with it, but maybe it will buy us some time. I shimmy out of this red abomination, knowing it won't matter now if they recognize me or not. I turn, surveying the rest of the room for a way out of this mess.

A wall covered entirely with weapons waits for me. It's covered from floor to ceiling with scythes. I weigh my options. I'm no good with these weapons, but I'm also no good without them. Maybe I can buy Mom some time to gather some strength and walk out of here, even if it's only because they are laughing at me.

Fists pound on the door. It won't be long before they get in. Breathe in. Breathe out. I shut my eyes and say a silent prayer, for help and for forgiveness.

I've already decided on a scythe. If I'm going to die, I want to die as death itself. I reach out for one, already worried about how long and cumbersome it will be.

Then, almost as if someone left it out for me, my eyes fix on a smaller curved scythe resting on a table. I think it's called a sickle. The handle is wrapped in leather and the blade is curved, sharp, and most importantly, portable.

The pounding suddenly gets quieter. I'm not comforted. I know they've figured out how to open the door. My right hand closes tightly around the sickle until my knuckles turn white. I move myself in between Mom and the door.

A hesitant creak, then four people flow in, scythes in hand.

Every last one is clad in the red hoods that have been plaguing my nightmares.

My eyes dart around the room, following their movements. They gather in a semicircle around me.

I shuffle, trying to keep all of them in view. Sweat rolls down my neck and my fingers shake. I ball my free hand into a fist and grip the sickle tighter, all too aware that I have no idea how to use it.

A woman's calm and stern voice rings out from the left. "That isn't for you." Her hood dips towards the sickle. Disdain drips from her very being.

"You're defiling it." A young man, maybe even a teenager, is practically leaning away from me. That same man from earlier, outside the door with Olivia.

"You. A child of Death." This voice belongs to a girl, decidedly not an adult. I cringe away from how young she sounds. Despite how menacing she might appear, I couldn't bear to hurt her. I know her voice from the laundry room. I think I'm going to have to hurt her, anyway.

I spare a glance for the fourth figure. Stocky and tall. He doesn't speak, merely twirls his scythe. I watch it rotate, one, two, three, four times, then come to a rest in both hands.

Four of them. One of me. I draw a deep breath in and readjust my grip on the sickle. I'll have to make the first move.

The young girl is speaking again, poison in her words. "You are not fit to wield a weapon of—"

I shove the hilt of the sickle into her jaw, cutting her off mid-sentence. She falls backwards, out cold.

A scythe comes straight for my head. I slide onto my front knee, slicing the back of the young man's calf as I turn into him.

He cries out in pain and stumbles as I scramble to my feet. I can hear the other two charging forwards. I slice diagonally across the man's back and he too falls to the ground, groaning in pain.

A faint metallic scent permeates the air. Before I can think too hard about the blood, or what I can see beneath it, I hear a scythe cutting through the air.

I slice across with the sickle, hoping against hope that I'll hit something before I see it. It hooks around the staff, and I push the blade away from me.

The silent man in front of me pauses a moment in shock.

Behind him, out of the corner of my eye, I can see the stern woman advancing.

I block the next swing from the man and duck under his scythe, slashing across his side. He stumbles, a free hand covering the cut.

I stop the first move from the stern woman, but I'm not as lucky on the next. The butt of her scythe rams into my stomach.

I double over, gasping for air. I'm choking, the world is spinning.

And a blade is coming for my throat.

I curse and lean back. A sharp pain stings through my upper left arm.

For a moment I think my old cut has re-opened. No. It's an entirely new cut in the same spot.

I press a hand over it in an attempt to staunch the bleeding, feeling the memory of the blade pass through my arm over and over again. I grit my teeth, trying to regain control.

I glance back at Mom, limp where I left her. I have to stay calm. I have to get her out of this.

The silent man is back up and the stern woman is advancing.

I'm lost in a flurry of scythe blades, dodging, ducking, slashing, blocking. My right arm lashes out wildly with the sickle as I try to figure out which scythe is coming for me next.

The air is ripped from my lungs by some force that knocks into my stomach. I don't know where from. A blade slices across the air in front of me. I dodge it just in time for it to only nick a few hairs from my scalp.

I'm trying to get closer, render their blades useless, but the swirling sticks and even more terrifying metal make it impossible. I can't find an opening. They're pushing me farther and farther back.

Mom groans somewhere behind me, her heartbeat growing louder and louder in my ears. So loud, I can't hear anything else. My legs shake, threatening to give way beneath me.

The pain of the young man on the floor somewhere is palpable too. I blink heavily, trying to regain my bearings.

Both scythes come towards me at the same time. My eyes clench shut of their own accord, bracing myself for the end.

My head is pounding, pulsing, and then, it splits open.

The blow never comes.

I peer through my lashes. The room is enveloped in a bright green glow. Both Red Reapers are frozen in front of me, scythes inches away from my throat.

A low whistle escapes my lips as I exhale. "Drop them," they whisper as I think it. The scythes clatter to the floor.

The young girl is stirring slightly. The young man doesn't appear to be conscious anymore and is in a pool of his own blood.

The silent man's wound is oozing blood onto the floor. And the stern woman's hood has fallen back, revealing greying hair and an impassive expression that I'm sure wasn't there before I took control.

I hook the sickle around my belt loop and throw my hands out, extending my control to the other two on the floor. Pain floods through me, some from my own injury, some from theirs.

I send them all onto the ground next to each other, frozen, and double back for Mom. I sling her arm around my shoulder. I don't know how much longer I'll be able to hold them. We don't have much time.

Mom's legs are heavy as lead. I lean even more of her weight on my good shoulder as my own blood drips onto the floor.

My control over them is wavering. Throbbing pain pulses in my upper arm in time with my heartbeat. I don't dare check it to figure out how much blood has been lost.

We only manage to turn one corner before I know this is the end of the line. At least forty Red Reapers are facing us down.

And I'm so tired. My head pounds. I can barely see. I'm half expecting the green glow to explode out of me, but I know that even if it does, I'll be even more exhausted afterwards.

There's no telling what has happened to Deanna or Esley. Maybe Jeremiah broke out his killing people with a touch power, maybe not. That's the only thing that could have kept them safe.

They have us cornered.

I am so, *so* stupid for thinking I could do this. Me, a mere nineteen-year-old girl with everything to lose.

Their scythes are at my throat, and it takes all of my strength to push Mom out of harm's way as I crumple to the floor. Not that it will matter.

"Do not kill her!" A voice rings out through the haze. It's that woman with the brown curly ponytail again, striding towards me like she owns the world. Some strange traitorous part of me is grateful for her. She nods at her red creatures, and they move without question.

"Come, Jillian." She pulls me to my feet and presses a hand over my cut. Warmth spreads through my skin, into my veins. Relief clouds my brain and I feel my hold on the Red Reapers a few doors back break.

My eyes drift to my arm. There's no more blood. No scar either. "We have a lot to talk about." She smiles.

Chapter Thirty-five

The woman leads me through the hallways, which are suddenly devoid of Red Reapers. "What are you going to do to her?" I manage to say.

"It was never our intention to kill her. Do not worry." She pats my arm lightly.

I'm mollified. My mind goes blank. The woman's hand briefly leaves my arm to open a door. Panic floods back through me. "My friends. Please—"

"The black-haired girl will be unharmed." Her hand is back on my arm. My shoulders slump forwards, and I relax. There is nothing to worry about. Nothing at all. We go down a flight of stairs. "Jillian, you're still in the dark about who we will and will not kill. Do you think we're ruthless creatures?"

I should answer honestly. It's what she wants. "Yes."

She smiles a strange wolfish smile at me. "You have much to learn about us." We're outside now, under the cover of night. The moon is barely a sliver in the sky, a scythe all its own.

We stride across the pavement, back to that yellow pyramid building. It's such a strange building.

"I always thought this building was strange too. But I've been living here since I was about your age. It's not as strange to me now." I don't say a word. "It didn't always belong to us. It used to belong to the government, actually. Quite a price tag came with it, I'm told."

She pushes a door open, keeping her hand on my arm this time. The ceiling isn't nearly as high as I was expecting. When we first enter, we're in a corridor that wraps around in both directions. She leads me off to the right.

Memories of Sundays and church, watching Father Rodriguez talk, flit up to the surface of my mind. And that smell again, old wood and incense. It sets my mind at ease.

The woman laughs shortly. "An odd thing to calm you."

We stop in front of a large painting. A black hooded figure carrying a scythe looms over the scene. People covered in boils are collapsed all over a dirt road. Their dead figures are all pointing towards a large hole in the ground, a mass grave. The work is simply titled *The Tragedy of Death* at the bottom.

"I'm sure you're familiar with the Black Death?" she asks, watching me closely. I nod. "Of course, Death was around for far longer than that, but this." She sighs heavily. "The toll on human life, the power that Death excised, just because Death could—" Her voice is filled with barely contained rage. I feel it too. I'm boiling. The unfairness that I felt when Nani Anisha died bubbles to the surface. She died young, and I barely got to know her. Death stole her from me.

She tugs me over to another, even larger painting. My rage dissipates.

This one is wider, stretching twice the length of the other. It depicts a lonesome figure draped in red walking through a graveyard. The figure rests a hand on the grave of a child. "That was our first member. A child of Life itself. Cursed to walk the Earth that Death ruled. We wear red for her. But she had a power," she says, leading me to the next painting.

A child now walks next to the figure, holding their hand. "A power to bring people back from Death." The child runs to its family in the next painting. They hold him close next to a warm hearth, crying tears of joy. "This power founded our group all those years ago. We are called Genesis, after the first with this power."

I notice that the painting itself is titled *Genesis*.

"That power was lost for hundreds of years after Genesis died. We struggled to keep each other alive. Many were claimed by Death without that power. Until me." Her chin tilts up with pride.

I glance at her, questioningly. "I too am a child of Life itself. I hold this power, the power to save others from Death. Of course, my power is futile if Death still sends their little Reapers out to do their bidding. I can't save everyone, not if your people continue acting as a living conduit."

"That's why you've been killing Reapers."

"Yes. A necessary evil. If you can't transport souls, they can't die permanently. Reapers are the only people we kill." Her grip on my arm tightens. "Tell me, how did you get your orders from Death?"

"I didn't," I whisper. "I never did."

"You never spoke with Death?" I hesitate before shaking my head. "Interesting," she ponders. "You have a power too, Jillian. When did you first become aware of it?"

I shouldn't tell her anything, but I want to. And I don't know why. "A few days ago." Her hand is still on my arm. "Will you please let go of me?"

"No." She smiles. I don't have the sense to be angry. "Do all Reapers get it?"

"No." I shake my head.

"Who gave it to you?"

"I think the Grim Reaper?"

"What do you mean, the Grim Reaper?" Her hand digs into my shoulder.

"I-I don't know. Just *the* Grim Reaper, you know?" Why am I telling her all of this? "What's your name?" I manage to blurt out.

"Lucia." Her voice is mild and thoughtful. "Lucia Rodriguez."

I recoil. "Rodriguez?"

"Yes. Finding out that my birth father was a priest was strange." This woman is Father Rodriguez's daughter. The world could not get any stranger than it is at this moment. I'm starting to see the resemblance, the hooked nose, the deep-set eyes. "But I suppose it makes sense that Life would go for people who are chasing everlasting life, doesn't it?"

"What?"

She glares at me, a warning almost. That I'm asking too many questions. "Blaise neglected to tell me how inquisitive you are." Her grip on my arm tightens. "When I say I'm a child of Life, I do mean it literally. Life carried me, gave birth to me, and then left me with him. This Father Rodriguez you love so much." Lucia's expression turns dark. "And he couldn't take responsibility for his actions."

This feeling is all too familiar. Coursing through my veins with an intensity that I haven't felt since I was fifteen. Abandonment and hurt. And why didn't he want me?

My gaze jerks to hers. Because she's about to speak. And I should be listening. "I could have let them kill you, Jillian, but I didn't. Do you know why?"

I want to tell her that my name is not Jillian.

"No," I say, both to her and to myself.

"I know what it's like to have powers and not know what to do with them. I can help you refine them. Show you their purpose."

Something is wrong. Something is very wrong. "And what could I give you?"

She merely smiles at me, that strange wolfish grin again. And I don't care that I'm not getting an answer. "What do you say, Jillian?"

I blink heavily at her. This is familiar. I can still move on my own, talk on my own. But—

I am not my own. Like with Desdemon, I can't move. But the weight isn't as crushing. Lucia's power is not as invasive or complete. Especially since she hasn't figured out that Jillian isn't my name.

I close my eyes, searching deep inside my heart for what isn't mine. Because this, whatever it is, is not in my head. There's a heated red spot inside my chest. Every attempt to push it out only makes it heat up. It keeps heating and heating until—

"Ow!" Lucia yanks her hand away.

My mind explodes with worry and hyperawareness. How did we get here? I don't remember the specific set of stairs or which door we came through. Where is Deanna? Mom? Esley? Jeremiah?

"Where are they?" I growl at her. "What did you do with them?"

She laughs lightly. "Fine. We'll do this the hard way." I watch her walk towards the wall. There's a door there. I didn't see it earlier. She pushes it open.

Chapter Thirty-six

The room before me is gaping and cavernous, like a cathedral, an amphitheater. The seats up and down are lined with figures cloaked in red. At least one hundred of them. I have no idea how many exactly. Murals similar to those paintings outside fill every spare bit of the ceiling.

I gaze up at them, faceless figures of fabric and weaponry. And I know that I will never ever be able to get into a single one of their souls.

My eyes flit downwards. Mom, Deanna, Esley, and Jeremiah are each standing far apart from each other, a Red Reaper assigned to each. My blood runs cold.

Lucia grabs my arm again. My thoughts are quiet. My heart rate slows. Nothing is wrong. We're all here to talk.

Lucia deposits me next to someone. A man. Familiar and tall. Lucia's hand leaves my arm as she walks forwards.

Blaise shifts uncomfortably next to me. Heat floods my cheeks. My teeth gnash together.

It would be so easy to strangle him right here.

"Jillian," he whispers.

I glare daggers at him. Why the hell is he still using that name? God, I hate that name.

His eyes widen momentarily. "Do what she says, and they'll live."

"Something was taken from us," Lucia announces. "A cure."

Mom's eyes meet mine. Confirmation. She did it. She took whatever they're after.

"Jillian, you've become fairly well acquainted with Blaise, yes?" Heat climbs up my face. "When do you think I made him immortal?"

I press my lips together, completely silent. Whatever game she's playing, I don't want any part of it.

Blaise nudges me. It takes everything in me not to punch him straight in the nose. "A year or two ago?"

"Blaise has been immortal since he was nine," Lucia says this as though we're merely in a science lecture of some kind. "Twelve years now."

I furrow my eyebrows. "He's still aging."

"Precisely the problem!" She beams at me as though I'm a small child. She reaches for a table in the center of the room, one I didn't notice before. The sickle from earlier is laid across it, wiped clean. "And he will continue to age for as long as he is immortal. Which, well, that will be forever. He'll keep aging forever."

Lucia turns back to Mom. "Vanessa stole the cure to that little snag right out of her own lab," she sneers. "You made it for us and then took it for yourself."

Lucia beckons to one of the Red Reapers in front of her. They drag Mom forwards. She at least looks more alert now. Some of that fire that I'm used to is back in her eyes. Lucia picks up the sickle. Blaise stiffens next to me.

"NO!" I shout, my feet springing into action. Blaise's hand shoots out and loops around my wrist as Red Reapers on all sides draw their scythes.

Lucia turns towards me, eyes wide in feigned innocence. She laughs. "I've been trying to make her immortal, not end her life. I'm not in that business."

"Aaron would beg to disagree," I spit.

"You're in that business, though, aren't you?" She runs a

cloth up and down the sickle slowly. "You killed the Ceremonial assigned to you. Drove her right off a cliff. For no reason." Mom's eyes widen.

"She was going to kill me!" I snarl. "She killed Aaron. She would have killed her." I gesture to Deanna. "If she hadn't been chasing us, I never would have—"

"So, you agree? Killing is necessary to save our loved ones?"

"You *made* it necessary."

"It's all we've been trying to do!" Lucia says. "*Save* our loved ones. Deep down, we want the same thing."

I shake my head. "It was an—"

"Oh, don't lie now and say it was an accident." Lucia rolls her eyes. "You know I already know. Blaise told me everything. I know everything about you."

"You don't."

"I do." She smiles.

My eyes flit between Lucia and Mom, trying to decipher her next move. Lucia beckons to me. I move forwards, closer to Mom.

"Death sent you to find out everything you could, didn't they?" Lucia turns to Mom.

Mom doesn't react. Did Desdemon send her? Is that why Desdemon was so worried?

"Your research was important to them, but *this* important?" She gestures to me. I furrow my brows. "Death handed you to me on a silver platter just to get her back. You are hopelessly outnumbered. Do the smart thing, Jillian. Join us."

I recoil in disgust. "What could you possibly want with a Reaper?"

"You are not just a Reaper. What you have? From the Grim Reaper himself? More valuable to us than killing you. You want to live? You want those people you love to live? Help us keep others alive."

Lucia stretches her hand out to me, palm up. It's my choice if I take it.

"You want me to be a traitor to my own kind."

"How long have they been your kind? A few weeks? What has Death ever done for you that is worth losing it all?"

It's Esley's hazel eyes that I meet this time. Not long, but long enough that I don't want her to die. I size up Lucia and the Red Reapers around us. Would she really let us live? Mom shakes her head at me. "If I do, will you let her go?"

"Let her go?" Lucia says. "Of course. Once she tells me where she put the cure, I won't need her any longer."

"I'm never going to tell you." Mom's voice comes out weaker than usual, but just as defiant.

Lucia growls and slams the sickle down onto the table.

I watch as she stalks towards Mom while a Red Reaper holds her steady. Lucia places one hand over each of Mom's eyes. A low humming fills the surrounding air, rattling my very bones. The red cloaked figures have taken up a chant, but I can't figure out what they're saying.

Mom screams.

My soul is on fire. My head is splitting open at the seams. Boiling blood courses through my veins. A thousand tiny needles pierce my skin. Slimy thread drags through me. Aaron is lying dead in the sand. I'm lying in the sand, my throat wide open and spewing blood.

Hands are covering my eyes.

Mom's screams ring through the air. My Reaper mark burns like a hot iron.

I clench my eyes shut, trying to hide from it all. My legs give out underneath me. Somewhere I can hear Deanna's voice. I have no idea what she's saying, but I can hear the desperation.

A hundred voices flood into me and are just as quickly silenced. Everything is quiet. All the pain is gone.

I open my eyes. My hands are shaking. They're spewing green

fog throughout the entire room. My eyes drift up to the sea of red before me. Tiny pinpricks of glowing green stare out at me from behind the hoods.

The whole world has come to a standstill. Deanna is frozen mid-struggle with a Red Reaper, both pairs of eyes glowing green. Esley is similarly frozen. Jeremiah's face is etched with worry, but he isn't moving. His eyes glow too.

My gaze drifts towards Mom. Lucia's hands cover her eyes, but Mom is still too, as though frozen in time.

My pulse thunders as Lucia moves. She examines her own hands, then turns to face me. Her eyes are untouched by green, still that same brown gaze.

I push myself to my feet, glaring at her. My mind is oddly quiet for the number of souls I'm holding.

Movement to my right draws my gaze. Blaise observes everyone frozen around him, an expression somewhere between fear and awe on his face.

"Leave her alone." I turn back to Lucia. My words are echoed by over a hundred people.

Lucia smiles and walks towards her sickle, as casually as if she were grabbing a snack. "Think carefully, Jillian. You're alone. How long can you hold this?"

I am alone. I've made myself alone. If I try to find Jeremiah, Deanna, and Esley in there, release their souls, what guarantee do I have that it won't all fall apart?

I glare at Lucia, sauntering around without a care in the world. The woman who gave the order to have Aaron killed, tortured my mom for weeks, and continues to torture Father Rodriguez even in her absence.

My hands shake and form tight fists. Lucia smiles a wolfish grin. She puts the sickle back down on the table. Opening her arms in invitation.

I accept, charging at her with everything I have.

My fist cracks against her jaw.

Her knee slams into my stomach, knocking the wind out of me. Her arms push me over her knee and towards the ground.

My hands catch my fall. I shake my head and bounce back up to my feet as quickly as I can. I charge at her again and miss.

Her fist slams into my jaw.

I stumble backwards. Pain radiates across my face, pounding in my skull.

Someone has slipped from my control. I search in a panic for who.

Deanna is charging towards us, tossing a scythe in my direction. My hand raises to catch it.

We slam the butts of our scythes straight into Lucia's stomach, sending her crashing backwards into the table.

Deanna charges towards her without hesitation. Lucia's hand wraps around the sickle and blocks the scythe before she's even had a chance to fully get up.

I'm running for her. Lucia kicks Deanna backwards as momentum to stand.

Another someone slips from my control as Deanna falls to the ground, but I don't have time to figure out who. I slice down with the bladed end, knowing it's pointless, and that Lucia saw it coming from a mile off.

She blocks with the sickle. I continue pushing forwards.

A memory flashes through me. Someone under my control sparred with her. Several people, in fact.

I draw on their muscle memory to dodge her next swipe, but I walk straight into her foot, and she swipes my legs out from under me.

My hands don't break my fall this time, my nose does. My sinuses are going to explode. Water fills my eyes. I pull my focus back, pushing the pain down. There's a spattering of blood on the floor in front of me.

I roll onto my back in time to see Lucia cry out in pain. Esley yanks her dagger back towards her, not wasting a second in striking again. Lucia just barely blocks her.

They are a whirlwind of flashing metal and limbs.

"Blaise!" Lucia cries out.

My gaze fixes on him momentarily. He's got a scythe of his own now, but his feet remain motionless. I watch long enough to see Deanna charging towards him.

Metal cuts through the air next to me. I lift my scythe to block in the nick of time. Lucia stands over me, her eyes wild.

My grip on the surrounding people is getting more tenuous by the second.

Jeremiah slips from my grasp, jumping into action immediately. Esley tosses him one of her knives and they charge at Lucia as if they've practiced this dance a hundred times before.

Lucia jumps away from me, on the defensive. She steps backwards, dodging, searching for an opening that doesn't come.

It won't matter. When my control slips, it won't matter. We won't win against all of them. Against these two maybe, but against them all?

I turn my own battle inwards, focusing on keeping the souls quiet. Only a part of me, nothing more. The mere idea is unnatural, separate people reduced to an extension of me. It's wrong.

No sooner has the thought entered my head than the three Red Reapers closest to us are free. They move to Lucia's aid.

I curse audibly. Mom's eyes stop glowing green instantly, as though a primal motherly instinct to chastise my language has taken over. Her skin is paler than ever, her eyes barely focused.

My control slips on a few more in the seats above us. They jostle the crowd in their efforts to make it down here.

I grit my teeth and reach back out for them. Green mist snakes through the air and straight into their eyes. Those closest to Lucia first, then the ones up in the seats. My whole body is shaking with the effort to keep them all still. A cool sweat trickles down my neck.

All around me weapons are clashing. A man's voice cries out in pain, but I have no way of knowing if it's Blaise or Jeremiah. Their side or ours. My vision is hazy, moving in and out of focus, darkening around the edges.

I hear Mom shout, "Jeremiah!"

It takes everything in me to pull my focus back into my own eyes and body.

Jeremiah whirls towards Mom, then follows her gaze towards me, crumpled on the floor and breathless.

In a single movement, he slashes across Lucia's thigh, leaving a deep gash behind. She falls to the ground, her sickle skittering across the floor towards me.

Blaise rushes towards her.

Esley is moments away from finishing the job when Blaise blocks her with his own arm.

Jeremiah pulls Esley by the waist and drags her away, towards Mom.

Deanna is beside me, tired but uninjured, thank God. Jeremiah scoops Mom into his arms.

The souls shake the bars of their prison. "We have to go now," I whisper, barely audible even to myself.

"Stop them!" Lucia screams at Blaise, her hand circled around her own thigh.

I meet his eyes. He doesn't move.

My heart clenches with indecision. Then his gaze darkens as Lucia grabs him for support.

I take Deanna's outstretched hand. She pulls me to my feet. My eyes alight on Lucia's discarded sickle and I scoop it from the floor in case she heals herself fast and follows.

Deanna tugs on me and I follow, sprinting after the rest of them.

We follow Jeremiah, his form surprisingly steady considering the load he carries. I barrel down the hill and towards what I can only hope is a nearby graveyard.

The world fades in and out around me until I can barely see where I'm going, led only by my grip on Deanna's hand.

Hundreds of voices echo through my head. The sound of our feet against the dead grass fades away until all I can hear is them.

"Murderer. Liar. Hypocrite. Devil!" they scream.

My hold breaks at the bottom of the hill. I barely squeak out the word, "Run," before crumpling to the pavement.

The last thing I hear is Deanna shouting, "We've got her, Vanessa, don't worry." And I know nothing more.

Chapter Thirty-seven

My head is pounding in time with a heartbeat. Not my heartbeat, someone else's. A strong hand squeezes mine. For one bizarre, hopeful moment, I think it's Aaron's hand.

I force my eyes open. Carl is at my bedside, his eyes bloodshot. "Carl?" My voice claws its way out of my throat, barely a whisper. "Where's Mom? What happened?"

"I'll go get some tea," Deanna says from my other side. Her hand leaves my shoulder. I didn't even realize it was there. My head whips towards her so fast I give myself a headache. "It's okay." Her voice is intoxicatingly calm. I have to believe her.

"Your mom's doing just fine. She's in another room. She was weak, but we got some food in her and she's doing better." Carl reassures me.

"Raina and Anisha?" I whisper.

Carl nods. "Worried, but fine." I exhale in relief, resting my head back on the pillow. The room around me is painted baby blue. There's a vase of cut flowers on the bedside table. "We're at my parent's place," Carl supplies. "Couple hours outside of Marbhaven."

Deanna returns with a steaming cup of tea laced with a hefty helping of honey. I gulp it down, the honey coating my throat.

"Jeremiah got us all to a graveyard, and I told him to take us here," Deanna says. "Took two trips, but we're all safe."

"Is he—"

"He left a few hours ago," Deanna says. "Said he had to talk to Desdemon."

"Can I see her?" I set the empty cup down. "Can I see Mom?"

Deanna offers up her arm. I wave her off and press my feet into the creaky wooden floor.

It's immediately disastrous. My legs give out and I crumple to the floor like a paper doll. Deanna and Carl pull me to my feet and this time I lean on her.

"Dad, can you make her some food?" she asks.

Carl nods and leaves the room. Deanna and I trudge down the hallway at a snail's pace. "This is stupid," I mutter. "I didn't even do anything to—"

"Not anything physical?" Deanna prompts. "I don't know. I don't think your soul was meant to hold a hundred others at the same time."

"But I should be able to walk."

"And yet, here we are."

"How long has it been?"

Deanna checks the clock hanging up on the wall. "Eighteen hours?" I groan. "They aren't going to find us. Not yet. We teleported here and unless they have a way of tracking that . . . "

She pushes the door at the end of the hall open. Mom is sitting up in bed, Raina and Anisha tucked under her arms.

When Raina and Anisha see me, they launch themselves from the bed towards me. I throw my arms around them, leaning against the bedpost for support.

Tears are streaming down my face before I'm even aware enough to stop them. "You're okay," I whisper. "You're okay. You're safe." I don't know if I'm comforting them or reassuring myself.

They are sobbing too, struggling to speak. Raina manages to spit something out about me being alive. Anisha isn't able to string more than a syllable at a time together.

"I didn't mean to worry you. I'm sorry. I'm so, *so* sorry. I—" And now I have the hiccups. Lovely.

Deanna helps me up onto the bed next to Mom and then closes the door behind her. I lay my head in Mom's lap and pull Anisha into a tight embrace. Mom's got Raina. We sit like that until long after the sun goes down, listening to the steady beating of each other's hearts. A constant reassurance that we are all alive.

At some point the smells of mulligatawny soup lure me up and out of bed. I'm surprised to find that my feet can take my weight now, barely. I bring bowls back up for Mom, Raina, and Anisha. We turn on the TV and watch Mom's favorite movie, quoting our favorite lines back to each other in increasingly ridiculous accents.

The twins drift off to sleep before the movie has ended. Mom stares at the end credits. I'm not entirely convinced that she's actually watching them.

"Were they scared?" she whispers into the darkness.

A steady rain patters against the window. "Yes," I answer honestly. "They tried not to show it, but yes."

"Were you?"

It's a few moments before I answer that one. "Of course."

"I'm sorry about"—her voice catches in her throat—"about Aaron. I—"

I nod. I don't know what to say. The fact that he's dead hits me again like a ton of bricks. We are silent as the movie ends, and we're brought back to the main menu. "What did you steal?"

"Medicine." Mom's voice is low in the dark. "I helped develop it, at Genesis. They wanted to test it on people. It was too soon. It was unstable. The side effects were"—she shivers next to me—"something was off. It wasn't helping them. Constant fevers, cold sweats, throat swelling, blood clots."

"What did they tell you it was for?"

"It was supposed to help with cell regeneration. Healthy cell regeneration. I assumed it was for cancer," she whispers. "They were testing it in small towns, where people wouldn't notice. Paid a lot of money to the participants, NDAs, the whole nine yards. I did some digging, found out what it was for and—" she stops.

"And what?"

"I took all of our samples and research files. It was only a matter of time before it killed someone. Worst part, it was addictive."

"What did you do with them?"

"I destroyed it. All of it. They took me before I could get back home."

"Jesus." I bury my face in my hands.

"I never imagined that it would connect to Desdemon or Reapers. Well, I suppose I had an inkling, but—"

"So, you do know Desdemon."

"Yes. When I was younger. They were"—she considers her words carefully—"there for me in a time when no one else was. You know that your Nani Anisha wasn't exactly happy that I was pregnant that young." I snort. "Desdemon offered me support. I'm very grateful to them."

I open my mouth to speak but freeze as a red glow erupts around the room. Father Rodriguez. Shortly followed by—

His unruly dark curls are even more messy. Dark circles surround his eyes. And those brown eyes . . .

God, I can't believe I ever liked his eyes. My hands are shaking.

"What is it?"

"Nothing." I shake my head. "I'm just tired."

"We should sleep." Mom kisses me gently on the forehead. "I love you, Jade."

"I love you too, Mom."

I lie down next to the three of them. Mom is out in a matter of mere minutes. I'm not as lucky.

The longer I look at him, the more that day in the forest plays through my mind. Over and over again. His lips on mine, soft kisses on my neck, a location spit out moments after. My stomach turns and my lips burn. I want to carve my lips off, purge every touch from my skin.

Him running in front of that car was planned. Asking me to meet him in the hospital room was a trap. Seeing me after I came back up from the Underworld was not a mere coincidence. He wasn't worried. Blaise told the Red Reaper that I was alive. That's how she found us. That's why she chased us.

The memory of Blaise's screams from that day plays through my mind on repeat. Our lips meeting over and over again. Him telling me to watch out for the Red Reaper on the day I jumped off the cliff.

Why? To gain my trust?

None of it was real.

My feet carry me down the hallway to the bathroom. I turn the shower water up as hot as it will go.

The water runs over me, scalding my skin. I scrub as hard as I can, over my neck, on my lips, relishing the revolting taste of soap in my mouth.

When I step out, his fingerprints and lip marks are finally cleansed from my skin. All that is left is a burning fire in the pit of my stomach. A fire that screams for revenge.

Chapter Thirty-eight

I'm sitting on our bench the next morning, watching the waves. The second Blaise woke up I left. Took one of the cars and drove back to Marbhaven.

I stare out at the sand, the spot where Aaron died. The red that stained the sand is gone now, but it's almost as if I can see the impression of his body. As though I can watch the progression of his footsteps down the path to the end of his life.

The waves roll over the sand in a steady beat. The same beat I've been hearing in my head. Mom's heartbeat. It's tugging me towards her again, even though I know exactly where she is now.

How I want to follow it.

"Thought we'd find you here," Deanna whispers, sitting beside me. Esley sits on my other side. Their eyes are on me.

I smile weakly. "Thanks for finding me."

Deanna clasps my hand. "Of course."

I turn back to the waves. "He was there last night, you know," I whisper.

"Blaise?" Esley asks.

"The man whose name we do not speak?" Deanna corrects, her gaze fixed on a point on the beach. Her jaw tenses.

I nod. "I'm gonna miss this place. The ocean." The sound of the waves drowns out my worries for a few precious moments. "But I can't stay here. He's going to figure it out wherever I go."

"We can't stay here," Deanna corrects. I turn to her sharply. "You didn't think we'd let you go alone, did you?"

"Come on." Esley chuckles, throwing her arm around me. "Perpetual road trip buddies!"

"Oh God," I groan. "Please tell me we'll have something more permanent."

"How does a short-term lease in Portland sound?" Deanna asks.

"It'll be fun!" Esley says. "You and I can split the wave of people dying in their sleep."

I roll my eyes. "I wonder which two of us will be sharing a room." They don't have any quips in return for that one.

"When do we leave?" Deanna asks.

"Tonight," I say. "Blaise is on a six-foot tether. If I leave before he falls asleep, he'll never know where your grandparents live."

Deanna nods. "We'd better get packed."

Esley pats her thigh. "Done."

"Good, you can help me." Deanna beckons to Esley. They start off down the beach together.

I gaze out at the ocean again. The colors blur into a mosaic of blues and sunshine. The ghost of a smile passes over my face.

Our spot.

The time for me to pack will come later.

Wind whips in my hair through the open car window. I drive up the winding cliffside, all the way to the church.

My feet pad along the grass lightly until I reach the edge, gazing out at the crashing waves below.

My heart beats loud in my chest, Mom's loud in my ears. I just got her back. The temptation to keep this, to take her with me, is almost too much to resist.

But I have something to give back. It's time to see the Grim Reaper.

Acknowledgements

Thank you, first, to EJ and the whole team at EJL editing. For everything from educating me on dialogue punctuation, to answering all of my questions on the minutiae of commas and dashes. You really made The Marbhaven Reaper shine! To my cover artist Sandra at Maldo Designs. I swear I cried when I saw how beautiful this cover was! Thank you so much for making a cover that I cannot stop staring at.

To all the folks at iN-TEA, thank you for the writing safe haven and the best gingerbread chai around!

To all my lovely beta readers, your insights were invaluable in shaping this story. To Jaya Zaveri, my friend, for allowing me to use her last name. Thank you!!! To Courtney and Amanda, my fellow authors. Thank you for making me laugh almost every single day. The struggle is real, but much more manageable with you two around.

To Haley, my best friend, and my sister. Thank you for everything that you are. Deanna is for you.

To Nona, for giving me everything I needed to make my first ever published book, "Ord is Sick" I still just *can't* stop writing.

To Tavi, for being my rock during this rollercoaster ride to publication. Thank you for the memes, the playlist, and for being the Meaperverse's first fangirl.

To Kathleen, my muse. The "Do you watch me while I sleep?" scene wouldn't exist without you. Thank you for being my sounding board, for helping me solve all of the plot holes, and for your absolutely unhinged comments on the side.

To Mom and Dad, I don't even know what to say. Thank you for everything it took to get this book and me where we are today. Mom, for proofreading the dang thing and almost definitely making a cake of the book. I can feel it happening as I type. Dad, for all of the hugs and talking me down from the ledge. Being your daughter has been one of the greatest honors of my life.

To Kyle, I couldn't have written the fight scenes without you. Thanks for being the best, most annoying, funniest, kindest brother out there.

To my husband, Luke, you're wonderful. From character art, to changing the plot entirely, to holding me when I'm having panic attacks about just about everything. I'm so lucky that you walked into my life. You're a bitch, and I hate you. :)

To my readers, oh what to say to you. Being an author has been my dream since I was six years old. You're more than readers, you are a dream realized. Thank you! Thank you! Thank you!

And lastly, to Lefty, Hazel, Paul, and Mike. I trust the afterlife is treating you well.

Maile grew up trying to wriggle her way into every single graveyard she passed. Now she writes stories about Reapers and witchy things to soothe her inner child. In her spare time, you'll probably find Maile engaging in way too many hobbies, but her favorites are painting, singing, and chatting with readers. She lives in Colorado, sipping hot chocolate in all two seasons with her husband.